A

WILLFUL

CORPSE

A WILLFUL CORPSE

AN ART OF MURDER MYSTERY

HELEN A. HARRISON

Back cover:

Jackson Pollock, Number 22, 1949

Oil on paper mounted on Masonite, 27 3/4 x 22 7/8 in.

© The Pollock-Krasner Foundation/Artists Rights Society (ARS), New York

Author Photo Credit: Roy Nicholson

First edition

ISBN: 978-1-68512-935-4

Cover art by Level Best Designs

This book was professionally typeset on Reedsy.
Find out more at reedsy.com

To Roy, always

Praise for A Willful Corpse

"Helen Harrison knows her way around—upstairs and down—what is generally called the art world. Her forensic examination of the convergence of big money, big egos, and high achievements is based on insider knowledge few could rival. Trust her, but watch your back as you venture into her perilous domain. It is a place where more than one person you'll meet deserves killing and is likely to fall victim to the intrigues that drew them and fellow denizens of the cultural mainstream and its backwaters like flies to a rotting corpse."—Rob Storr, former Dean, Yale School of Art

"A rich cast of characters with all the complexities and charm one could want…informed by a true insider's eye. The writing and plot work [are] excellent."—Bronwen Hruska, author of *Accelerated*

"Another entertaining mystery from Helen Harrison! Skillfully weaving fact and fiction, *A Willful Corpse* will keep readers engaged from beginning to end."—Carrie Doyle, author, Hamptons Murder Mysteries; co-founder, Hamptons Whodunit

"The mix of fact and fiction in this art-world thriller by insider Helen Harrison is as fun, fast, and complicated as trying to decipher the missing Jackson Pollock paintings at its core and figuring out which are real and which are fake."—Jonathan Santlofer, bestselling author of *The Lost Van Gogh* and *The Last Mona Lisa*

Friday, May 2, 1986

His blood was boiling. Two hostile encounters within ten minutes had left him furious and emotionally exhausted. *Calm down,* he told himself as he descended the steps to the 68th Street IRT subway station. *They won't persuade me to change my mind, no matter what they promise.*

He inserted a token in the turnstile and stepped onto the platform. It wasn't too crowded. There was a vacant space on a bench, so he sat, pulled *The New Yorker* from his pocket, took a deep breath, and settled down to wait for the train.

Almost immediately, the platform began to fill with raucous students from Hunter College's elementary and high schools, horsing around and exploiting the station's echo-chamber effect. Fortunately, he had long ago perfected the fine art of blocking distractions, so he was less disturbed by their high jinks than he had been by the shouting matches he'd had on the street. Immersing himself in the magazine helped quiet his nerves, until he read the poetry.

He did not need to interrupt his rumination on the deplorable state of contemporary verse to know that the train was approaching. The rush of air in the tunnel and the vibration under his feet told him that the downtown Number 6 would soon arrive.

He folded the magazine, rose from the bench, and crossed the crowded platform, dodging and weaving to avoid the boisterous youngsters. Being sedentary by nature, he hoped to get a seat. The first on board stood the best chance, so he worked his way close to the edge. As the train entered the station and his fellow subway riders jostled for position, he felt a hand on his left hip. It pushed him off the platform and into the path of the oncoming local.

His body triggered the train's emergency braking system, but not before two cars had passed over it. He was pronounced dead at the scene.

iii

One

Friday, March 21

"**N**O!"

Ellen winced as Francis' fist slammed down on the table, hard enough to make pencils and water glasses rattle, to emphasize his negative vote. She tried not to show how startled she was. This was her first meeting since being appointed to the board that authenticated artwork by Jackson Pollock and Lee Krasner, and she was determined to maintain a professional demeanor. Sitting opposite her, Charlie threw her a discreet wink, as if to say don't worry, we're in this together.

All too familiar with Francis' outbursts, Bill closed his eyes and exhaled a puff of cigarette smoke that barely camouflaged an exasperated sigh.

Equally experienced, Gene rearranged his lips into a nearly undetectable frown. *I don't need that,* he thought, *especially in this case.*

"Perhaps we should have it brought in for examination," he suggested reasonably. "Judging by even the best transparency isn't always reliable."

Francis scowled. "Dammit, Gene, I don't have to see it in person to know it's not a Pollock. It's as dead as a dodo, absolutely no juice in it at all." He grabbed the eight-by-ten transparency, neatly mounted in a black mat, waved it in the air dramatically, and plopped it back down on the light table. "Even in the film, it's obvious."

"The situation is a bit delicate," said Gene. "I wanted it considered without prejudice, so I didn't mention it earlier, but the owner is a client of mine, and a personal friend. If she had come to me for advice before she bought it, I would have recommended that she submit it to us first. But she didn't, so calling it into question now puts me in an awkward position."

Glaring at Francis, Bill leaned across the table and snatched the transparency. "It looks all right to me. Not the best Pollock I've ever seen, but not the worst, either. And it has a perfectly good provenance. Sold by Betty Parsons in forty-nine to a woman who passed away last year, leaving it to her son, who sold it to the present owner."

"Then why isn't it in Betty's gallery records?" Francis' voice, an odd amalgam of elocution-lesson diction and his native Brooklynese, rose sharply. With each word, he jabbed his index finger at a ring binder marked Betty Parsons Gallery 1948-1982.

"It could be one of the miscellaneous items that carried over from Peggy's inventory," said Bill, referring to Peggy Guggenheim, Pollock's first art dealer and patron. "You know how vague that is. Five gouaches. Ten drawings. Four works on paper. Her lists are full of things like that. And Betty wasn't the most accurate record keeper, either." He sniffed meaningfully. "So inconvenient of her to die before we could ask her if she recognized it."

"And so foolish of the owner's son to have had it reframed before he sold it," added Gene. "There might have been a gallery label on the back. People don't realize how important such things can be."

"Labels can be faked," said Francis dismissively. "Anyway, not only no label, but no bill of sale, no exhibition history, no publication. Why didn't the original owner submit it to us in the seventies?"

Gene's patience was wearing thin. "According to my client, the son said his mother knew nothing about the art world, so she wasn't aware that there was an authentication process, much less a reason to question the picture's bona fides. She bought it on a whim when a friend took her to the gallery. Small paintings on paper like this weren't expensive. As Betty's records show, they were priced at two hundred and fifty dollars. Just another impulse purchase by someone who, the son said, was a champion shopper. She fancied it, so she bought it, took it home, and hung it on her wall. The son remembered that his father wasn't too pleased."

With Francis and Bill, Gene had been a member of the earlier authentication committee established by Lee Krasner, Pollock's widow and the executrix of his estate, to create the Jackson Pollock catalogue raisonné—the documentation of all his known works. There were also plenty of imitations, homages, copies, misattributions, and downright forgeries that had to be weeded out. Krasner was the ultimate arbiter, though by relying on a panel of experts to back her up, she couldn't be accused of personal bias in favor of, or more pointedly, against Pollock hopefuls.

The four-volume treatise had been published in 1978. As an inevitable consequence, predicted by the editors in the introduction, pieces that had been overlooked appeared, as did a new round of fakes. So the committee continued to meet from time to time, anticipating an addendum to the catalogue and continuing to protect the integrity of Pollock's legacy.

As far as the integrity of Krasner's own oeuvre was concerned, she needed no outside authority. But after her death, the committee was revived as the Pollock-Krasner Authentication Board, and possible Krasners also came under its purview.

* * *

Pollock's work not being her specialty, Ellen Jamieson sat silent through the argument. Her job on the board was to opine on Krasner's work, now being vetted for a catalogue raisonné of its own. She'd been the artist's part-time personal assistant for five years and was intimately familiar with the oeuvre, which she had meticulously documented as new pieces were created, exhibited, sold, and reproduced in catalogs and art magazines. And she had tracked the whereabouts of earlier works as they went to auction, were sold through galleries on the secondary market, or were acquired by museums.

Charlie also listened to the exchange without comment. Vice-president of the Pollock-Krasner Foundation, a charity established by Krasner's last will and testament, Charles C. Bergman was responsible for overall administration, but not for authentication matters. His affable demeanor

3

and background in non-profit philanthropy made him an ideal supervisor of the board, but as an ex-officio member, he had no say in its deliberations. For him, as for Ellen, this was the first meeting. A perceptive judge of character, he had sized them all up long before the discussion got heated.

He already knew Eugene Victor Thaw, the foundation's president, who had hired him the previous fall. A respected private art dealer who had managed the Pollock estate very profitably for a dozen years before Krasner's death, Gene was renowned for his tasteful wardrobe, impeccable manners, astute connoisseurship, and uncanny ability to place his blue-chip inventory with just the right discerning, well-heeled collectors. It was said that he had the best eye in the business, but Charlie wondered whether, just this once, Gene was letting his judgment be clouded by his desire to save face with his important client.

No such consideration would have crossed the mind of Francis Valentine O'Connor, Ph.D., the maverick art historian who had written his doctoral dissertation on Pollock and was the co-editor with Gene of the Pollock catalogue raisonné. Even if his own mother had spent her life savings on the picture in question, if Francis believed it was phony, he would say so and to hell with the consequences. Compromise was alien to him. His larger-than-life persona was contained in a body of medium stature and slightly rotund proportions, crowned by a head of luxuriant auburn hair and matching mustache. His contrary nature made him a difficult colleague, but as maddening as he often was, no one could fault his meticulous research or impugn his integrity. As far as Charlie was concerned, he was a pompous pipsqueak who nevertheless was an invaluable asset to the board.

Like Francis, William Slattery Lieberman, chairman of the Metropolitan Museum of Art's department of 20th-century art, was a temperamental cuss but equally vital to the board's credibility. Roughly the same height as Francis, his erect bearing and air of superiority made him seem taller. He had been a close confidant of Krasner's since his days as a curator at the Museum of Modern Art, where they had conspired to build a comprehensive collection of Pollock's work. Serving with Gene and Francis on the original authentication committee, he had often run interference when Krasner became problematic, which was not uncommon. Charlie saw him as imperious and snobbish, and disapproved of his patronizing attitude toward Ellen. He had agreed to her appointment to the board, but obviously had no intention of welcoming her as an equal.

She had only recently gotten to know the avuncular and sympathetic Charlie, but she had encountered the other three men many times before, as a bystander when they visited Krasner on business. As the artist's employee, she had always addressed her as Miss Krasner, and was not invited to her cocktail parties or the domestic gatherings of art-world insiders, though she sometimes accompanied her to gallery receptions and to meetings with her dealer. Their relationship was strictly professional, and Ellen preferred it that way.

After Krasner died, in June 1984, Gene had asked Ellen to stay on to work for the estate, continuing to document the oeuvre during the transition to the foundation. When Krasner's apartment was sold, her files were moved from Ellen's small office, a converted closet adjacent to the artist's studio, to a slightly larger space in Gerald Dickler's midtown law firm, where at least she had a window. A distinguished specialist in art and entertainment law and senior partner in Hall, Dickler, Lawler, Kent & Friedman, Gerry Dickler was well known to Ellen as Krasner's longtime legal advisor; he had written the will that established the Pollock-Krasner Foundation, of which he was now chairman. When Gene recommended that the foundation publish a Krasner catalogue raisonné, Ellen was the natural candidate for the editor's job, so she continued as a part-time employee, with a pay raise, flexible hours, an expense account, and a seat on the authentication board.

Charlie had taken an immediate liking to Ellen, a petite, blue-eyed blonde who dressed well and smiled often. At age thirty-eight, with a prominent career in fashion illustration, she was mature, diligent, and easy on the eye. Outgoing without being presumptuous, she was thoroughly conversant with Krasner's work and had a sense of humor that Charlie appreciated, which is to say that she laughed at his jokes. After she was appointed to the board, he resolved to ease her as gently as possible into the troika of competing egos. He hoped she would be the fourth wheel needed to stabilize that rocky vehicle.

The only downside was that the board now had an even number of members, and he was not authorized to be a tiebreaker. Not that he would have wanted the role, since he lacked the necessary knowledge and experience. He had hoped that his diplomatic skills could forestall that eventuality, but here it loomed in front of him, and on the very first occasion.

No one had asked Ellen's opinion, and she didn't offer it. She had quickly grasped the situation and decided that she'd let the Pollock experts settle it among themselves. It was looking like two against one, with Francis the insistent holdout, when Bill picked up on the idea of examining the piece in person.

"Let's take a look at the damned thing itself," he grumbled. Turning a world-weary gaze on Gene, he asked, "Is your client in the city? Perhaps we can send a messenger to pick it up and bring it to the next meeting," mentally adding, *and by that time, Francis will have cooled off and might just come around.*

"I think that's a splendid suggestion," said Gene gratefully. "She lives on the Upper East Side, not far from me. Once we know when we'll be meeting again, I can make the arrangements. I'm sure she won't mind waiting a few more weeks." With the announcement of plans to publish a Krasner catalogue and a Pollock supplement, the number of submissions had swelled considerably. The board had several other items on today's agenda, and would no doubt be meeting again fairly soon. Tabling this problem would unclog the bottleneck it was causing.

* * *

Francis' scowl returned. "Oh, very well. Let's move along." He let his expression soften and reached for another folder. "We have a potential Krasner here that Ellen needs to consider." He opened the file and removed an eight-by-ten black and white photograph in a Mylar sleeve and handed it to her, politely turning it so it was properly oriented, and gave her a curt little nod to indicate his approval. She wondered if he was being condescending, but changed her mind when he added, without irony, "she knows the oeuvre inside out."

What a nice thing to say, she thought. She wouldn't be there if she weren't an expert on Krasner's output, but Francis' words were more than just a compliment. They signaled his endorsement of her role, and even hinted that he might defer to her on Krasner issues. It nicely counterbalanced Bill's hauteur, with its unspoken suggestion that she was not up to the task. Here was her first test, and in spite of Francis' encouragement she couldn't help feeling unsure of herself as she approached it.

But she knew immediately that the work was genuine. It was one of a group of collages Krasner made in 1953 from torn-up drawings, either her own or Pollock's or both. There were about a dozen, and Krasner had photographs of most of them in her files, though unfortunately not this one. Nevertheless, Ellen was sure it belonged in the series. She flipped the photo and saw a familiar stamp on the back: LIGHTHOUSE PHOTOSHOP / 54 Newtown Lane / East Hampton, N.Y.

An accompanying letter from the owner, Carol Braider, explained that it had been given to her and her late husband Donald, the former owners of an East Hampton bookstore where Krasner had had a solo exhibition in 1954; it was both a Christmas gift that year and a thank-you for presenting the show. The signature and date, "LK-53" in block printing at the lower right, would have been easy to fake, but the composition and technique were distinctively Krasner's, as was the material. It fit right in with the others, which were well documented. This one had been overlooked because it was given away so soon after it was made. The Braiders must have had it photographed before they left East Hampton and moved upstate in 1957.

Ellen studied the picture, wanting to show that she was deliberating carefully, not jumping the gun, and not appearing nervous. In fact, she was feeling quite calm and confident, but well aware that she was being scrutinized. So she took her time, and when she spoke, it was with measured directness.

"I'm sure this is right," she told the others, and explained how it fit into the 1953 collage series. "I've heard Miss Krasner talk about the Braiders," she added. "Donald died some years ago, but she kept in touch with Carol. I used to put through calls to and from her occasionally."

"You make a very convincing case, Ellen," said Gene. "I'm familiar with those collages. I bought one at auction several years ago, and Lee told me the story behind them. She had done a group of ink drawings on paper and was so dissatisfied with the whole batch that she tore them up and threw them on the studio floor, walked out and slammed the door. She didn't go back in for a couple of days, and when she did, the mess on the floor looked kind of interesting. She remembered how her teacher, Hans Hofmann, used to tear up and rearrange drawings, so she started recombining the fragments and before she knew it her work was off in a whole new direction."

Ellen passed the photograph to Lieberman, seated on her left, and asked, "What do you think, Bill?" The use of his first name was intentional. When he deigned to notice her, he pointedly addressed her, with exaggerated formality, as Miss Jamieson.

He stiffened slightly and exhaled smoke in her direction as he took the picture from her, just bordering on grabbing it from her hand. Charlie resisted the temptation to scold him for his bad manners, and Ellen, a non-smoker, silently accepted the punishment for her insolence and resolved to ask Charlie to rearrange the seating at the next board meeting.

Bill also took his time over the photo, even resorting to a magnifying glass. The collage looked authentic, and the provenance was entirely plausible. Not wanting to say directly that he agreed with Ellen, he equivocated.

Addressing Charlie, he advised, "This appears to be a good candidate for inclusion in Lee's catalogue raisonné. We should follow up with Mrs. Braider, don't you think?"

Charlie concurred. Since board meetings were confidential and no minutes were taken, he jotted a note on the folder to ask his secretary to call Carol Braider—her telephone number would be in Krasner's address book, which was in the foundation's files—and ask for any additional documentation she might have. Perhaps she had kept Krasner's thank-you note, or she might have lent the collage to an exhibition with a catalog in which it was illustrated. And, as with the purported Pollock, examining it first-hand would be advisable, especially if there were no paper trail.

The rest of the meeting proceeded uneventfully. A couple of likely genuine but minor early works by Pollock were added to the list for further research, which was Francis' province, and four obviously bogus ones were dispensed with by common agreement. One was a copy of a known but missing painting from his Equine series of the mid 1940s; the others were drip paintings with forged signatures. To forestall lawsuits, the board would not label them as fakes, but simply decline to include them in the catalogue supplement.

As far as the Krasner research was concerned, Ellen reported that she was making good progress compiling an inventory of all known works, a job that was complicated by the artist's habit of recycling her paintings and drawings, as she had done with the Braider collage. Matching the fragments to known but destroyed pieces or figuring out which canvases had been partially or totally reworked demanded a keen eye and persistence, and Ellen had both.

Two

In her day job as a fashion illustrator—her drawings, signed "Jami" with a distinctive flourish, often graced full-page ads in *The New York Times* and spreads in *Vogue* and *Harper's Bazaar*—Ellen had a reputation for delivering the goods on time and to the client's satisfaction. It was said that her warm personality could melt the frigid hearts of even the most formidable art directors.

Her ability to get along with cantankerous characters had been an invaluable asset to her as Krasner's assistant. Her job had been largely clerical, mostly record keeping and dealing with correspondence. By the time she was hired, in the fall of 1979, the artist was already suffering from painful arthritis, as well as chronic colitis and circulatory problems caused by years of heavy smoking, none of which improved a naturally prickly disposition.

She went to the East 79th Street apartment one day a week and worked in a tiny office in what had been the master bedroom, now serving as Krasner's studio. Originally a walk-in closet, the windowless room had just enough space for a desk with a telephone and electric typewriter, a chair, and a row of filing cabinets along one wall. When Krasner showed it to her, she thought, *good thing I'm not claustrophobic,* and was relieved when she was told she could leave the door open.

Krasner had offered her the job on impulse, and she had surprised herself by accepting. The offer came when she finished interviewing the artist for her Hunter College senior thesis. After several years as a professional illustrator, but with only a high school education and her art school training, she had decided to get a college degree.

When she graduated from high school in 1966, Ellen had no clear idea of her future, except that she wasn't going to follow her mother's example and get married immediately. Not only was her steady boyfriend going off to college in Chicago, but she wouldn't have accepted if he'd proposed. Independent by nature, she had no intention of settling down right away. College was not an option for her, however, since her parents wouldn't support her, so she got a job at the Automat on West 57th Street, opposite the Art Students League—a move that, though she couldn't know it, would change her life.

The dead-end job was boring, but she got to know some of the League students who came in for the Automat's cheap and filling fare. When she asked them what went on across the street, one of them offered to show her around and suggested she take an evening life class. Although she enjoyed visiting art museums, she'd never contemplated being an artist herself. But the class wasn't expensive, the art students were a gregarious bunch, and she had nothing in particular to do after work, so she signed up.

It was in Edward Laning's Thursday evening Life Drawing, Painting, and Composition class, in the fall of 1967, that she met her future husband, Timothy Juan Fitzgerald, known as TJ. And it was Laning who encouraged her to switch to Dagmar Freuchen's fashion illustration class, where, much to her surprise, she found her true calling.

League instructors were known for being not simply art teachers but also respected art world professionals. Freuchen was among New York's top illustrators, in demand by the major magazines and fashion houses. Her approval could open doors for outstanding students who wanted to enter the field, and Ellen was among them. After a couple of years' training, she was asked if she'd like to earn a small fee for helping Freuchen with a magazine layout she was working on.

"I think you are ready," said Freuchen through the smoke from her Sobranie Black Russian. "I need some accessories, which you may draw."

Flattered, Ellen tackled the job enthusiastically. It involved rendering hats, handbags, gloves, and shoes as alternatives to the ones shown on the model. She arranged them in a dynamic swirling pattern around the figure, animating an otherwise static illustration. Impressed by her ingenuity, Freuchen became her mentor, steering assignments her way and introducing her to the network of advertising agencies, fashion editors, and art directors responsible for hiring the illustrators, most of whom worked freelance. It wasn't long before she was as busy as she wanted to be.

Despite her professional success, Ellen had been self-conscious about her lack of further education. Most of her colleagues were college graduates, and many even had master's degrees in fine art. In her single days, her roommate Michele had been a theater major at Hunter College, a branch of the tuition-free City College of New York, which had a highly rated arts curriculum. She decided to investigate, and found that, though she'd been out of high school for ten years, her academic diploma and the school's open admissions policy qualified her for enrollment. Unfortunately, the tuition was no longer free, but the $925 annual price tag was affordable.

When she broke the news that she wanted to go back to school, TJ, who had a master's degree in forensic psychology from John Jay College of Criminal Justice, was all for it. As a partner in a private detective agency, he was making good money and had no problem with her need to cut back on her illustration work. So she dropped a few clients, juggled her schedule, tabled her plan to rent a separate studio space near their East 15th Street apartment, and became a college freshman at age twenty-eight.

* * *

Entering her senior year at Hunter, with a double major in studio art and art history, she'd been told by her advisor, Rosemary Strauss, that she needed to decide on a thesis topic. She proposed "Lee Krasner in the Nineteen Thirties." Strauss thought it was an excellent choice, since it dealt with Krasner's career before Pollock came into the picture, when she was a leading member of the American Abstract Artists, a small but active group devoted to exhibiting and promoting their brand of modern art.

"Why did you choose Krasner?" Strauss had asked. Ellen explained that her husband's family and Krasner had friends in common, so she had met the artist socially several times out on eastern Long Island and in the city. And she already knew something about the Works Progress Administration's Federal Art Project, which had employed Krasner during the Great Depression.

"One of my instructors at the League, Edward Laning, used to talk about the WPA a lot," said Ellen. "According to him, it was a godsend for the artists. The government paid them to do their work and donated it to public buildings, and the women and men got equal pay for equal work. Mr. Laning did the big murals at the main library on Fifth Avenue, and others on Ellis Island."

"I know," said Strauss. She rose from behind her desk and pulled a book from her shelf: *The New Deal Art Projects: An Anthology of Memoirs*, edited by Francis V. O'Connor. She handed the book to Ellen. "This will give you the overall story, as told by those who were there, including your friend Laning, whose piece on the mural program is quite entertaining. You may borrow my copy. Rosalind Bengelsdorf Browne's piece on the American Abstract Artists is of special interest.

"When Francis was doing his New Deal research," she continued, "he found the manuscript of *Art for the Millions*, a planned book of essays by WPA artists, written in nineteen thirty-six. It was supposed to tout the project's accomplishments and stimulate further federal support, but publication plans fell through at the time. Francis got it published a few years ago. I don't have it here, but I'll get the library to put a copy on reserve for you. They also have some of Lee's exhibition catalogs, which I'll reserve. The ones from the Whitney and the Corcoran are good for biographical information."

Strauss made it clear that these secondary sources were not going to be enough; she insisted that Ellen interview the artist. "As Francis would tell you, there's no substitute for first-person testimony," she said. She also recommended additional reading for historical context. "You must be thoroughly familiar with the social and political background. Lee's not patient with people who don't know their stuff."

Ellen had a twinge of misgiving. "I know she has a reputation for being difficult. As a matter of fact, I once witnessed one of her outbursts. Do you think she'll agree to talk to me?"

"Oh, I'm sure she will," Strauss reassured her. "I'll call her first to see if she'll approve, but I know what she'll say. She's always delighted to talk to anyone who's interested in her and doesn't just want to hear about Pollock. By sticking to the thirties, you'll be fine." She grinned and added, "Of course, their paths did cross once during that time. She told me the story herself, when we were discussing the Artists' Union, another group she was active in. They used to picket for more jobs for artists, and once even had a sit-down strike in the art project office. You'll read about it in the memoirs book.

"Anyway, they would get together in somebody's loft, have their business meeting, and then put on some records and dance. Lee was dancing with her boyfriend, and a guy who was clearly not sober cut in, stepped all over her feet, and propositioned her. No small talk, he got right to the point. He asked her, 'Do you like to fuck?' She said he was good-looking, but too rude and crude, so she blew him off. She didn't know his name and didn't want to.

"When they met up again five years later, under very different circumstances, she recognized Jackson Pollock as the jerk at the dance. He'd completely forgotten the incident, and she enjoyed making him squirm by reminding him. But she told me all was forgiven when she saw his work, which she said just bowled her over."

"I certainly won't bring that up, Professor Strauss," said Ellen, "though I do want to know more about the Artists' Union, as well as what it was like to work on the WPA and earn a living wage as an artist. And get paid the same as the men. That's pretty hard to imagine."

Three

At two in the afternoon of September 17, 1979, armed with a cassette tape recorder and a steno pad for backup notes, Ellen had announced herself to the doorman at 180 East 79th Street and was directed to apartment 12-C.

When she wrote to request the interview, she had reminded Krasner of their encounters over the years, so she expected to be met with some recognition. And with Rosemary Strauss as her thesis advisor, she also hoped to be seen as a serious art history student, not merely the daughter-in-law of the New York City police officers who had cleared Krasner's late husband of homicide, or the wife of the private detective who solved the murder of Alfonso Ossorio, Krasner's one-time close friend and confidant.

She had chosen a conservative but fashionable navy-blue worsted pantsuit—the sort of business attire she would wear to meet a client—as appropriate to convey her maturity. Straightening her back and taking a deep breath, she rang the bell.

Presently, the door opened to reveal Krasner, decked out in an unflattering orange velour leisure outfit, with baggy trousers and a loose cowl-neck top that failed to disguise her sagging breasts and belly, and bright red suede slippers with turned-up toes, like the kind sported by Santa's elves.

As she introduced herself, Ellen hoped her face didn't betray her impression. In her youth, Krasner was known for her alluring figure and chic wardrobe. She'd worked as a nude model for art classes, and as a fashion model for illustrators like Ellen, who now wondered whether Krasner, seventy years old and in poor health, had simply given up caring how she looked around the house.

"Well, come in," said Krasner tersely as she turned and led the way down the hall to the sunken living room. "You can hang your coat in the closet on the left." Ellen noticed that the artist's gait was stiff, probably owing to her advancing arthritis, and that she was shorter than she remembered. When they first met in the late 1960s, Krasner had been a couple of inches taller than Ellen, who was five foot three. But now, in her two-inch heels, it was she who was five foot five, while Krasner had lost at least an inch, maybe more.

A parlor suite and coffee table were grouped in front of a functional fireplace, one of the many charming features of the pre-war building. Krasner plopped down in one of the armchairs, reached for the cigarette box on the coffee table, and gestured to Ellen to take the couch.

She wondered if Krasner was going to clam up on her, thinking, *maybe she's having a bad day. Maybe I should ask if we can postpone this,* but then decided to proceed.

"It's very good of you to see me, Miss Krasner," she began. "As I explained in my letter, I want to learn about your early career directly from you. It may seem like ancient history to you, but I think an artist's formative years are fascinating, particularly in your case, since you've revisited them yourself in the collages you made from your Hofmann School drawings." Krasner's 1977 exhibition at Pace Gallery, composed of canvases onto which she'd glued cut-up figure studies done forty years before, had been the latest example of her penchant for cannibalizing earlier work.

As she spoke, Ellen removed the tape recorder from her briefcase and set it on the table, as close to Krasner's chair as she could. "I hope it's all right for me to record our conversation. I want to be sure I'm accurate when I quote you. I'll take notes, too, but my shorthand is terrible," she said, adding an apologetic smile.

Krasner took a drag on her cigarette. "Your letter said you wanted to record, and I have no objection. Let's get on with it."

Guided by Strauss, Ellen had prepared a list of questions, starting with Krasner's family background. They covered her training at The Cooper

Union and the National Academy of Design, her government employment, the artists' organizations in which she was active, why she returned to art school in 1937, and what she was doing during the WPA's decline. It was a long list, and Ellen doubted they'd get through it all in one session, but if she could put Krasner at ease and gain her confidence, she could probably come back again.

She took out her steno pad and pen, reached over and activated the machine, and spoke the preliminaries—the location, date, and purpose of the interview. "Please tell me," she asked, "when you first knew you wanted to be an artist. Was it when you were a child in Brooklyn?"

"It certainly was," Krasner replied emphatically. "My parents had no interest, but my brother Irving encouraged me. He was the oldest of the six and the only boy. I'd be drawing at the kitchen table, copying fashion illustrations from magazines, and he'd admire my little sketches."

Disregarding Strauss's strict instructions to let Krasner do the talking and avoid off-topic conversation, Ellen decided to interject. "I don't think I mentioned it in my letter," she said, "but I'm a fashion illustrator by profession. I trained with Dagmar Freuchen at the Art Students League."

Krasner thawed just a bit. "Really? How interesting. I'm at the League in twenty-eight, only for a month in the summer, taking anatomy with Bridgman. Then I move to the National Academy in the fall. I want more structure, more intensive study. You can't imagine how serious I am!"

"I kind of fell into illustration by accident," said Ellen, "a very happy accident. But let's get back to your story. I understand you went to Washington Irving High School. Why there, and not a high school in Brooklyn?"

* * *

The scheduled hour came and went. As she questioned Krasner about the past, Ellen noted her curious tendency to slip into the present tense, as if she were still in the places and with the people she was describing. Once she warmed up, she held forth in great detail, painting a vivid picture of the

New York City art world during the Great Depression. Having read the books and articles recommended by Strauss, Ellen knew the general history, but Krasner's insider account, complete with incisive character studies of the various players, brought the scene to life for her. This intimate material was going to make her thesis much more than just a dry academic exercise.

As the interview progressed, she became aware that her subject occasionally tried to trip her up, more or less checking to see if she'd done her homework. For example, when Krasner got to the story of her arrest during a rowdy Artists' Union demonstration outside the art project headquarters, she said, "When they're booking us, we all give false names of famous artists. I forget what mine is."

"Wasn't it Mary Cassatt?" said Ellen, recalling the account of the incident in Gerald Monroe's dissertation on the Artists' Union, which she'd gotten, at Strauss' suggestion, from the NYU library. Krasner confirmed that she was right and went on to describe with relish her night in jail, where she met fellow artist Mercedes Carles, who became a close friend. "Mercedes is Rosa Bonheur," she told Ellen with a grin.

When side B of the ninety-minute tape clicked off, they had reached the time of Krasner's study at the Hans Hofmann School of Art, where she learned the principles of Cubism and produced figure drawings and still life paintings according to the master's dictates, which she said took her a while to decipher. "For the first six months, I can't understand a word he's saying. His thick German accent is incomprehensible. The class monitor has to translate for me."

Her evolution from a figurative idiom inspired by Matisse and Cézanne to a more abstract approach was the crux of her development during the decade in question, and Ellen was eager to delve deeply into her motivation, as well as her relationships with the like-minded members of the American Abstract Artists. But she realized that Krasner was tiring and decided to try to make a follow-up appointment.

To her surprise, it was Krasner who suggested that she return another day to get the rest of the story. "I'm sorry to cut you off," she said, "but I have another appointment at four and I need to lie down for a bit. Would you like to come back next Monday at the same time?"

"Yes, of course, if that will be convenient for you," said Ellen gratefully. "I apologize for taking so much of your time, but I've been so fascinated by your story that I'm afraid I didn't realize."

While Ellen packed up her recorder, Krasner rose from the armchair with difficulty, wincing as she took a moment to straighten up. Instinctively, Ellen reached out to help her, but Krasner waved her away. "I can manage," she snapped. "You can find your way out. I'll see you next week."

Four

The following Monday, Ellen arrived back at Krasner's apartment with her recorder, notebook, and a typed transcript of the previous week's interview. Through TJ's connections, she had found a court reporter who moonlighted and was glad to have a diversion from the monotonous legal fare.

This time Krasner, wearing a nondescript schmata as unflattering as the orange velour, greeted her more cordially. "Hello, Ellen. Come on in. I made us some tea."

Stepping down into the living room, Ellen saw a tray with a teapot, cups, and a little dish of lemon slices on the coffee table. "That was very thoughtful, Miss Krasner," she said. "Shall I pour?" She preferred tea with milk and sugar but was happy to drink whatever the artist provided.

Once the tea was served, she offered the transcript to Krasner. "I had last week's tape transcribed so you could review it and make any changes or corrections you like," she told her, hoping it would prove her commitment to accuracy. "I'll leave it with you, and you can take your time looking it over."

But Krasner made no move to accept it. Instead, she said, "Read it to me."

Ellen groaned inwardly. *Good Lord, this will take the whole time. I expected to finish today, but I'll have to come back yet again.* Resigning herself to the situation, she agreed, trying to hide her dismay.

The tedious process went smoothly enough at first. They sailed through Krasner's childhood and early training at Washington Irving—the only New York City high school that offered art classes for girls, which was why she'd gone there—but when they reached her Cooper Union and National Academy days, things quickly bogged down. She had described some of her fellow students in less than flattering terms and was particularly scathing about a few of the hidebound instructors, but now insisted that all those colorful details be deleted.

"I really should be more generous," she told Ellen. "The teachers were very old-fashioned, and we often did not see eye to eye," (*I'll say you didn't,* said Ellen to herself as she dutifully crossed out line after disparaging line) "especially about my enthusiasm for the brand-new Museum of Modern Art, but they did give me solid technical training." Not that those instructors were likely to complain about her opinion of them, since they all were long dead.

What she didn't mention was her realization that many of the students she had belittled were still very much alive and would no doubt resent her judgments if they found out about them. Who knew if Ellen might use some of the interview in an article for one of the art magazines, which those people would read?

She even second-guessed her treatment of her former live-in lover, Igor Pantuhoff, who had drunk himself to death a few years before. Igor had been the Academy's golden boy in the early 1930s, and their ten-year affair had lasted all through the period in question. She had candidly discussed her ambivalence about the relationship, marked by his serial infidelity, but decided that those issues were irrelevant to the topic of her artistic development and demanded that Ellen remove them.

And so it went throughout the hour and beyond. References that might anger her fellow WPA and Artists' Union alumni were also expunged, and with each deletion, Ellen felt the life draining from the narrative. She was sure that, when they finally got around to the Hofmann School and the American Abstract Artists—for which she'd probably have to wait another week—Krasner's account would be more circumspect and therefore much less engaging.

When the marathon revision was done, Ellen sensed that Krasner had run out of steam. The mantle clock said it was nearly half past three, and her tape recorder, with its blank cassette, was still in her briefcase. Once again, she apologized for staying so long and asked if she could return to finish up next Monday. Somewhat wearily, Krasner agreed and remained seated as Ellen packed the eviscerated transcript and let herself out.

* * *

In conference with Professor Strauss, Ellen showed her the document and unloaded her frustration.

"She wouldn't look it over herself, made me read the whole damned thing to her, and insisted I take out all the best parts," she complained. "All the human interest, all the personalities behind the ideas they were debating. I'm going to have to discuss the conflicts in general terms, instead of crediting them to specific people. Even her boyfriend Igor, a really interesting character, turns into just another fellow student tentatively exploring modernism in defiance of the Academy's traditional approach."

Strauss gave her a knowing look. "Can't say I'm surprised. Privately, Lee has no qualms about criticizing her old friends—she does a wicked imitation of the late Harold Rosenberg at his most grandiose—but going on the record is something else again. Still," she added, "you have it all on the tape. Hang onto it."

"I already knew a lot about Igor," said Ellen. "I didn't bring it up, since it wasn't relevant and I didn't want her to get off track, but my husband was the detective who cracked the Ossorio murder case three years ago. My married name is Fitzgerald, as in Sweeney and Fitzgerald, Private Investigations."

"What an amazing coincidence," said Strauss, "though it helps explain Krasner's appeal as your subject." She leaned over the desk, resting her chin on her hands and adopting an expectant look. "Apropos of human interest, I want to hear the inside story."

* * *

On Monday, October first, Ellen returned to the apartment determined to finish the interview and escape within an hour. There were only a few years left to cover, from Krasner's 1937 enrollment in Hans Hofmann's class, to 1940, when, after working as an assistant on other artists' WPA murals, she finally received her own mural assignment.

Once again in the unfortunate orange velour, Krasner actually appeared pleased to see her, and said so as she let her in. "You're very punctual," she remarked as they headed down the hall, "I appreciate that. Many people seem to think I have nothing better to do than to wait around for them."

She had set out the tea tray again, and Ellen poured for them both. Making small talk as she unpacked the recorder, she mentioned that Professor Strauss sent her regards, as well as gratitude for her cooperation.

"I like Rosemary," said Krasner, "a very smart lady. She wrote a perceptive essay about Hans Namuth's photographs of Jackson for a book that was published in France last year. She read it to me before she sent it to be translated. I was quite pleased by her insights."

This was the first time Pollock's name had been mentioned, and Ellen decided to ignore it, unless Krasner brought him up again. But they were already past the time of the Artists' Union dance fiasco, which she had not described, so he was unlikely to make another appearance.

Ellen turned on the recorder. "At the end of our first interview," she began, "you were telling me about your early days studying with Hofmann in Greenwich Village. What made you decide to go back to school after years as a practicing artist? And why Hofmann's in particular?"

As expected, Krasner's reply was far more focused on Hofmann's theories and the school's practical aspects than on the personalities of her fellow students. Even Hofmann's well-known eccentricities were downplayed in favor of his appeal as a transmitter of the modernist principles he had embraced in Paris, where he fraternized with Picasso, Braque, Matisse, and other innovators, and which he had taught at his Munich school before the First World War. Only twice did she display an emotional response to her experiences with him.

First, she said how angry it made her that Hofmann would correct students' drawings by working on them himself, and even tear them up and tape the parts together, to show how the composition or proportions could be improved.

"I couldn't stand that," she fumed. "He had no right to interfere with my work. Yes, I wanted his criticism—that's what I was there for—but not for him to touch what I was doing, much less literally rip it to pieces. That was just too much, and I told him to keep his hands off!"

She had a more nuanced reaction to Hofmann's critique of a still life painting she made after a couple of years of study with him, by which time she had thoroughly absorbed the neo-Cubist approach that was the foundation of his teaching. As she recalled, he examined the picture, turned to the class, and remarked, "Dis ist zo goot, you vout not know it vas done by a voman."

"To Hofmann, this is the highest compliment, but as you can imagine, it lands with a thud on me," she said with feeling. "He has no idea how patronizing it is, and I have to take it as praise. Coming from him, such enthusiasm is rare, so I just smile and thank him while I'm seething inside."

By the time Krasner had finished describing her abortive mural project for the New York City Municipal Broadcasting studio, which was cancelled when the WPA was winding down, the hour had passed, and Ellen had all the material she needed for her thesis. She was glad that this time there had been more emphasis on Krasner's aesthetic motivations, as they illuminated the aims and intentions of a generation of aspiring modernists striving to surpass the School of Paris. That goal wouldn't be achieved until after World War II, but the seeds were sown in the thirties, and it was clear to Ellen that Krasner had played a vital role in that process.

As she put away her recorder and notebook, she thanked the artist for being so generous with her time and so articulate in her responses. "Would you like to have me read a transcript of today's tape?" she asked without enthusiasm, sure that even though Krasner had been much more discreet than before, she would say yes. She was surprised when the reply was negative.

"That won't be necessary," said Krasner. "I think you understand my position. The art comes first, that's what it's all about. Don't you agree?"

"Certainly, Miss Krasner. That was my concern from the start, and you've given me so much in that regard, I can't thank you enough." She hoped she didn't sound obsequious, but she really meant it.

Krasner not only took her gratitude at face value but shocked her by making a proposition that could only have been prompted by an astute assessment of her sincerity.

"How would you like to come work for me? I need someone honest and reliable as a personal assistant. Just one day a week. I had a young woman, also an art history student, working for me for a couple of years, but she got married and moved to the West Coast."

Ellen was astonished. Also, speechless. She stared at Krasner—two blue-eyed women reflecting each other's gaze.

Krasner broke the silence. "How much do you make for a day's work as an illustrator? Whatever it is, that's what I'll pay you."

Hesitantly, Ellen found her voice. "I, um—it depends on the assignment. I usually charge twenty-five dollars an hour. When I need to go to the designer's place or a showroom, or meet with the art director, they give me cab fare."

"How much is that a day?" asked Krasner. "I'm not good at arithmetic."

"An eight-hour day would be two hundred dollars. That's working straight through, but I take a break for lunch, so it's really only seven and a half hours."

"Good grief, Ellen, you don't have to be that honest! I'll pay you two hundred, and you can have an hour off for lunch. How about it?"

"What would you want me to do?"

Krasner rose from her armchair, again with some difficulty but refusing Ellen's help, led her into the bedroom-turned-studio and showed her the closet-turned-office.

"It's mostly correspondence, keeping track of appointments, telephoning, record-keeping, inventory," she explained. "I devote one day a week to the business side of things. I don't need to tell you that being an artist isn't only about creativity. I have to manage my career, and also handle the Pollock estate. I inherited all his remaining work, and for twenty-plus years, I've spent a great deal of time and effort cultivating the market for it. And the sharks are always circling."

Five

March 21, 1986

When the board meeting broke up just before noon, Gerald Dickler's personal assistant asked Ellen to stop in to see the attorney on her way out.

"Mr. Dickler needs your signature on a non-disclosure form," Carla Evans explained as they walked down the hall. "It's just a formality, really. I'm sure he trusts you not to discuss board matters outside the meetings."

From behind them, Charlie interjected, "The only person Gerry trusts is his wife, and then only with looking after their three beautiful daughters."

"I heard that, Charlie," said Dickler, who had stepped into the hall to greet Ellen. "Very unfair, but you're partly right. My daughters are beautiful." With a broad smile illuminating his round face, he led Ellen to a well-upholstered armchair opposite his imposing walnut desk.

"Thank you for agreeing to serve on the authentication board," he began. "I know how invaluable you were to Lee during the last years of her life. She often told me how much she appreciated your help, though I doubt she told you. Gratitude wasn't her style."

"It's true that she didn't often say please and thank you," said Ellen. "She could be impatient if I was slow and would bark at me if I made a mistake, but I didn't resent that. After all, I wasn't a volunteer. She was paying me to do what she needed done, and she had every right to expect it to be done to her liking. And she was often in pain, which would make anyone short-tempered."

Dickler's smile returned, and his shrewd eyes crinkled behind his horn-rimmed glasses. "A very sensible attitude. I was also paid to look out for her interests, and I was often on the receiving end of her outbursts—usually something to do with the perfidy of the art world—but I learned not to take it personally." He leaned back in his chair. "She was a very complex woman, fiercely independent yet terribly needy. Charlie was teasing when he said I don't trust anyone, but that was certainly true of Lee, with two exceptions, Gene Thaw and me. Frankly, she could even sometimes be suspicious of Gene, though she never had cause. As a dealer, he always had that whiff of commerce around him, and she was profoundly cynical about the art market."

He opened a folder on his desk, removed a document, and handed it to Ellen. "As Miss Evans told you, I need you to sign this non-disclosure agreement. Precisely because information about works under authentication board consideration might affect the market, and also might expose the board to litigation, members must agree to keep all deliberations private and confidential."

"I understand completely," said Ellen, taking a pen from the holder on the desk. "Charlie told me it would be required. Let me just read it through before I sign."

"Not only sensible, but smart, just as Lee said you were. I don't suppose she told you that, either."

"Well, not in so many words. I did sometimes overhear her tell someone that I was efficient, or knew what I was doing, even that I was her good right hand. I took those remarks as compliments." She read the form, signed it, and handed it back. "Here you are, Mr. Dickler."

"Please call me Gerry. I'm grateful for your willingness to serve, and I hope those three prima donnas won't give you too much grief. I gather you've already had a taste of Francis' temper. My door was open, and I heard him from here."

* * *

Back at home, busy at her drafting table by the north window that overlooked East 15th Street, Ellen heard TJ's key in the door. Not that he needed a key. He was an expert lock picker, a talent that had helped him solve numerous cases but was never acknowledged in his reports to clients or in court, where evidence so gathered would be inadmissible.

She stood up, stretched, and went to greet him as he removed his coat and hung it on a hook behind the door. The gesture reminded her of the first time they had made love, nearly twenty years ago, after arguing about visiting Andy Warhol's Factory, where TJ, then a budding detective, hoped to find out who killed an artist at the Art Students League. She had wanted to go with him and grabbed her coat off the hook. He said it was no place for a nice girl, which made her see red, and she told him off. When he approached her, she assumed he was going for his coat, but instead he embraced her, and they settled the argument in bed.

The memory made her welcoming kiss extra sweet, and he returned it with equal ardor. "Hey, I like that," he said. "Let's do it again."

"I have a better idea," she suggested, running her hand down the front of his trousers and squeezing gently. "Not just better," he replied, "brilliant."

Half an hour later, having agreed that they were famished, they rose and washed and headed to the kitchen. As he sliced carrots and put them on to simmer and she brushed olive oil on a couple of veal cutlets, he apologized for forgetting to ask how the meeting went.

"You're very thoughtless, but I forgive you," she teased. "You had other things on your mind."

"I certainly did. And it's all your fault, you sexy lady. Still hot after all these years."

"Please don't remind me how many. And you haven't exactly cooled down. It's a good thing I'm on the pill, or this apartment would be crawling with brats."

They had agreed at the outset to wait to start a family until they were both well established in their careers, but even after that had happened—or, more accurately, because it had happened—they kept postponing getting pregnant. Then Ellen enrolled at Hunter College, so the prospect was further delayed, and still further when she went to work for Krasner. While friends their age now had teenage children, they were still childless, and time was running down on Ellen's biological clock, which couldn't be rewound. It would have to be soon or not at all.

Their respective mothers had almost given up hope of a grandchild or two, and since neither Ellen nor TJ had siblings, they were the only hope. But like many couples who were childless by choice, they were reluctant to take responsibility for another life in an already overcrowded world. And they had settled into a loving and companionable relationship. When they talked about it, which wasn't often, they had to admit that they dreaded the disruption, the intrusion, the distraction that caring for children would entail. Naturally, the burden would be borne largely by Ellen, who worked at home most of the time, while TJ worked odd hours at the detective agency and was sometimes away for days on an out-of-town case. Even if, in theory at least, he was willing to share the parenting duties, he'd be unlikely to fulfill that commitment on a fifty-fifty basis. But with just the two of them, he was a more or less equal domestic partner. He had surprised her by taking on the role without her expecting it, which she found both remarkable and endearing.

"Potatoes or rice?" he asked, and she opted for potatoes, which he fetched from the vegetable bin in the fridge and rinsed under the tap. "Fried or mashed?"

"Whichever you prefer," she replied.

"By the way," he said as he heated the frying pan, "how the hell *did* the meeting go?"

Before answering, she mentioned her promise not to divulge the details of the board's deliberations. "I know you understand why I need to take that seriously. Unlike Gerry Dickler, I would trust you not to blab, but I signed a legal agreement to keep board deliberations confidential, so my conscience won't let me tell you about authentication matters."

"I don't care about what's real and what's fake, unless someone hires me to find out if the painting he lost in a divorce is a valuable original or a worthless copy. What I want to know is how you got on with them in your new role. I hope they were respectful."

"The only one who was less than collegial was Bill Lieberman, who seems to regard me as the help. Oh, he's got the background, but also an attitude a yard wide. That said, he had to agree with me, very reluctantly and ungraciously, about a genuine Krasner that was submitted for the CR. I guess there's no harm in telling you about a real one that'll be in the book. Gene Thaw accepted my judgment without question, even before Bill weighed in to confirm it. Of course, I would expect Gene to be sympathetic, since he's the one who hired me to work on the catalogue and invited me to be on the board."

She seasoned the cutlets, slipped them under the broiler, and continued. "Charlie Bergman isn't a voting member, but as the foundation's administrator, he runs the meeting. He's very nice and supportive, and so is Francis O'Connor—supportive, that is, but not so nice. No, I shouldn't say that. It's just that he's volatile. I never heard him talk back to Miss Krasner, but a few times when she contradicted him or gave him a piece of her mind, I could tell he was holding it in. He showed no such restraint in the meeting."

"He'd better not let loose on you, or I'll track him down and knock his block off."

"It was a Pollock matter, so I was on the sidelines. He erupted like a volcano when the other two Pollock experts disagreed with him. Gave me a start, I can tell you."

Six

Tuesday, April 15

Ellen's office in Hall, Dickler's suite on the 20th floor at 460 Park Avenue, was on the building's south side, overlooking 57th Street. Even so, if it hadn't been furnished as the headquarters of the Lee Krasner catalogue raisonné project, she would have found it an excellent place to set up her drafting table. When she first moved in late last year, she had considered asking Gerry Dickler if she could rent a vacant office down the hall for her own use, but decided against it. Even though it was close to her midtown clients, the fact that it was inside a law firm somehow didn't seem appropriate.

From the time she'd begun working as an illustrator, her studio had been in the combination living-dining room of her three-room apartment. It was both convenient and practical, but it meant that she had no privacy, and her materials and work in progress dominated the décor. TJ joked that they didn't live *over* the shop, they lived *in* it. When she fretted about how much her work intruded on their domestic arrangements, he told her not to be silly, it didn't bother him at all, but it bothered her.

On this particularly lovely spring morning, as the daylight flooded the office and she wondered again whether any adjacent space was available, the intercom buzzed, and the receptionist told her that there was a call for her from Dr. O'Connor. She pressed the flashing button on the outside line and was connected.

"Hello, Ellen. Francis O'Connor here. Do you have a moment to chat?" His manner of speaking made him sound a bit like someone doing a music-hall imitation of a minor English public school headmaster, which could be either amusing or intimidating, depending on one's mood. Ellen decided to be amused. She was also pleased to have the opportunity to acknowledge his backing.

"Of course, Dr. O'Connor. But first, I want to thank you for the boost you gave me at the board meeting. I really appreciate what you said."

"Bill Lieberman needs to go to charm school. His arrogance is insupportable. You're just as well qualified as he is—he only has a bachelor's degree, you know—and while he did study briefly with Paul Sachs at Harvard, his real education was acquired on the job at the Modern and the Met. There's no substitute for direct experience of the art, and you have that in your specialty, working for years with the artist herself. Of all people, Bill should respect that."

Ellen was quite touched by his vehemence. "I don't know what to say, Dr. O'Connor, except how grateful I am that you have such faith in my judgment."

"You can say that you'll have a drink with me after you finish today. There's something I'd like to discuss with you, and I'd prefer to do it in person. And you can say that you'll address me as Francis. Are those requests acceptable to you?"

"I'll be glad to accept both requests," she said, thinking, *He can be quite amiable when he wants to. I wonder what he has on his mind.* "Where, and what time, would you like to meet?"

"You're at Fifty-Seventh and Park, so let's meet in the King Cole Bar at the St. Regis. You tell me what time."

"I should finish up by five-thirty. It will only take me a few minutes to walk over."

"I shall be there at half past five, eagerly awaiting your arrival."

His formality brought a smile to her lips. "I won't keep you waiting, Francis."

* * *

The King Cole Bar—a storied oasis where the likes of Ernest Hemingway, Marilyn Monroe, John Lennon, Marlene Dietrich, and Salvador Dalí had often indulged and regularly overindulged—took its name from a Maxfield Parrish mural depicting the merry old soul and his entourage. It had adorned the lounge since 1932, when its installation heralded the repeal of Prohibition.

"I've never been here before, though I've certainly heard about it," said Ellen as Francis escorted her to a table with an excellent view of the painting, which ran the length of the thirty-foot wall behind the bar. "I'm not a fan of Parrish's illustrations. His technique is amazing, but they're too lurid for my taste. This mural is more conventional, and quite delightful."

"I thought you'd appreciate it," said Francis as he held her chair. "I'm researching a book on mural painting in America, and this one has an interesting backstory. John Jacob Astor the Fourth commissioned it in nineteen-oh-six for the bar in his Knickerbocker Hotel. It was moved here after the Knickerbocker closed. Parrish, a teetotal Quaker who disapproved of cocktails, was reluctant to take the job, but he was persuaded when Astor offered him the princely sum of five thousand dollars."

A waiter appeared and took their orders. Ellen asked for a white wine spritzer.

"I shall have a Bloody Mary, the establishment's signature concoction," announced Francis, and resumed his story. "Astor, who fancied himself akin to royalty, insisted on his own likeness, sans moustache, for King Cole's face, and what Astor wanted, Astor got. But Parrish added a twist at his patron's expense. Notice the expressions of the courtiers surrounding the king, who looks not so old—Astor was in his early forties—and less merry than mischievous. The joke is that His Majesty has just rather pungently broken wind."

"Oh, my goodness!" said Ellen, examining the painting with new eyes. "I see what you mean. Do you think Astor knew?"

"Even if he didn't spot the clues himself, no doubt his cronies would have pointed them out to him and had plenty of laughs at his expense. But whatever ribbing he got didn't last long. He died on the *Titanic* in nineteen twelve."

Their drinks arrived, and Francis raised his in a toast. "To you, my dear Ellen, and to the success of the Krasner catalogue raisonné. Not an easy task, but you're up to it."

"I've finished the inventory of what's left in her estate," Ellen told him, "and I think I've located most of the works that were sold, though I'm sure there are some still out there. The biggest problem is identifying things she re-worked or destroyed, and of course, weeding out any fakes that may be submitted. There are bound to be some once the word gets out."

Francis agreed. "Gene says the foundation is planning a big ad campaign in the art press, just as we did for the Pollock catalogue. My own experience tells me it will open the floodgates to spurious claims, but the only way you'll find the missing pieces is through publicity. And the occasional stroke of luck."

He took a bite of celery stalk and continued. "As I told you on the telephone, there's a matter I'd like to discuss. Something has come to my attention that may have serious implications for the Pollock estate, but at present, I'm not prepared to take it up with the foundation. I need more information, that is to say, evidence, before I do."

Ellen sipped her spritzer and asked, "Is it something I can help with?"

"Not you," he replied, "your husband. I understand he's a private investigator. I should like to hire him. How much does he charge?"

Interesting, she mused. *What could be so sensitive that he can't share it with the foundation?* "Well, it depends on what he has to do. You really should ask him directly. He's a partner in Sweeney and Fitzgerald. The office is on West Forty-Ninth."

"Yes, of course, but I don't want to go to his office. I'd be obliged if you would arrange for me to meet him at your apartment."

A concerned look crossed her face. "I'll be glad to set up a meeting with TJ—that's Timothy Juan Fitzgerald—but why not see him at the office? Is there a problem for you if someone finds out that you're talking to a detective?"

"Possibly. Let's just say I prefer to keep my inquiries sub rosa for now. Consulting with Timothy Juan Fitzgerald, a wonderful hybrid name, will help me decide what steps to take."

"He's named after his Irish grandfather on his father's side and his Cuban grandfather on his mother's side. He has his dad's bright red hair and his mom's brown eyes, kind of a striking combination. His partner, Pat Sweeney, who's as nondescript as they come, insists that he wear a hat when he's doing surveillance."

"I look forward to meeting another red-headed Irishman," said Francis, acknowledging his own auburn locks. "Please let me know when it will be convenient for me to call on him."

Seven

Saturday, April 19

"Come in, Francis," said Ellen, "and welcome. I see you navigated the stairway successfully."

Winded from the four-story climb, Francis nodded and caught his breath as Ellen helped him out of his coat. "I'm glad you warned me," he said. "Its precarious condition made me question the wisdom of my request to meet Mr. Fitzgerald at home."

"It's been the same since I moved here twenty years ago," she told him. "Originally, I shared the apartment with a roommate, before I met TJ. We called it the Up 'n' Down—a walkup that's rundown—and the building's condition hasn't improved with age. The models who come up to pose for me are always complaining about the stairs. We keep talking about moving, but the rent's really reasonable and we're used to the place. When it finally does fall down, they'll probably find our bodies in the rubble."

"The landlord keeps promising to renovate," said TJ as he advanced to greet his guest, "but we're not optimistic." He introduced himself and led Francis to a comfortable chair in the combination living room-dining room-studio, where Ellen's drafting table and materials were on prominent display.

Always self-conscious about the confusion of living and working space, Ellen apologized. "I'm sorry it's so cluttered. We have only one bedroom, so I have to work in here."

Francis tut-tutted tolerantly. "Almost all the artists I know live and work in the same room. Several of them are in lofts right down the street on Broadway, in buildings far more rundown than this one. And you have steam heat. Count your blessings, my dear."

"I'm with you, Francis," said TJ. "We looked at a couple of those lofts. All the appeal of the sweatshops they originally were. What can I offer you? Coffee? Tea? Or would you rather have a beer?"

"Coffee, if it's not too much trouble. Or whatever you prefer."

"I'll make it," offered Ellen, "while you two get acquainted. And once it's ready, I'll head out and run some errands. I know that what you want to discuss with TJ is not meant for my ears."

"I appreciate your discretion," said Francis. "If you had not volunteered, I would have suggested that you leave us. When all is eventually revealed, you will understand why."

* * *

"As Ellen has no doubt told you," Francis began when they were alone, "I am in charge of compiling a supplement to the Pollock catalogue raisonné. That work entails not only locating genuine works that have come to light since the original publication eight years ago, but also eliminating counterfeits, of which there are many.

"It is absolutely vital," he insisted, his voice rising, "that no fakes find their way into Pollock's officially documented oeuvre. Not one single entry in the original catalogue has been challenged or refuted, and I shall see to it that the supplement is equally authoritative!" His pride was evident in his tone, as was the intensity of his commitment.

"I can see why that's so important," said TJ, "both for the sake of your reputation and as a purely practical matter. I have only a passing acquaintance with the art market, but it's clear that when the integrity of an artist's legacy is compromised, its monetary value is, too."

"That's not the issue," Francis retorted, as if such a consideration were insulting. "What's at stake is the essence of what makes a work of art *aesthetically* valuable. That has nothing to do with its selling price. And

Gene Thaw, the art dealer par excellence, will support me when I insist that aesthetic value is determined, not by the market, but by connoisseurship, the judgment of the educated eye!" Once again, a fist descended to emphasize his point, but this time it landed quietly on his chair's cushioned arm.

Although prepared to wait patiently for Francis to get to the point of the meeting, this rant caused TJ to wonder whether someone was questioning his qualifications, or perhaps his incorruptibility, and he needed a detective to find out who was after him.

He decided to lay it out. "So what's at stake here, Francis? Is it your reputation?"

The question was received with an incredulous grunt. "Certainly not! On the contrary, my adversaries know all too well that I can't be warned off or bought off. Both have been tried and have failed."

TJ's next question was obvious. "Then why do you want to hire me?"

"To catch a counterfeiter," was Francis' answer, on which he elaborated.

"As soon as the foundation announced the supplement, dealers and collectors started contacting me. Some have documented works that were originally catalogued as unlocated but have since turned up, and a few have pieces that were unknown the first time around. There are, however, a number that fill certain gaps we had identified and published, literally, as blank spaces in the oeuvre. Five of them, all poured paintings from the prime period, nineteen forty-eight to nineteen fifty, have been submitted. The current owners claim to have acquired them in various ways, similar to the plausible stories told by some owners of real ones."

He paused and took a sip of his coffee. "But these are not real ones. They are the work of a very clever forger who has no doubt made a great deal of money selling them to unsuspecting buyers, using the blank spaces to convince them that they have the missing paintings."

Mindful of Francis' keen sense of his own expertise, TJ realized he had to be careful how he phrased his follow-up. "Do you detect a fake by connoisseurship alone, or are there other ways of verifying it?"

"I am confident that my judgment, based on experience and discernment, is correct, but it's important to have as much substantiating evidence as possible. Authentication, the saying goes, is a three-legged stool: connoisseurship, provenance, and technical analysis. If one of the legs is weak or missing, the stool won't stand up. But that rule is not hard and fast.

"For example, a work that has no documentation at all may have been a gift from the artist to a friend, then changed hands, perhaps more than once. But without good provenance, analysis of the materials is extremely valuable for verification. Unfortunately, in the case of the only fill-in-the-blank fake we've been able to test, both the paint and the support—the canvas, that is—are of the period, so the forger was able to obtain the right stuff for the job. He, or possibly she, has clearly done the research."

"Then what convinces you that it's a fake?"

"Like handwriting, Pollock's technique of applying liquid paint created signature forms unique to their author. And like a handwriting expert, I can identify those forms. Even using the same type of paint, applied by the same facture to the same type of canvas, the results are not the same."

He leaned forward for emphasis. "Moreover, because this type of mark-making is so distinctive, I believe all five fakes in question were painted by the same hand, though there are almost certainly one or two others involved in passing them. If you can find the accomplices, they will lead you to the painter."

"That's the kind of work I do," said TJ, "but I don't understand why you personally need to hire me. Isn't this something the foundation should be handling? After all, you're compiling the catalogue under their auspices."

The only answer Francis would give was, "I have my reasons."

* * *

An hour later, after shopping for art supplies at Utrecht on Third Avenue and a fruitful detour to Strand Books on Broadway, Ellen returned home to find Francis gone and TJ washing the coffee mugs.

"Did you two come to an agreement?" she asked.

"Yes, I think so."

"That sounds kind of tentative. Did he have a problem with your fee?"

"No, he was fine with fifty an hour, plus expenses. The problem is that I don't see why he needs me. He could do what he wants me to do, but he wouldn't say what's stopping him, so I don't know what he's up to. What I do know is that there's a lot of money involved."

Eight

Number 5, 1949

Monday, April 21

"Art forgery, huh? That's a new one." Patrick Michael Sweeney fired up a Chesterfield and leaned back in his chair. "Any leads?"

Seated on the other side of his partner's desk, TJ reached into his jacket pocket and fished out a sheet of paper. "O'Connor gave me a list of the five owners, but he thinks they bought the paintings in good faith. My first step is to find out where they got them. Apparently not from any of the art galleries that deal in this sort of stuff. That was the first thing he checked. Then he decided not to pursue it himself, so he hired me."

"How does he know they're phony?"

"He's the number one expert. Says he can tell just by looking at them. But that's only his opinion, which unfortunately isn't backed up by the test results on the materials. They had one analyzed, and it passed."

"They all here in town?"

"Three of 'em are. One's in Chicago, one's in Boston. I'm leaving them for last." He folded the paper and returned it to his pocket. "Tell me something, Pat. Why do you think he wants a private eye on the job?"

"You tell me," said Sweeney. "You got a theory?"

"He's already figured it out, or at least thinks he has, but he doesn't want to be the one to blow the whistle. And he needs evidence he can't get without giving himself away. His colleagues only know about the one they took to the lab—that was the first one that came in. But when others started turning up and he recognized what he calls the artist's hand in them, he smelled a rat."

Sweeney smoked in silence for a few moments, considering the implication. "You said O'Connor told you he's not the only one who decides. They have a committee. Why not leave it up to them? If the others like the fucking things, let the majority rule."

"You can guess the answer to that," said TJ. "Actually, two answers. For one thing, he's stubborn and opinionated, and he's dead certain he's right. No way he'd just go along. But even more important, I think he doesn't trust the others. Maybe they're in on the deal. If the paintings are genuine Pollocks, they're worth plenty, a real treasure trove. Once they're in the catalogue, with the foundation's seal of approval, no one will question them."

* * *

Francis had suggested that TJ pass himself off as an art collector who was in the market for a Pollock. It was not uncommon to bypass the galleries and auction houses, which charged hefty commissions, and approach an owner privately, so it wouldn't raise concerns if he were to contact the people on Francis' list.

He decided to go first to Mr. and Mrs. Peter Stanley, the owners of the canvas that had passed the forensic tests, reasoning that they would be confident the board would accept their painting. The couple lived in one of the venerable residential buildings on Central Park West. Francis had told him that the Stanleys were members of the Museum of Modern Art's contemporary art committee and owned a modest collection that they were actively expanding, hence the purchase of the purported Pollock.

TJ's call found Mrs. Stanley at home. After introducing himself as Timothy Fitzgerald, a fellow collector of modern art, he said, "I understand that you and your husband own a Pollock painting that was missing for many years. What a thrilling discovery!"

Gloria Stanley was a bit wary of this stranger who had telephoned out of the blue. "Where did you hear that?" she wanted to know.

"A friend of mine, a conservator, works for the firm that did the paint test. He knew I was in the market for a Pollock, so he told me one had just turned up. My friend gave it such a buildup that I persuaded him to tell me who owns it." He pretended to be trying but failing to hide his enthusiasm. "Please pardon my calling you like this, but I'd be ever so grateful if you'd let me see the picture, just to satisfy my curiosity. I promise not to take up much of your time." He was hoping his feigned excitement was both flattering and effective.

Like most collectors, Gloria enjoyed displaying her acquisitions, especially when she had snagged something special that other collectors coveted. "Well, I'll have to talk it over with my husband when he comes home this evening," she said. "Where can I reach you tonight?"

TJ thanked her profusely and gave her his home number. "I'll be waiting by the phone. I live just off Gramercy Park," he said, exaggerating slightly, "and I can hop in a cab and be there in twenty minutes."

Gloria giggled. "My, you are eager. I didn't mean to imply you could come right over if Peter agrees. Let's just see what he says and take it from there."

"Of course," he said with an apologetic sigh, "please pardon me again. But I don't have to tell you how exciting it is to find something like this. I'll have my fingers crossed until I hear from you."

Assuring him that she wouldn't keep him waiting any longer than necessary, Gloria ended the call. He hoped he hadn't come on too strong—he was aiming for just the right balance of earnestness and impatience, such as any avid collector might express. He'd laid the groundwork; now all he could do was wait.

The call came at 9:30 p.m., inviting him to cocktails on Wednesday evening. "There will be a few others joining us," said Gloria, "I hope that won't be a problem."

"Certainly not," he assured her, hiding his disappointment. *Smart girl,* he said to himself, *or maybe it was the husband's idea to have witnesses.*

* * *

At seven-thirty on Wednesday, TJ's taxi dropped him at The Brentmore, a vintage 1910 twin-façade pile at the corner of Central Park West and 69th Street. The doorman announced him and directed him to the elevator, where he pressed the button for the tenth floor.

Preparing for his role, he had drawn on his experience growing up amid the art collection of his family's friends, the artist Alfonso Ossorio and his companion Ted Dragon, whose East Hampton estate, The Creeks, had been renowned for its wide-ranging assortment of modern art and all manner of exotic artifacts. Much of it had been disbursed since Ossorio's murder ten years earlier, but it remained vivid in TJ's memory. In case he was questioned more closely about the source of his information, Francis had supplied the names of the company that had tested the painting and one of its employees.

Gloria Stanley greeted him warmly at the door and escorted him into the living room, which faced east overlooking the park, and introduced him to her husband and another couple. With windows on two sides, the room had little hanging space, but there were a few small paintings by twentieth-century abstractionists. Evidently, the prize Pollock was elsewhere.

Peter Stanley invited TJ into the dining room, where a well-stocked bar and trays of hors d'oeuvres occupied a long sideboard. "What are you drinking, Tim? May I call you Tim? If so, please call me Pete," he said affably.

"Thanks, Pete," said TJ, eyeing the collection of bottles. "I'll have a glass of the La Lagune, please. I'm not partial to spirits."

As Pete poured the red wine and refreshed his own scotch and soda, TJ took in a few more examples from the Stanley collection. A row of Sunset screen prints by Andy Warhol hung on the west wall over the sideboard, and a large, exuberant Norman Bluhm canvas from 1973 occupied the wall facing the windows.

"I admire your arrangement," said TJ as he took the wineglass from his host. "Sunrise in the front room and sunset in the back. I'm sure that's quite deliberate."

Pete raised his glass. "You're very perceptive, Tim. I'll show you some of our other treasures—one, in particular, will have special interest for you—but you must tell us about your collection. Wait, I hear the doorbell. I believe the Millers have arrived."

Another couple came in and were introduced, taken to the bar, and served drinks. Meanwhile, the others had gravitated to the dining room. Rather than wait to be quizzed, TJ decided to take the initiative.

"Your Bluhm is a beauty," he began. "Norman really came into his own in the early seventies, and this is a prime example. I have an acrylic on paper from the sixties, got it directly from him. I try to avoid the dealers, and I hate bidding at auction. I'd much rather go right to the source." What he was actually describing was a 1964 piece that had belonged to Ossorio. And this deception gave him an excuse to establish his aversion to the orthodox art market.

"So you know Bluhm?" asked Gloria.

"Not well, but I met him socially and visited his studio a couple of times. He used to have a place in East Hampton, near where my family and I summered for many years." That was the truth; Ossorio had taken the Fitzgeralds there.

He turned to the wall of Warhols. "Have you been out to Eothen, Andy's place in Montauk? That's where he got the idea for the sunsets. Even though the property faces the ocean on the south, you get a panoramic view east to west from the bluff." Again, it had been Ossorio who took TJ and his family to meet the artist at his seaside compound, dubbed "from the east" in Greek.

His blatant name-dropping was having the desired effect on his audience. *Careful,* he told himself, *better not lay it on too thick. Maybe one more for good measure, then back off.*

"I think I spotted a Krasner in the living room. Am I right?"

Pete smiled and nodded. "Yes, one of our more recent acquisitions." The party moved into the front room, where a Little Image painting from the 1940s hung over the fireplace.

"Wonderful, a real gem," TJ gushed. Here he was on very firm ground. "This is from Lee's breakthrough series, her first all-over abstractions, done right after they moved to East Hampton. She was quite proud of them."

"Good grief," said Pete, "did you know her, too?"

"She's another of the artists I used to see out there," he replied truthfully, omitting his wife's more intimate connection. "A real character, not easy to get along with. But she took a shine to me and let me buy one of her collages, from the group she did in the early fifties. That was another turning point for her." The 1953 collage in question had belonged to Ted Dragon and was indeed acquired directly from Krasner's studio.

"Don't tell me you also knew her husband," said the man he'd been introduced to as Fred Miller. The note of skepticism in his voice warned TJ not to embellish his answer.

"Well, no, not exactly. That's to say, I never met him, but I was there when he died. My parents and I witnessed his fatal car crash in fifty-six. I was eight years old."

Six jaws dropped simultaneously. Now they were hooked, but good.

"Speaking of Pollock…" TJ let the sentence hang.

"Come with me," said Pete, pushing open the double doors to an adjoining room. It was furnished as a library, with comfortable armchairs and floor-to-ceiling bookshelves on the walls with windows and doors. Along the only unbroken wall was a low cabinet, over which hung a single painting.

It was not terribly large, perhaps three by four feet, TJ guessed, but it had all the earmarks of a classic Pollock drip painting—or, more correctly, a poured painting, the descriptor Francis preferred. To him, and to Krasner as well, "drip" sounded arbitrary, while "poured" connoted deliberation. It was also the term Ossorio had favored, and TJ was inclined to follow his lead.

The Stanleys stood back and let their guests take their time with the painting. It was a few moments before anyone spoke. TJ had decided not to be the first, wanting to see how the others reacted.

Miller broke the silence. Turning to the Stanleys, he said, "I owe you a dinner at Lutèce. I bet you wouldn't be able to get a Pollock, and I lost. Congratulations!"

Gloria was grinning like a funhouse poster, and Pete looked equally pleased with himself. "Not just any Pollock, Fred. One that's been missing for years, and we found it." He went to one of the library shelves and pulled out a large volume bound in beige Buckram. He opened it to a bookmarked page and laid it on the cabinet under the painting.

"This is volume two of the complete catalogue of Pollock's work," he explained. Everyone gathered as he pointed to a blank rectangle on the left-hand page. "*Number Five, Nineteen Forty-Nine.* The folks who compiled the catalogue knew it was out there, but they couldn't find it, so they left room for it. And here it is, on our wall."

Suddenly, everyone was talking at once. Words like astonishing, fantastic, incredible, and amazing were tripping over one another, Gloria was embraced and kissed, Pete's hand was pumped, and toasts were proposed.

True to his persona as a collector who coveted such a painting, TJ posed the question that was on everyone's mind. "Where on earth did you find it? I've been hunting for something like this for months—make that years. I've hounded the dealers, even though it's against my religion, and I know it didn't come up at auction, or I would have held my nose and bid on it."

Pete raised his hand in an apologetic gesture. "Sorry, Tim, but that information's confidential. What I will tell you is that I wasn't strictly accurate when I said we found it. Really, it found us."

Nine

"Well, I've laid the groundwork," TJ told Ellen. He was back home by nine, and she had dinner waiting. As they ate, he described the cocktail party and the guests' reactions to the painting.

"No one questioned its authenticity, but why would they? First of all, it looks very convincing. It's not all that colorful, mostly black, white, and silver, which fits with others of the period, and the material is obviously enamel paint, applied with the kind of sweeping gestures you think of as typically Pollock's. Second of all, the idea of it filling a gap in the catalogue is really plausible. Pete Stanley showed us the book with the missing entry. Pretty persuasive."

"Any idea how much they paid for it?" asked Ellen.

"No, but Francis thinks if a real one that size were on the market, it wouldn't go for less than a quarter of a million, probably more. It's from the most desirable period, there's nothing like it left in the estate, and there hasn't been anything comparable at auction in quite a while, so they're very scarce."

Ellen frowned and took a sip of red wine—a Chianti several notches below the Bordeaux TJ had been served at the Stanleys'. "Based on my first and only experience with the authentication board, I have to ask why they didn't take the painting to the experts before they bought it. There was just such a case, which of course I can't discuss, at the meeting. The owner bought it in good faith, but the board is doubtful." She didn't mention that it was only Francis who had rejected it.

"That would have been the prudent approach," said TJ. "I can't imagine that the Stanleys didn't know about the foundation and the board beforehand. After all, they're involved with the Modern, so they're hardly naïve."

Then he had a thought. "I wonder.… Maybe they don't own it. Maybe they have it on approval, pending authentication."

Ellen scoffed at that notion. "You'd have to be a pretty brazen forger to take that risk. Okay, so you paint a picture that looks like a Pollock to most people, you use the right materials, and you make up a believable background story. That could work if there's no formal authentication process. But in this case, there is. Suppose, in spite of the evidence in its favor, the experts don't like it? For liability reasons, they wouldn't call it bogus, they'd just decline to put it in the catalogue, and there goes your sale."

"Point taken," said TJ, "though, by your reasoning, you'd have to be a pretty daring collector to risk buying an unauthenticated Pollock."

"But the seller could argue that it *has* been authenticated," she countered. "It's documented in the original catalogue. *Number Five, Nineteen Forty-Nine.*"

* * *

TJ phoned Francis on Thursday morning to make his report and outline his plan. The call was picked up by an answering machine:

"You have reached Dr. Francis O'Connor and Raphael Research. You may leave a message after you hear the little chime."

TJ identified himself and started to ask for a return call when Francis picked up.

"Hello, TJ. I take it you have news for me. Please pardon the automated response. I always monitor my calls."

TJ wondered if that was his standard procedure, or if he'd started screening callers after the fakes began appearing—maybe another sign of his desire to distance himself from the investigation. Either way, it was a small but telling aspect of Francis' personal protectiveness that TJ would have to work around.

"An understandable caution, Francis," he said. "It's good to know who's on the line before you answer."

"I'm glad you appreciate that," said Francis. "Did you see the Stanley picture?"

TJ filled him in on the previous night's visit.

"When I call Gloria Stanley to thank her for inviting me to see the painting, I'll tell her how envious I am and try to persuade her to let me in on the source, in case there's another one available. I'm sure they believed my story, so they won't be surprised when I try to find out more about where they got it."

"They'd probably be suspicious if you didn't," said Francis. His long history of working with both Krasner and Thaw had given him a fine appreciation of the way collectors' minds worked, often with the complexity of a Swiss watch. "As a matter of fact, her reply may give you the answer to whether or not they own it. If they do, she might be willing to steer you in the right direction. If not, she'll be afraid you'd outbid them, and you won't get anywhere."

"According to your notes," said TJ, "the paperwork that came with it said only that it had been in private hands for decades, but no indication how it got there, or how the Stanleys found out about it. Pete Stanley said something enigmatic about its having found them. I have no idea what he meant by that."

"One of two things, I think," said Francis. "Either they had a chance meeting with the owner or owners, maybe went to their home and saw it, recognized it, and induced them to sell it—those things happen, you know— or more likely they were approached by the purported owner's agent who knew they were in the market. From what you tell me of the rest of their collection, they're mid-level collectors aiming higher, shooting for the big time."

Francis was warming to his speculations. "It could be a combination of the two, and this scenario works for the other related fakes, too. An accomplice pretends to be an elderly eccentric who's a bit gaga, and the agent takes Stanley to meet him. The old crock babbles on about how he used to drink with Jack and Bill and Franz and their pals, how he bought their stuff when no one else was interested, just for beer money, when the dealers' backs were turned. The agent explains that the fellow has to go into a home, so everything is being liquidated. He's afraid that if his relatives find out what he has, they'll want a cut, so it's being done quietly.

"By now, Stanley is salivating. Yes, says the agent, there's a Pollock available, quite a nice one, and well documented before it went missing forty-five years ago. The old crock could probably get a bundle for it if he sent it to auction, but his family would descend like locusts, so he's willing to cut a deal."

"I can see how seductive that would be," said TJ, "but why only the Pollock? If this guy has de Kooning, Kline, and others, too, why not go for them as well? Get all the high cards in the deck?"

"I understand you have a degree in forensic psychology," said Francis, with a slightly peeved tone that brought Brooklyn out of hiding, "so use your noodle! They don't have any fake de Koonings or Klines. That's just part of the yarn to make it more believable. As far as we know, they're only forging Pollocks, though frankly that remains to be seen. Suppose Stanley did ask about the others. He'd be told they're already spoken for."

"You're right, Francis, I should have thought of that. It's the same with any con game, always leave 'em wanting more. If they pull it off with Pollock, they can always try again later with Kline, and say the deal didn't go through."

"They may be doing that now, with other marks, for all we know, though I have my reasons for doubting it. De Kooning is still alive, if not fully compos mentis, and his wife and lawyers are quite vigilant, so he might be too risky. Kline is another story. He's been dead for twenty-five years, there's no catalogue, and none in the works. Believe me, there are a lot of fake Klines out there already—almost as many as there are fake Pollocks. Nevertheless, I shall ensure that Pollock's legacy is rigorously protected."

To TJ's ears, the authentication board notwithstanding, Francis Valentine O'Connor, Ph.D., considered himself to be a one-man bulwark against the ongoing attack on the oeuvre's integrity. But his comments on the vulnerability of artists' estates raised a question.

"I understand what you say about de Kooning being too risky, but isn't that true for Pollock as well? Okay, he's safely dead, and so is his wife, but the foundation is a pretty formidable watchdog—thanks to you," he added diplomatically. "Surely that's a strong deterrent."

"Yes," replied Francis, "but there are also strong incentives. The money, for one, though I don't believe that's the primary motive here."

"Then what is the motive?"

"Revenge."

Ten

I n roughly twenty years of dealing with the Pollock estate—first as a doctoral student working on his dissertation, then compiling the chronology for the first major Pollock retrospective, held at the Museum of Modern Art in 1967, which led to the formation of the original authentication committee, and now serving on its successor—Francis had seen scores of purported Pollocks that turned out not to be genuine. They fell into three basic categories: copies of known works; works mistakenly believed to be by Pollock because they looked similar to his; and works made deliberately to deceive.

The copies were relatively easy to detect and dismiss. The mistakes were more problematic, since some of them were done during Pollock's lifetime using his technique, so the dating was correct. But false signatures were often added later, and the provenances tended to be sketchy, clear indications that the paintings weren't as advertised.

Where actual forgeries were concerned, they were usually accompanied by fake documentation and sometimes even genuine exhibition and publication histories. They might be exposed by checking the phony letters, bills of sale, and testimonials, or by materials analysis, but Francis insisted that connoisseurship was the first and most important line of defense.

In his long experience, however, fakes had always appeared singly. An auction house would approach the committee for verification of a piece they wanted to offer for sale. A dealer would submit something he or she had taken on consignment or bought from an estate. Someone cleaning out a deceased relative's house would find one and hope for a bonanza. Yard sales, flea markets, and thrift shops were also sources of such finds. Or, as was the case with the disputed painting on paper by Gene Thaw's client, collectors who had what they assumed were real but overlooked ones would submit them for publication.

Francis' internal red flag went up immediately when he saw the photograph of the Stanleys' painting; he just didn't like the look of it. But Gene and Bill had been inclined to accept it, so he had recommended the testing, if the owners approved. They were very much in favor, agreed to pay the $500 cost, and were delighted when it turned out to be money well spent. Francis had demurred, still sure that his eye hadn't failed him, and asked to postpone the final vote pending provenance research—a reasonable request that the others had okayed.

Then another one turned up, with a similar story attached: it filled one of the catalogue's blank spaces. A third one soon followed, then a fourth and a fifth, and Francis' red flag turned into an alarm bell. It wasn't so much that the coincidence was improbable—after all, the whole point of creating a supplement was to locate pieces that were missed the first time around—but that he was sure all five had been painted by the same person. Of course, that was to be expected if the person was Pollock. But he was also sure it wasn't.

"You must understand," he told TJ, "that my reasoning is more than mere speculation. But I need proof, or if not, then enough evidence to prompt a formal investigation, preferably by the police, that will expose the scheme. I have chosen to seek professional help because it seems the best way to succeed. I am the foremost authority on Pollock, but as a detective, I would be a rank amateur."

"All right, I see that," said TJ, "but I could use more to go on. You say the motive is revenge, not money. What makes you think that?"

For a few moments, there was silence on the other end of the line. "I should not have said that so decisively. It is a guess on my part, but I'm confident I'm right. When you get closer to what I believe is the source, you'll understand."

TJ was finding his client's evasiveness tiresome. "Dammit, Francis, why don't you let me in on where you think this will lead? Give me more to go on if you have it. That could save me a lot of time and you a lot of money."

Again, there was hesitation. "It is just possible…" another pause, "that I am wrong, so I do not want to prejudice your investigation."

Boy, that was hard for him to admit, thought TJ, *and he has a point. If his suspicion isn't justified, I could go down a blind alley.*

"But I will tell you this," Francis continued, "not only are all five paintings the work of the same person, but they were all painted at the same time, right after the catalogue was published."

"Why wait until now to sell them?"

"Because now Lee Krasner is dead."

* * *

After finishing his conversation with Francis, TJ made his courtesy call to the Stanleys.

"Hello, Gloria, it's Tim Fitzgerald. I can't thank you enough for yesterday evening. You have a beautiful view of the East Side and the park, your friends are delightful, and the wine was excellent."

"Is that all you enjoyed?" she asked coyly.

"Did I forget to mention your collection? Well, that goes without saying," he teased. "Seriously, Gloria, I'm deeply impressed by what you and Pete have put together. I'm sure the Modern's trustees are hoping you'll remember the museum in your will." He skipped a couple of beats to let his flattery sink in, then added the twist. "But, just between us, one of your paintings disappointed me."

"No, really? You seemed so enthusiastic about everything. What was it?"

"The Pollock."

"The Pollock?" she gasped, her dismay audible.

"Yes, the Pollock. I'm deeply disappointed that it's on your wall and not mine."

"Oh, Tim, you are a naughty boy! You had me going for a moment. But I guess I can't blame you for being envious. Maybe we shouldn't have let you see it after all."

"I'm very grateful that you did. It gives me hope that I'll get as lucky as you. By the way, you wouldn't consider letting me make an offer, would you?"

Gloria pretended to be surprised, though she was expecting that. "Absolutely not! We wouldn't think of parting with it."

TJ bluffed, certain he wouldn't be called. "If you tell me what you paid, I'll double it."

"Not even tempting, Tim. We'd never replace it, even for twice what we paid."

"Then perhaps you'll take pity on a poor, bereft soul and tell me where you got it. Maybe there's more where that came from."

"I very much doubt it. But I don't suppose there's any harm in telling you, if you promise to keep it to yourself." TJ untruthfully assured her that it would go no further.

"Peter was approached by an attorney acting for the estate of an artist who was a friend of Pollock's back in the old days. His name was Joseph Meert, the artist, that is. I'm sure you've never heard of him, and neither had we. To make a long story short, Meert once saved Pollock's life, and this painting was his reward. Later he dropped out of the art world, moved upstate to Cragsmoor, and died a couple of years ago, leaving everything to an animal shelter. The attorney, a friend of Meert's, was helping to liquidate the estate."

"Why didn't he take it to a gallery, or sell it at auction?"

"You're a fine one to ask that. Like you, he's skeptical of the art market, and he didn't want to pay the commission. He thought a private sale would be quicker and cleaner, and we were happy to oblige, since it was obvious why the painting hadn't been seen in decades."

The story sounded pretty good so far, though TJ wondered if there really had been a friend named Joseph Meert. That could easily be checked, and he assumed the Stanleys had done so. But how had the attorney made the connection?

"How did the lawyer know you were looking for a Pollock?"

"That's the really interesting part," said Gloria, eager to share the remarkable coincidence that had led to their purchase. "His practice is in New Paltz, and we have a weekend place there. We love the Hudson Valley, so much more relaxed and unpretentious than the Hamptons. Anyway, the local state university campus has an art gallery that they're hoping to expand into a proper museum, and they've been courting us to get involved. So we loaned them a few things, and at the opening reception, we happened to mention that we were looking for a Pollock. Somehow, that always seems to come up whenever we're asked about our collection—at least it did until now—and the lawyer was there and overheard us. The next day he gave Peter a call, and here we are."

"Why couldn't something like that happen to me?" TJ lamented.

Gloria was sympathetic. "Maybe it will, Tim. After all, it really was just luck. Like Peter said, we didn't find the painting, it found us. If you keep putting the word out, one may find you, too."

"Thank you again for your hospitality, Gloria. Please pass along my gratitude to Pete. If you change your mind about selling, you have my number. Then I'll be the luckiest man in New York."

Eleven

"You've done an excellent job learning the cover story," said Francis, once again on the line with TJ, who had repeated Gloria's account virtually word for word. "This placement has been very carefully engineered."

He gave TJ the background. "Meert met Pollock at the Art Students League in the early nineteen thirties, and they remained friends for the rest of Pollock's life. He lived on Cooper Square, I think—anyway, very near Pollock's old apartment on East Eighth Street. After Pollock moved to Long Island, he would sometimes stay with Meert and his wife Margaret when he came to town.

"One winter night, after hours of drinking at the Cedar Tavern on University Place, Pollock headed for Meert's but collapsed in a pile of snow in front of the building. He would have died of exposure if Meert hadn't looked out the window, spotted him, dragged him inside, and warmed him up. Another artist who lived in the building told me the story. So he really did save Pollock's life, but there was no mention of a thank-you gift.

"I don't remember if we contacted Meert in the seventies. He must have moved upstate by then. We tried to get in touch with all Pollock's old friends who were still alive, and a few of them did have early sketches and things from their WPA days, as well as holiday cards and some interesting correspondence, but nothing major turned up. I'll have to check the files to see if we wrote to him. If we did, and he replied, he would have told us he had a missing Pollock."

"Are you sure about that?" asked TJ. "It's only his word that Pollock gave him the picture. Suppose Krasner claims he stole it? Or finagled it out of him when he was drunk? She's got a high-powered New York lawyer and he's got some hick in New Paltz, so how's that gonna work out for him?"

"You're quite right, that could have been Meert's thinking. He would not have been able to sell it while Lee was alive, so better to keep it hidden. Then she dies, and before he can sell it, he dies, too. But, as you know, it's my belief that it's not a Pollock. The question is, could it be a Meert? That would be the natural conclusion. Meert's admiration for Pollock's remarkable achievement might have prompted him to experiment with the pouring technique. But if he exhibited such work, he'd be accused of simply imitating Pollock, so he never showed it to anyone. It only came to light after he died." He paused. "But that's not the answer."

"Why not?"

"For one thing, using Pollock's technique doesn't guarantee the result will look like a Pollock painting. Anyone can pour house paint and come up with something distinctively his own. I've seen plenty of examples. Also, Meert had too much respect for Pollock literally to copy him. Moreover, I think if he had tried, he would have failed. The painting in question is an outright forgery, not an homage or a technical experiment. The person who painted it intended it to be accepted as a Pollock."

Francis was satisfied with his own reasoning. "No, I don't think it was Meert. But whoever it was knew exactly how to position it. What Mrs. Stanley thinks was an amazing coincidence was anything but. Which leads me to ask who would know enough to pull off such a scheme. And what of the other four paintings? Do they all have such elaborate, and entirely plausible, hidden histories?"

TJ had the list in front of him. "Any idea who I should hit next? There are two more with city addresses, and the two out of town. Have you checked any of their stories?"

"I told you I've eliminated the dealers. None of the galleries that handle modern paintings on the secondary market have seen any of them. I contacted those in Chicago and Boston as well, a much smaller pool, but also with negative results. That's as far as I've gone. As I explained when I hired you, I don't want to take it further myself."

Still in the dark about the reasoning behind Francis' tactics, TJ tried to draw him out. "But isn't it your job to research the provenance? Surely the owners would expect you to be making detailed inquiries as a natural part of the authentication process."

"Under normal circumstances, yes. But this is not normal. The mastermind behind this scheme has exploited a loophole in the original catalogue, something that, frankly, I should have anticipated. I blame myself for not foreseeing that this could happen, but even in retrospect, it seems far-fetched."

TJ could hear the frustration in Francis' voice and appreciated his dilemma. By leaving spaces to be filled, he had believed he was diligently recording known but unlocated works. They appeared on inventories or exhibition checklists but couldn't be found. They might have been destroyed or repainted, or they might be out in the world waiting to be rediscovered. In fact, several missing pieces had turned up over the years—including some of Pollock's WPA canvases that had disappeared from public buildings or were sold for scrap when the project closed down—but they had been photographed when they were new, so they were reproduced in the catalogue.

When there was no photo, however, the entry was a blank. By doing that, Francis had left the door open for the lost works, but also for fakes tailored to fit the bill.

"Far-fetched in what way?" asked TJ. "Surely the reason to do the supplement is to find the missing pieces."

Francis was becoming testy. "My dear boy, there are *five* of them, all from the most desirable period. That would be a wonderful outcome if it weren't for the fact that Pollock didn't paint them! And may I remind you, all are the work of one artist, who happens *not* to be Pollock. You must understand how the process works. Many fakes have been submitted to us, but they do not come in groups. Mind you, these have been cleverly salted in various collections, not submitted by a single individual, but when they are compared, it's obvious to an expert that they are related."

"It's obvious to you, but how about the other experts? Ellen says you and the other two don't always agree. Is that the case here?"

Another uncomfortable silence. "The others have only seen the Stanley picture. I have held back the rest."

* * *

TJ's next call was to the New York Public Library's information desk, requesting a list of attorneys in New Paltz, New York. There were three law offices listed in the Ulster County Yellow Pages, and he took down the numbers. He dialed the first on the list and was told that the firm specialized in criminal law and the late Joseph Meert had not been a client. So he tried the second number.

"John G. Sisti, Esquire. How may we help you?" said the female voice on the other end of the line. TJ identified himself, falsely, as an agent for the late Joseph Meert's family, asked to speak to Mr. Sisti. The secretary asked him to hold, so he assumed he had the right attorney. A few moments later, he was connected.

"I understand you are acting on behalf of the Joseph Meert estate," said TJ.

"What is your interest?" was Sisti's reply.

"My client has only just learned of Mr. Meert's death and would like to know the terms of the will," TJ explained.

"The document is on file at the county clerk's office in Kingston," Sisti told him. "You may consult it there." He wasn't going to discuss the details over the phone with a total stranger. TJ decided to try a more straightforward approach.

"I appreciate your discretion, but I hope you'll answer one question. I know that Mr. Meert was a close friend of the artist Jackson Pollock. Was a Pollock painting found among Mr. Meert's effects?"

Sisti snorted derisively. "I get it. Joe's family disowned him when he decided to become an artist, but now that they think he had something valuable they want a piece of it. Well, you can tell them not to bother. There was no Pollock, and if there had been, the proceeds from its sale would have gone to the Ulster County SPCA. That's the beneficiary of his will, which I wrote, so I know it will hold up if any of his people try to contest it."

"The reason I ask, and the reason I was hired," TJ told him, "is that a Pollock painting recently turned up with a provenance of Meert's estate, reportedly a gift to him from Pollock. I'm sure you understand why my client would want inquiries to be made." That part, though evasive, was true.

"I can assure you, Mr. Fitzgerald, that there is no such painting on the inventory, which I myself made, of the art in Joe's collection. All of it is his own work, with very little market value. I'm afraid the SPCA won't be getting a windfall from him."

"I'm disappointed, but not surprised," said TJ. "I had a feeling that the story wasn't true, and I thank you for confirming my suspicion. Would you mind answering one more question?"

"Depends what it is."

"How many partners are in your firm?"

"You're talking to all of them."

Twelve

Number 23, 1950

Back on the phone with Francis, TJ reported his conversation with the attorney. "So, apparently, someone impersonating Sisti offered the painting to the Stanleys. How hard would it be to pull that off?"

"Not hard at all, I should think," said Francis. "Print up a fake business card, put the painting in storage in Manhattan, so they never have to visit the New Paltz office, tell them the very believable tale, show them the catalogue, and quote a bargain price, though not so low that they get suspicious. Even sophisticated collectors could fall for it, and evidently did."

"What about the others? Who should I hit next?"

"The second one to contact me is an elderly gentleman who lives in Greenwich Village. He's one of those types who scour the antique shops and second-hand stores looking for hidden treasures, and by his account, he's found some over the years. He says he bought the painting from the Salvation Army thrift store on West Eighth Street. It's supposed to be *Number Twenty-Three, Nineteen Fifty*, a small but classic work that's been missing for thirty-five years. Of course, it isn't *Number Twenty-Three, Nineteen Fifty*, but that's the story."

"If it was just lying around the thrift store," said TJ, "how could the forger be sure that someone who knew about the catalogue would buy it? Anybody who fancied a drippy abstract picture could have picked it up. And if he bought it from Sally's, whoever planted it there got nothing for it."

"Yes, it would have had to have been a donation, so this time it wasn't about the money. As I told you, I don't think financial gain is the primary reason these fakes are appearing. But it's also possible that this packrat owner, whose name is Richard Wagner, is part of the scheme. I think you should check on him next."

* * *

After ringing the bell of the basement apartment at 113 Washington Place, TJ could hear the yapping of a small dog. When he had called Wagner to ask for an appointment, he'd been warned that Magpie, who turned out to be a terrier of dubious pedigree, would greet him enthusiastically. "He's a collector, just like me," said his owner with a raspy chuckle that signaled a pack-a-day habit.

As promised, Magpie gave TJ a hearty welcome, while his owner unsuccessfully admonished him to get down and shut up. Wagner, whom TJ had expected to resemble a character out of Dickens but turned out to look remarkably normal, like the retired postal clerk he was, then escorted him into an apartment that smelled of tobacco, with undertones of dog urine.

The front parlor was overflowing with furniture of all periods, in states of repair that ran the gamut from functional to decrepit, heaped with an equally eclectic mixture of ceramic, glass, and silver housewares. One wall boasted an ornate floor-to-ceiling bookcase housing a random assortment of publications, small sculptures, and art pottery. Paintings and works on paper, mostly abstract, covered every inch of the remaining wall space, and a few pieces of statuary stood guard over them. Odd shoes, dismembered dolls, and other evidence of Magpie's personal collection littered the floor.

Proudly showing off his acquisitions, Wagner took TJ on a tour of the other rooms, which were equally chock-a-block. His living quarters could well have been his own private jumble shop, given the amount and variety of his holdings. But it was unlikely that anything in this hoarder's paradise would be for sale until his estate was auctioned off after his death.

Returning to the front parlor, Wagner offered his guest a seat. "Take any chair you like," he said, though none of them were vacant. TJ gingerly removed a toppling pile of magazines from a threadbare armchair and sat, while his host took similar action to clear a Regency carver detached from a long-defunct dining set.

Wagner got straight to the point. "You're here about the Pollock, you said."

"As I told you on the phone," replied TJ, "I've been hired to research the provenance of your painting." He had decided on a more straightforward approach than he'd used on the Stanleys, but without revealing his client's identity, though he figured Wagner would assume it was the foundation.

"You mean where I got it? I told that O'Connor fella I bought it at the Salvation Army, the one around the corner on Eighth. I have a standing order with the management to let me know when something interesting comes in, and soon as they got it, they called me. They didn't know what it was, 'cause it isn't signed or anything, but it's splashy and colorful, just the kind of thing I'd go for."

"That's not what I meant," said TJ. "I'm trying to establish its history from before you bought it. When was that, by the way?"

"I guess I've had it for about a year. Must have been last spring. Paid twenty bucks for it. I probably have the receipt somewhere." Since Wagner appeared never to throw anything away, TJ thought it likely that he could lay his hands on it, if necessary, but for the time being, he was more interested in the artwork itself.

"Would you mind showing me the painting?"

"It's in the back. Follow me." With Magpie at his heels, Wagner led the way through the dining room to a room at the rear of the building, where a door led to a long, narrow garden, bordered by St. Joseph's Academy on one side and a six-story residential building on the other.

In the back parlor, several framed paintings were stacked against one wall, which was already filled with pictures. "I ought to start thinking about thinning out the collection," said Wagner wistfully. "Either that or get a bigger apartment." To TJ, it was already quite large. If it hadn't been in the basement, he'd have considered it perfect for Ellen's studio and their domestic needs.

Leafing through the stack, Wagner removed a painting about a foot square, with a simple wood frame typical of the 1950s. Like many Pollocks of the period, it was composed of interlacing layers of fluid enamel paint on a solid background, in this case a dark red, which enhanced the vibrancy of the black, white, green, and silver overlay. He handed the painting to TJ.

Other than the Pollock-style abstract imagery and technique, there was nothing to identify it, so TJ turned it over to examine the back. He saw that instead of canvas, the support was Masonite, a pressed-wood material that Pollock was known to use. And not just Masonite, but a board printed with a green and white baseball diamond design. It was mounted on one-by-twos, to which the frame and hanging hardware were attached. Stuck to the mount was a label from the Betty Parsons Gallery.

"Did you send in a photograph of the reverse?" he asked Wagner, who replied no, he had sent only a color picture of the front. "I saw the back didn't have a signature or date, just the gallery label, which I mentioned in my letter, so I didn't bother."

"What do you make of the baseball design? I've never seen anything like it."

"I figured it was a game that Pollock got tired of playing with and decided to recycle. From what I read in the biography that came out last year, he and his wife were very frugal. Never threw away anything they could re-use. Folks after my own heart."

"Would you mind if I took photos of it?"

"Go right ahead. Take it out back where you have good light." He opened the garden door, through which Magpie made a beeline for the little ginkgo tree in the far corner.

While Magpie relieved himself, TJ took the painting out and propped it against the wall. His Canon 110 Subminiature camera was loaded with color film. He photographed the front and the back, as well as details of the framing, mounting, and label. As he returned the painting to Wagner, he asked, "How did you know to send the photo to O'Connor?"

"I read about the new catalogue in *Art News*. There was a blurb in the January issue, and it gave his name as the one to contact, in care of the foundation." Judging by Wagner's extensive magazine collection, that was entirely plausible. It seemed to TJ that, like the Stanleys, Wagner was an unwitting conduit, not in on the forgery scheme.

"I appreciate your taking the time, Mr. Wagner," he said as he returned the painting to the stack. "I hope it will be possible to trace it back to previous owners, which will be a big help in the authentication process."

Wagner's eyebrows went up. "Oh, I don't think there's any doubt that it's one of the lost Pollocks," he said with assurance. "I went to the library and looked it up in the catalogue. It's in the second volume, on page one twenty-six. *Number Twenty-Three, Nineteen Fifty.*"

* * *

A two-block walk up Sixth Avenue took TJ to West 8th Street and the Salvation Army Donation Center and Thrift Store. He asked to speak to the manager and was directed toward a large African American man named Isaac Henry. TJ introduced himself and explained his mission.

"Mr. Wagner called and told me to expect you," said Henry, "but I don't think I can help you. The picture came in over a year ago, and I don't remember who brought it. All I can say is, it wasn't a regular donor, or I would remember."

"Don't you give donors a receipt?"

"Yes, so they can take a tax deduction for charity, but we don't put their name on it. We just write what it was. Every month, we send the duplicates to divisional headquarters up on West Fourteenth, but I doubt they'll have kept them this long."

"So you're saying that, even if they did still have the duplicate receipt, it wouldn't tell me who the donor was."

"That's about the size of it, Mr. Fitzgerald. When Mr. Wagner told me what you're after, I tried to think back, but I couldn't even say if it was a man or a woman, or both. Sometimes couples come in together. And I can't recall if it was a single item or with a bunch of stuff." He shook his head and apologized.

TJ handed Henry his card, the one with his home telephone number, and no mention of his affiliation with a detective agency. "If you do remember anything about the donation, please call me. It would be a big help to Mr. Wagner, and we'd both be very grateful." Without saying so, there was the implication of a reward.

Henry smiled broadly and took the card. "I'll be happy to help if I can. Mr. Wagner is our best customer."

* * *

On the way back uptown to his office, TJ took the film to be processed by Duggal, the photo lab on West 24th Street where Sweeney and Fitzgerald had an account. They did the job while he waited, so he decided to call Francis from the pay phone and offer to take the prints to him.

At first, his client was reluctant, but TJ reassured him. "I don't wear a uniform, you know, and my credentials are in my wallet. No one looking at me would peg me for a detective. And I might be visiting anyone in the building. Only the doorman will know which apartment I'm going to. There's something peculiar about this painting, and I want to hear what you have to say when you see it."

"What's peculiar about it is that it's bogus," said Francis testily.

"I defer to your judgment, but that's not the only thing. You'll know what I mean when I show you the pictures."

"Oh, very well. Two Fifty, East Seventy-Third, eleven-C."

"I'm at Duggal, on Twenty-Fourth off Sixth, waiting for the film to be developed. Won't be too much longer. I'll grab the F and be with you in, say, half an hour."

Thirteen

TJ changed to the uptown 6 at Lexington, got off at 68th Street, walked up to 73rd and turned right. This part of the Upper East Side was well known to him. He had had a few clients who lived in the neighborhood, and he and Ellen were members of the Whitney Museum of American Art on Madison at 75th. They had gravitated there since their days at the Art Students League, when the museum had featured in the murder case that had fueled their romance.

In the lobby of Francis' building at the corner of Second Avenue, the doorman, whose nametag identified him as Louis, told him he was expected. He rode up to the eleventh floor, where the door at the end of the corridor stood ajar. He announced himself before pushing the door open and stepping inside.

"Come in, come in," Francis responded from the kitchen, "I'm just making us some tea. Or would you rather have coffee? Or something stronger?"

"I'd love a beer, if you have it."

"Splendid. I'll join you," said Francis, and presently emerged into the hall with two Michelobs, two glasses, an opener, and a dish of mixed nuts on a tray. He led TJ to a round table in a small dining area that boasted a bay window wrapping around the alcove, affording views of both 73rd and Second.

"You have a great spot here," remarked TJ as he took a seat at the table. "I bet these corner apartments are highly sought after."

"I was lucky to get this one when I moved here from DC in seventy-two, though they're not as desirable as you might think. Some people don't like them because of the traffic noise on two streets, but I have the fortunate ability to block out such distractions when I concentrate on my work. And the light, as you can see, is wonderful." He opened and poured the beers. "Let's drink to the success of your investigation."

"Well, the Stanley inquiry was productive, but today's has hit a dead end," TJ reported. "I couldn't trace the thrift shop donor, though I have hopes that the manager may remember something and get in touch. But I want you to see what you make of the back of the painting. I told you there's something odd about it."

"The back? You didn't tell me that."

"Didn't I? Sorry. Here, let me show you." He took the Duggal envelope out of his pocket and spread the prints on the table.

"Hah!" said Francis as he picked up a print that clearly showed the baseball diamond pattern. "I know exactly what this is, and it makes me even more certain that my suspicions are correct." He went to one of his many bookshelves, returned with well-worn copies of volumes one and two of the Pollock catalogue raisonné, and opened the second volume to page 100.

"As you see," he pointed out, flipping through the next several pages of black-and-white illustrations, "these small paintings on Masonite are all the same size, twenty-two and a quarter inches square, and all were created in nineteen fifty. There are sixteen of them. Although not illustrated, some have the baseball-diamond printing on the verso. If Mr. Wagner's painting were not a fake, it would be the seventeenth."

TJ was perplexed. "How do you know for sure that it isn't?"

"As I told you, this scheme has been extremely well planned and executed. Only someone with inside knowledge could carry it out, and frankly, I am the only impediment to its complete success."

Jeez, what an arrogant character, said TJ to himself, *but then, what the hell do I know?* He pointed to the photo of the painting's back and asked Francis, "Would you mind clueing me in?"

"Ah, yes, the baseball diamond. Pollock had four brothers. The one closest to him in age, Sanford—known as Sande—was also an artist. He and his wife lived with Jackson in the Eighth Street apartment, and he and Jackson both worked on the WPA. When we entered the war and the project was on the way out, Sande's wife got pregnant, so they left the city and moved up to Deep River, Connecticut, where he opened a commercial silkscreen business, printing signs and circuit boards and the like.

"In nineteen forty-eight, a company in that area hired him to print the boards for the Autograph Baseball Game, which is what you see here. Facsimile signatures of well-known players of the day are printed around two of the margins. They're partly hidden under the wooden mounting, but you can see some at the bottom and on the right side."

TJ picked up one of the photos and looked closely. "Oh, yeah, I see them," he said.

"After the job was finished," Francis continued, "there were many pre-cut boards left over. Some were fully printed like this one, some were partially done, and others were blank. Sande, who now had two kids and had given up the idea of a career as an artist, asked Jackson if he could use them. Remember, these people came of age during the Depression. They never discarded anything that was remotely useful.

"In fact, Jackson liked to work on a hard surface, and had already painted several pictures on Masonite, so he told Sande he'd be glad to take them. He had recently become friendly with Alfonso Ossorio, a wealthy artist and collector who had bought a large one on Masonite from nineteen forty-eight, and—"

TJ interrupted him. "Alfonso and Ted were dear friends of my family, and I'm still close to Ted, though we don't see much of each other since he sold The Creeks and moved into East Hampton village. It was my parents who investigated the Edith Metzger killing—we were in East Hampton on vacation at the time—and I'm the detective who solved Ossorio's murder."

Francis looked at TJ in astonishment. "My God, I had no idea. I wasn't around when Pollock died. I was still an undergraduate. You must have been a child."

"Yes, I was eight. After the whole business was settled, we used to spend our summer vacations at The Creeks. When Alfonso was killed, I was twenty-eight, and Sweeney had just made me a partner, so naturally Ted turned to me to investigate."

"Mr. Fitzgerald, you amaze me. I did not know Alfonso well, though I visited The Creeks several times to see his Pollocks when I was working on the catalogue. I never went in the summer, however, as I was not there to socialize, so I see why our paths did not cross."

Francis took a swallow of beer and continued. "The point is that Jackson had no way of getting the game boards from Sande. His broken-down Model A Ford coupé had no room to carry such a load, and in any case, it never would have survived the trip to Deep River and back. But Alfonso had a station wagon, and he offered to drive Jackson to pick them up, so they took the ferry to Connecticut and brought back scores of the things. Alfonso took a few for himself, and Jackson kept the rest. He used many of them as floor tiles when he had the studio and house renovated in nineteen fifty-three, by which time he was no longer painting on them. All the game-board Pollocks were completed in nineteen fifty. Betty Parsons showed a group of them that winter, which explains the phony gallery label. Or it may be a genuine label taken off a work by someone else who showed there."

He opened volume one of the catalogue raisonné to the plates at the front. "Here are three examples in color. He used the rough side of the Masonite, which has a canvas-like texture that is distinctive if you know what to look for. As you can see, they're quite varied, and this one," he said as he turned to Plate 34, "like Mr. Wagner's picture, is neither signed nor dated. There are others like that as well."

TJ's puzzlement showed on his face. "I don't get it. How would a forger even know about the game boards, let alone get hold of one after all these years, assuming there are any unpainted ones still lying around?"

Francis let out an irritated huff. "I told you I believe the fakes were painted by someone in Pollock's inner circle, or at least someone with access to the same materials as he used and knowledge of his practice. There really is no other explanation."

"That narrows the field quite a bit," said TJ. "Even I can think of a couple of people who might qualify. But why would they want to get even with him now? He's been dead for thirty years."

Francis turned his gaze toward the east window and seemed to be studying the vehicles moving downtown on Second Avenue. After a few moments, he turned back to face TJ and spoke.

"That, Mr. Timothy Juan Fitzgerald, is a very good question. One that I expect your investigation to answer."

Fourteen

"The man is exasperating," said TJ as he prepared the ingredients for a recipe he was trying out. It was his turn to cook dinner. While uptown, he had stopped into Citarella on Third Avenue and picked up a nice salmon fillet for two, Parmesan cheese, and some fresh garlic and herbs.

"He insists that he more or less knows who's responsible, but that's as far as he'll go," he told Ellen, seated on the kitchen stool with a glass of wine.

"Funny, he wasn't at all reticent about expressing an opinion—make that a certainty—at the board meeting," she said, grinning.

"Wish I knew what's holding him back," said TJ as he filled his own wine glass. "Anyway, I think he's right about the forger being an insider. Everything about the Stanley picture screams nineteen forty-nine, and the photos and descriptions of the other four are just as convincing."

"I suppose it could be a coincidence that they fit the empty spaces, couldn't it?"

"One, maybe, or even two, but not five. And he hasn't given up on his theory that a single forger is responsible for all of them. That makes sense, because if the person had the right materials for one, it stands to reason that there could be enough for more. If five different people were doing them independently, they'd all have had to find period ingredients, and how likely is that?"

"You can buy enamel house paint and Masonite in any hardware store, and Utrecht still stocks the same standard canvas they've been selling for decades."

"Yes, but the paint chemistry has changed since the forties, and Masonite and canvas age over time. Those things can be detected by testing. Besides, according to Francis, the style of paint application—what he calls the facture—is the same in all of them. If different forgers did them, they wouldn't be consistent like that."

Ellen nodded. "Right. So, how does he figure it now?" She set her wine glass on the counter and took salad fixings out of the fridge.

"He thinks the forger had the materials all along, maybe even since before Pollock died, but didn't use them until after the catalogue was published. When he saw the blanks, that's what gave him the idea. So they were painted in the late seventies or early eighties and kept under wraps until after Krasner died."

"Why not start releasing them earlier? They could have been sold quietly, one by one, with no one the wiser."

"Suppose Krasner knew who Pollock gave the materials to. He gave some of the game boards to Alfonso, and maybe to other artist friends as well. Maybe she'd given away some of his unused stuff herself. If a buyer took one to her for approval and she pegged it as a fake, she might be able to identify the faker."

Ellen didn't accept that argument. "But like I said, anyone could buy that stuff off the shelf. It didn't have to come from Pollock or Krasner. Let's say someone was a big Pollock fan or a close friend, like that guy Meert. He could pick up a few cans of house paint and a roll of canvas and experiment with the technique. He's not happy with the result, so he dumps it and puts the materials away. Twenty years later, the catalogue comes out and he sees dollar signs. He dusts off the supplies and has another go."

"Yeah, but what about the game board? Sure, the game was commercially available, but who would know that Pollock painted on the leftovers? That had to be an insider."

Then Ellen had an idea. "You said they were printed by his brother, Sande. He's as insider as they come. Maybe he had more of them than what he gave Jackson. Lee once told me that Jackson left nothing to any of his brothers. She said they were bitter about that, after all they'd done for him. Especially

Sande, who'd tried to keep him on track when they lived together in the thirties. You say Francis thinks the real motive for these forgeries is revenge, not money. Who had more reason to want to get even than Sande? And make money doing it."

TJ poured more wine for Ellen and himself. "After Francis told me where the game boards came from, I thought he was pointing me in that direction. Sande was an artist, he was intimately familiar with his brother's technique, and he had access to all the same materials. He had the motive and the means. Suspect number one, right?"

"Damn right!" said Ellen, thrilled that TJ agreed with her.

"Only one problem," he said. "When I suggested that to Francis, he told me Sande died in nineteen sixty-three."

* * *

TJ had asked Francis for copies of the photographs of the Stanleys' painting and the three he hadn't seen, and volumes one and two of the catalogue raisonné. They arrived by messenger the following day, addressed to Ellen Jamieson at home.

"Boy," said TJ to her as she handed over the package, "he doesn't even trust the delivery service, in case they're in cahoots with the forger. I wonder if he's not just a bit paranoid."

"He must think he has good reason to be careful," said Ellen. "You know what they say: if you think someone's following you, they probably are. He may already have been threatened."

"Come to think of it," recalled TJ, "something like that came up when we first met. He said he couldn't be warned off or bought off, and that both had been tried. I assumed he was talking about the past, but maybe not."

* * *

TJ took a taxi to the office and set up a folding table as a dedicated workstation for the case. As he was opening the package, Pat Sweeney knocked and entered.

"Still on the O'Connor job?" he asked.

"Yeah, two down and three to go. Hope I have better luck with those." TJ pointed to the photos.

Sweeney frowned at them. "You say somebody would pay a bundle for one of 'em? Not me, no sir. Looks like leftover linguine."

"I knew you were a connoisseur, Pat. Course the point is that these aren't Pollocks, at least not according to O'Connor, so when we prove they're fakes you can pick one up for a song."

"No thanks, not at any price! But if you run across a fake Norman Rockwell, let me know." Wishing TJ good hunting, Sweeney retreated to his office and left his partner to study the evidence.

TJ opened volume two and found the spaces where *Number 5, 1949,* and *Number 23, 1950,* were supposed to fit. The first, now property of the Stanleys, had the sketchiest information—the medium, date, signature, and owner were unknown; only the size, 36 x 39 inches, was recorded. It had been shown at the Betty Parsons Gallery the year it was painted, after which it dropped from sight. The Wagner picture was better documented. Parsons had shown it in 1950, and it had been in several other shows before it disappeared two years later. The other three—*Number 8A, 1948, Number 22, 1949,* and *Number 32, 1949*—had exhibition histories but had also been missing since the early 1950s. TJ wondered why, when Pollock began showing at Parsons, he stopped giving his paintings titles and started numbering them. He figured Francis would know, so he jotted down a note to ask him.

Leafing through the book, TJ counted eleven blank spaces, covering the years from 1948 through 1951. The forger had chosen astutely. All were either medium unknown or on canvas, not on paper, and were small or medium size, like most of Pollock's paintings. His most famous works were the mural-size canvases like those in the Met and the Modern, but they were the exceptions. Of the 382 paintings in the two volumes, TJ found only 25 that were more than eight feet in either height or width, and several of those were long frieze-like compositions only three feet tall or less.

Among the missing works, the largest was *Number 35, 1949*, which measured 70 by 62 inches. Although it would have been the most valuable, it would also have been the most conspicuous, as well as the hardest to fake convincingly. The smaller ones were made with arm and hand gestures, while the big ones are frozen choreography. If the movements of a supremely gifted dancer could be recorded on canvas, they would be analogous to Pollock's compositions, which he called "energy and motion made visible." He described his spontaneous creative process as "memories arrested in space," so singular and so personal that only someone working from inside his head could produce them.

That was what Francis claimed he could recognize, so anyone trying to fool him would be wise to steer clear of a major canvas and hope that lesser ones would slip past him—all the more so if confounding the experts, rather than financial gain, was the primary motivation.

Fifteen

Number 32, 1949

The final New York City prospect was a Park Avenue matron, Mrs. Gordon Fairfax, who claimed to have *Number 32, 1949.* TJ found the space on page 78 where it fit, then turned his attention to the letter that accompanied Mrs. Fairfax's photo of the painting.

She said she bought it from the son of the late George Loper, an East Hampton carpenter and handyman who had done some work for Pollock in the fifties and took it in lieu of cash payment. It was common knowledge that the artist had often tried to barter his work for goods and services, but it was also well known that he seldom succeeded. Still, there were exceptions. The owner of the local general store in Springs had taken a 1948 canvas to settle the grocery tab, and a lawyer friend had accepted a small early painting as payment for writing Pollock's will. Those trades, however, were documented.

TJ decided to use the Wagner tactic, presenting himself as a researcher tracing the painting's provenance on behalf of the foundation, without saying so in just those terms. That was true indirectly, except that he was acting privately for Francis, but in the end, it amounted to the same thing. So he called Mrs. Fairfax, explained the purpose of his inquiry, and asked for an appointment. She said she'd be pleased to see him on Monday morning.

Promptly at ten, he arrived at 1185 Park Avenue, a magnificent pre-war monument entered through neo-Gothic arches leading to a spacious central courtyard with a circular driveway, a rarity in Manhattan residential properties. The doorman announced him and directed him to the private penthouse elevator, where he noticed that, though the building had 15 floors, the Fairfaxes were on 16. As in many multi-story buildings, superstitious tenants wouldn't rent or buy on the thirteenth floor, so there wasn't one.

As he emerged from the vestibule, the maid took his coat and directed him to the living room, where Beatrice Fairfax was waiting for him. The apartment was as impressive as he had anticipated. Its tastefully conservative décor contrasted agreeably with contemporary works by Ellsworth Kelly, Robert Rauschenberg, and Jasper Johns, as well as earlier abstractions by Philip Guston, Arshile Gorky, and Willem de Kooning.

Notwithstanding the surroundings, Beatrice Fairfax, a tall, slender woman in her mid-sixties, proved to be outgoing and unpretentious. "Call me Bea," she chirped as she shook his hand politely but with a firm grip. She asked whether he wanted tea or coffee, got coffee for an answer, and transmitted the order to the maid. Directing TJ to a comfortable armchair by the fireplace, she installed herself on the couch.

"I'm sorry to say that the Pollock isn't here," she began. "It's down at Orrin Riley's being cleaned—it really was quite filthy, after hanging in old Mr. Loper's workshop all those years, but otherwise it's in excellent condition."

"I saw the color photograph you sent to Dr. O'Connor," said TJ. "I assume that was taken before it was cleaned."

"Yes, and you can see how dingy it looks. Susanne assures me it will be much brighter once the grime is removed."

"Susanne?"

"Susanne Schnitzer, the late Mr. Riley's partner. She's taken over the restoration business since his death in January. He was at the Guggenheim for years, you know. He's worked on a few of our other pictures. If you're looking for a restorer, I highly recommend his studio."

"Did you by any chance have the back of the painting photographed?"

"No, we didn't bother. It's covered with cardboard, which is a good thing considering the conditions it was kept in."

"Were there any labels or other marks on the cardboard?"

"Just a number, thirty-two, in pencil."

The coffee arrived, accompanied by a plate of shortbread cookies. "Please help yourself," said Bea as she poured, and TJ took her advice.

"Your letter said you bought the painting from Loper's son," he said. "What I'm trying to do is trace its history to confirm the chain of ownership. Can you tell me how Loper came to have it, and why his son sold it to you?"

"Our buying it was purely a matter of chance," she told him. "Gordie and I have a summer home off Lily Pond Lane in East Hampton." TJ pictured a palatial so-called cottage hiding behind the hedges on that upscale residential street south of the highway. "I stay out all season, right through Labor Day, but Gordie's on Wall Street, so he comes out on weekends. We go year-round, weather permitting. It's quite lovely in the winter, and we often have the children and their families there for the holidays.

"One Friday late last September, we arrived to find that the wind had overturned the grill on the deck and damaged the railing. We're right on the ocean, so it can get pretty rough sometimes, especially during hurricane season. We should have secured the darn thing, but we forgot. Anyway, when we'd picked up the mail, I'd found a business card in the mailbox—we often get them from local tradesmen looking for work. This one was from George Loper, Junior, Custom Carpentry, so Gordie called him. He came over right away, assessed the damage, and said he'd be back the next day with an estimate for repairs."

Bea paused to refill his coffee cup and continued. "Sure enough, he showed up on the Saturday morning with a price for the job, and it was very reasonable, so we told him to go ahead. At lunchtime, I took out a tray of sandwiches and some lemonade, and we had lunch together. That's when he told me about some of the interesting people he and his dad had worked for over the years, including Jackson Pollock."

* * *

As far as the painting's history was concerned, the story was that Loper senior had helped Pollock renovate his barn studio in 1953. When it came time for him to get paid, Pollock asked if he'd take the painting, which had just come back from a traveling show. It had been priced at $300, which was what Loper was owed, and he kind of liked its loopy shapes, so he took it. But according to the son, who was seven at the time, when his dad brought it home, his mom had a fit, told him to return "that worthless scribble," as she put it, and get the three hundred in folding money. Loper refused, said he wouldn't shame Pollock by going back on the deal, and hung it in his workshop where the missus wouldn't have to look at it—though she made him swear never to pull such a stupid move again.

Decades pass, old man Loper retires, the son takes over the business, and the picture is still hanging over the tool bench. Not a clueless Bonacker, George Jr. knows who Pollock was and how valuable his work has gotten, but his father is very attached to the painting and doesn't want to sell it. Then, two years ago, George Sr. dies, and George Jr. inherits the workshop and its contents, so he decides to find out what he could get for it.

First, he goes to Guild Hall, the local art museum, and shows it to the curator. She gets all excited, pulls out the catalogue raisonné, and looks up *Number 32.* There are two of them: a big one from 1950, roughly nine by 15 feet, in a German museum collection; and a small 1949 work, 31 by 22 and a half, medium unknown, marked "collection unidentified." Like Pollock told Loper's dad, it had been in a show that toured around the country from 1951 to '52, so now he has a solid ID. He asks the curator how much it's worth, but she says it's not ethical for her to evaluate it, and besides she doesn't know what they're going for these days, though it's bound to be plenty. Then he takes it to a local art gallery, where the dealer assumes he is, in fact, a clueless Bonacker and quotes him a price he's sure is way too low.

Meanwhile, Bea is getting very curious. She and her husband have a respectable art collection, but nothing by Pollock. While Loper is complaining about what an idiot the dealer is, thinking he'd fall for such a ridiculous offer, she's wondering what kind of figure he has in mind. She asks if he'd be willing to tell her what the offer was, and he says, fifty thousand, give me a break, it's got to be worth double that. On impulse, she says bring it over, and if Gordie and I like it we'll give you a hundred thousand cash. No kidding, he says, and she says how about tomorrow? We'll be back from church by half past eleven.

Sure enough, around noon on the Sunday, Loper's pickup pulls into the driveway and he's got the painting, wrapped in brown paper, on the passenger seat. The Fairfaxes show him into the dining room, and they unwrap the parcel on the table. The canvas is face down, in a wood strip frame typical of the period, and Loper points out the number penciled on the cardboard backing. Before turning it over, he warns them that it needs a good cleaning after all those years in the shop, but he didn't want to do it himself in case he messed it up. Quite right, they say, and try not to show how eager they are to see it, while he spends a little more time apologizing for not taking better care of it.

TJ listened respectfully as Bea described the transaction. *Playing them like a fiddle,* was his silent assessment of Loper's tactics.

Finally, he flips the canvas, revealing a classic poured Pollock, as dirty as promised but otherwise intact. After asking the owner's permission, Gordie moistens his handkerchief on his tongue and rubs a blob of paint at the upper right. What looked like light gray is actually a rich creamy white, and the trio marvel at the transformation. Pollock used house paint because of its flowing viscosity and chromatic brilliance, and it turns out to be remarkably durable as well. They're thinking it won't take much to make this baby as vibrant as the day it was painted.

Now they get down to business. Loper says he wants to buy his mother a condo in the village now that she's on her own, and it's going to cost around a hundred thousand, so he won't take less. Bea and Gordie are thrilled. They know one like it fetched $200,000 at Christie's a year ago, and they're still kicking themselves that they dropped out at one seventy-five. But this is the vindication. It's like digging up buried treasure, and they didn't even have to hunt for it.

They arrange to meet Loper at East Hampton Library on the Monday morning to look it up in the catalogue, which checks out. Then they go up the street to Chase Manhattan Bank, where they transfer the funds to Loper's business account and take possession of long-lost *Number 32, 1949.*

Sixteen

"Even more elaborate than the Stanley deal, and equally effective," said Francis in response to TJ's report. "Just as there was a real Joseph Meert, there probably was a real George Loper, though the son, like Meert's attorney, is likely an impostor. He waits until the Fairfaxes are away, walks in from the beach, smashes the grill against the railing and sticks his phony business card in the mailbox. How hard would it be to set up a bank account in a false name at the East Hampton branch of Chase Manhattan?"

"All you need is a photo ID, like a driver's license, and a taxpayer number, and those can be faked. In my line of work, we see them all the time. By now, if Loper junior doesn't exist, I guarantee you the account has been closed. Easy enough to check."

"That can wait. You say the painting is at Orrin Riley's? Go take a look at it and get plenty of photographs."

TJ was hesitant. "Wouldn't it be better if you went? I don't know what to look for, and surely a first-hand inspection would be the way to go at this point."

Once again, he heard Francis' short-tempered bark on the other end of the phone. "My dear boy, that's out of the question! How often must I impress upon you that I don't want to be involved?"

"Look," said TJ, still wondering why his client was so reluctant to pursue inquiries himself, "it's one thing to have me follow the false trails of these pictures, because I'm an expert at that sort of thing, but when it comes to the pictures themselves, you're the expert, so that's where you need to pick up the investigation. You do see that, don't you?"

"Yes, yes, of course," Francis grumbled, "but there are circumstances of which you are not aware. It is not, ah, wise for me to appear in person."

He wasn't going to budge, and TJ decided it was pointless to argue. After all, Francis was paying for his time and effort, so he might as well go along. "All right, have it your way. I'll call Bea Fairfax and ask her for permission to photograph the thing at Riley's studio. I don't think it'll be a problem."

* * *

With Bea's approval, TJ made an appointment to visit Orrin H. Riley Ltd. Fine Art Conservation, at 361 West 36th Street. Susanne Schnitzer greeted him at the door and led him to a worktable where a young man wearing a headband magnifier was cleaning the painting in question. The strip frame had been removed, revealing the heads of the tacks that had been used to attach the canvas to the stretcher. A powerful gooseneck lamp was focused on the lower right corner. Next to it was a pile of used cotton swabs and a dish of liquid.

Schnitzer introduced the technician. "Rufus, this is Mr. Fitzgerald, who's researching the Pollock's provenance. Mrs. Fairfax says it's fine for him to examine it."

"It's pretty much done," said Rufus, adjusting the lamp so it illuminated the whole surface evenly. The interlacing tendrils of white, black, yellow, and green enamel, punctuated by dabs of crimson, were as bright as new. "You should have seen it when it came in. Dull as a dishrag, covered in dirt, but it was all superficial."

"How did you clean it?" asked TJ as he photographed the rejuvenated canvas, both full shots and details.

"We have an extra-gentle mini vacuum cleaner that lifts off the loose particles without disturbing the paint," Rufus explained. "Then we use these swabs, moistened with our own specially formulated solvent, to remove the rest." He picked one up and demonstrated. "You work it with a rolling motion, like this."

"Looks pretty tedious. Must take lots of patience, as well as a light touch."

"This one took longer than an ordinary painting of the same size, due to the character of the material," said Rufus. "A lot of the paint is raised a bit and rounded, like a string, so it's not just a question of cleaning a relatively flat surface. You must be careful not to dislodge it. Fortunately, there are no loose flakes, cracks, or other damage. And the pigment has really held its color. Looks great, don't you think?" He was clearly proud of his work.

"Sure does," said TJ, and studied the painting for a few moments. Knowing Pollock's identification with the forces of nature, he couldn't help imagining the crimson patches as the rosa rugosa that grows wild on eastern Long Island, amid a thicket of brambles. He very much doubted that the artist would have been trying to depict anything so literal, but when he was a youngster, both fascinated and confused by Pollock's abstractions, Ossorio had assured him that his own interpretation was perfectly valid. Then he reminded himself that, according to Francis, this painting wasn't a Pollock at all.

"No signature, I see. Is there one on the back?"

"Unfortunately, no," said Rufus as he turned the canvas over. "I hoped to find something when I removed the backing, but no such luck. There's a partial label on the stretcher, but that's all." In the upper right corner, a fragment of discolored paper showed the letters BETTY PAR and the number 15—presumably part of the gallery's address, 15 East 57th Street—printed in blue. It also contained the price: $300.

"I'd better get a shot of that," said TJ, and deployed his Canon 110 again. Although he had grown up studying the Pollocks in Ossorio's collection and was familiar with those in the New York City museums, he had never seen the back of one, so he had no idea whether what he was looking at was what you'd expect to find. The canvas and the stretcher appeared to have some age on them. The mark left by the backing board was clearly visible; the wood was darker where it had been exposed to the air.

If this was made since the catalogue was published eight years ago, he thought, *whoever did it really knew his stuff. Not only does the back look right, but the front is pretty convincing, too. Damn, I wish Francis had come along.*

"I understand the cardboard backing has a number on it. May I see it, please?"

Rufus reached under the workbench and took it off the shelf. It had been attached to the stretcher with staples, which he had carefully pried out and placed in a little dish. "It's illustration board," he said, turning it over to show the maker's stamp, Bainbridge, on the back. TJ nodded in recognition. Ellen had boxes of the stuff in various sizes.

"It was probably put on to protect the picture when it traveled," said Rufus. "Or maybe the previous owner added it later." He reversed it. "Here's the number you're looking for." He pointed to a pencil notation near the top edge: No. 32. TJ shot the whole board, front and back, a close-up of the number, and even the dish of staples.

Seventeen

Number 8A, 1948

After another trip to Duggal, a call to Francis, and a subway ride uptown, TJ entered the lobby of 250 East 73rd Street with a second package of photographs. Francis had brought in lunch from the deli on Second Avenue, and the two sat at the table in the sunny nook to eat their sandwiches while they examined the pictures.

To TJ's surprise, Francis was more interested in the illustration board than in the painting itself. "In 1949, Pollock made a series of paintings on paper which he mounted on illustration board like this," he said. "The manufacturer's stamp is on the backs. This reinforces my belief that the forger has intimate knowledge of Pollock's methods and materials."

"The technician said it could have been put on by someone else, when it went on the road, or by Loper. He's planning to replace it and reinsert the heavy-duty staples in their original holes. He considers that to be an important part of the restoration process, which is quite an operation. I'm glad I got a first-hand look, but I wish you'd been there with me."

TJ half expected Francis to bite his head off again, but this time the response was more sympathetic. "I agree that direct inspection is preferable to even the best photographs, but I cannot afford to be personally involved in the process at this stage. Your investigations are proving very fruitful, which bears out the wisdom of my decision to bring you into the case."

"I'm glad you're pleased with what I've come up with so far," said TJ, "but I hope that at some point you'll explain why it's me and not you who's doing the digging."

"Yes, of course," Francis assured him. "And when I do, you'll understand my caution." He rose from the table. "Now let's have a look at our two remaining candidates."

On the large desk in the adjoining living room, which doubled as his study, Francis had laid out documentation of the paintings purported to be *Number 8A, 1948,* and *Number 22, 1949.* As with the other three, to TJ's eye, they looked remarkably convincing.

"Alfonso told me that Pollock used numbers instead of titles because he wanted people to look at the work as pure painting, not pictures of something else," he said. "Is that right?"

Francis nodded. "Yes, he stopped giving them titles when Betty Parsons took over his contract, though he went back to it later, at the insistence of Sidney Janis, who started representing him in nineteen fifty-two. It was too confusing, you see. He started with a new number one each year, and Betty was not the most methodical record-keeper, so the inventory got out of hand. It certainly made my work on the catalogue more complicated. See this one," he pointed to the photograph labeled *Number 8A, 1948,* "it has an A after the number, which would lead you to believe that there's a number eight as well, but there isn't. At least not anymore. He may have painted over it, or perhaps it never existed. Most frustrating."

TJ snickered. "Maybe that's another one waiting to be rediscovered. Or counterfeited."

"Heaven forfend!" Francis rolled his eyes. "I'm having enough trouble dispatching the duds I know about." He picked up the paperwork that accompanied the photograph. "This one was sent in by the director of the Smart Museum of Art at the University of Chicago, who claims it was found in a closet in the office formerly occupied by Harold Rosenberg. Harold was based in New York City, but in the mid-sixties, he got a teaching job in Chicago, so he was back and forth."

"The art critic? I met him a couple of times at Alfonso's. He has a place in East Hampton, not far from Lee's."

"Had is the operative word. He died in seventy-eight, though I believe his wife, May, still owns the house in Springs. In fact, they were there before Jackson and Lee, which was part of the attraction. Lee had shared an apartment with them for a while in the thirties, when she and Harold were on the WPA, before she met Jackson, and they were close friends in the days before Jackson got famous.

'That all changed in nineteen fifty-two, when Harold wrote an article that Lee believed denigrated what Jackson was doing. That, and the fact that Harold became de Kooning's champion, caused a rift that never healed. Those were the days when people took sides—you were either for de Kooning or for Pollock, who had Clement Greenberg touting him. Such rivalries seem petty and foolish in retrospect, though at the time they were deadly serious."

"But you say that, before they fell out, Rosenberg and Pollock were good friends, so he might well have bought a painting to help Jackson out when he was hard up."

"He and May did own one from the 1946 Accabonac Creek series, but they didn't get it directly from Jackson. It originally belonged to Peggy Guggenheim. Under the terms of her financial support for Pollock, she owned almost all his output from that period. According to our records, she donated it to a charity auction, and Harold bought it. It's called *Constellation*. Pollock was still using titles then, and several of them allude to celestial phenomena. But there's no record of Harold's having owned one from forty-eight."

"He must have known about the catalogue. Surely, he would have wanted his picture to be in it."

"Of course, he knew, and he submitted *Constellation*. It's one of the few that's illustrated in color. That's why I'm even more doubtful about this one." Francis pointed to the photograph. "The letter explains that the professor who occupied the office after Harold's death retired last year, and the cleaners found it tucked away in the closet when they were moving his stuff. They assumed it belonged to the university and took it to the museum. The curator had read about the supplement, so here it is."

Francis fetched his heavily annotated copy of the catalogue raisonné volume 2 and turned to page 36. The blank square identified the painting—medium, size, and other identifying marks unknown—as having been sold through the Museum of Modern Art's art lending service to an untraceable buyer.

"I must admit respect for whoever pulled this one off. The forger would need to know where Harold's office was and that his successor was getting ready to leave, get the painting to Chicago, gain access to the office, and tuck the thing away in an inconspicuous place—maybe behind some file boxes—so it would look like it had been there since Harold's day. A remarkable feat of planning and execution, and it worked."

"But why would Rosenberg have left it behind?"

"He took a medical leave of absence in the spring of seventy-eight, no doubt expecting to return in the fall, but he died in July, so he never went back to collect his effects. They probably found other things of his in the closet as well. The perfect setup for a plant."

"It wouldn't even have to be planted," offered TJ. "Someone posing as a cleaner could have just taken it to the museum, not gone into the office at all. He could say he found it in the closet, drop it off, and leave. He'd still need to know which office it was, and that the occupant was gone, but that's all."

Francis nodded. "You're right. It could have been a simple handoff. At some point, you'll want to check the details of the curator's account, see if that's what happened. At the moment, it's not necessary."

A sly smile crept onto his face. "In this case, unlike the other three you've investigated so far, we have an advantage. Harold is deceased, but his widow, May Natalie Tabak Rosenberg, is very much alive and domiciled in Greenwich Village. Here's her telephone number. I suggest you show her this evidence and see what she makes of it."

* * *

Mrs. Harold Rosenberg lived on the parlor floor of a charming brick townhouse at 117 East Tenth Street. Like TJ's own building not far away, it had been divided into apartments. He was met at the door of #2 by a slightly disheveled woman in her mid-seventies, her square face topped by a mass of grey curls. When he had called, she told him she was free that afternoon.

She invited him into the front parlor, where every available surface was laden with publications and manuscripts. Groaning bookshelves lined the walls, and overflowing filing cabinets stood between the windows. Apologizing for the disorder, she gestured to a vacant chair and found one for herself.

"I've been trying to get Harold's papers in shape," she explained. "He wanted everything to go to the University of Chicago, and they need it to be sorted and boxed. I really must get that done." Remembering that Francis had told him Harold had died eight years ago, TJ wondered what was holding her up, when she added, "I'm having a hard time separating my material from his. I'm a writer, too, you know."

"No, I didn't know that," TJ admitted. "I hope I didn't interrupt your work."

"Not at all," she said tactfully. "I don't mind a bit of distraction. I'm working on an article for *The New Yorker*. Harold was the magazine's art critic for years, and they occasionally publish one of my pieces. It's nothing major, just a few observations about the New York art world, which is in a sorry state these days. Harold would be disgusted by the superficiality and commercialism."

"I won't keep you long," said TJ. "As I mentioned on the phone, I've been asked to verify the provenance of a painting that's been submitted to the Pollock catalogue raisonné supplement." He opened a manila envelope and handed her an eight-by-ten color photograph of the painting in question. "Do you recognize it?"

May's sharp brown eyes focused on the picture, and she shook her head. "I've never seen it before, though I've seen many like it." She turned over the photo and read the information on the back. "Jackson was at his peak in nineteen forty-eight. He was sober then, being treated by a local doctor in East Hampton, who kept him on the wagon for two years."

She looked away wistfully. "He was so sweet-tempered when he wasn't drinking. He used to come over and play with our daughter, Patia. He loved children, wanted to have a family of his own, but Lee wouldn't hear of it. I don't blame her. She wasn't going to take care of him *and* a kid. It was hard enough for her to carry on with her own work under the circumstances."

It occurred to TJ that May was obliquely commenting on her own situation, having to balance her writing career with marriage to Harold, a large man with an equally oversized ego, and motherhood. According to Francis, their union was a fractious one.

When he told her that the painting had reportedly been found in Rosenberg's former office at the university, there was a moment of silence. Then she went off like a Roman candle.

"That no-good son of a bitch! He was holding out on me!" She stood abruptly and started pacing around the room. "He wanted a divorce so he could shack up with that piece of tail who latched onto him in Chicago, and if I'd known he had the painting, he'd have been forced to sell it and give me half. We had an earlier one, which I sold right after he died. Where the hell could this one have come from? Not from Jackson, or I would know. And certainly not from Lee. She had a big fight with Harold in the fifties, and after that, he was persona non grata. She and I would get together for drinks or coffee sometimes, but never with him."

TJ let her go on, hoping she'd drop a clue that would lead him to the source, but evidently she was as much at sea as he was.

"He wouldn't have bought it from Sidney and paid the commission. He was a cheapskate. He must have gotten it from some collector in Chicago and kept it there, where I wouldn't see it. I knew all about the students he was screwing, so I stayed away. I wanted nothing to do with his pretentious academic cronies and their boring wives, whose husbands were just as unfaithful. The last thing I needed was their sanctimonious sympathy."

TJ decided to interject before she waded too deeply into self-pity. "From what you say, there was no mention of this painting in your husband's will. Were you his executrix?"

"Yes, and his primary heir. Apart from a bequest to Patia, his entire estate came to me. He left instructions about his papers—as I told you, he wanted them to go to the university—but he didn't leave them outright. It's up to me to carry out the bastard's wishes. I'm still under his thumb." Her bitterness was palpable.

"The museum submitted the painting because it was taken to the curator, who probably assumed that, since it was found on school grounds, it was the school's property. But they should have contacted you. As your late husband's heir, you're the rightful owner."

May stopped pacing, and her eyes widened. "You're right."

"I'm not saying they deliberately tried to cut you out. Your husband passed away nearly a decade ago, and someone else occupied his office. According to the museum, it was found in the closet when the next guy retired. The folks at the museum must not have realized that it belonged to Professor Rosenberg, much less that he had a living relative."

"They damned well should know! They're always after me to send them Harold's fucking papers. As if I have nothing better to do than organize them. Why don't they get a graduate student or an archivist to help me deal with them?"

"I'm guessing that the library and the museum don't talk to each other. I'm sure you know how territorial academia is. Nevertheless, if the painting belonged to your husband, it's now yours, and the university will be notified."

May looked introspective, and TJ figured she was calculating how much it would sell for. As a genuine 1948 Pollock, its price would amply compensate for her resentment. He decided not to spoil her satisfaction by raising the question of its attribution.

Eighteen

Number 22, 1949

Back at his office, TJ phoned in his report to Francis, who was gratified by May Rosenberg's reaction.

"I knew she wouldn't recognize it," he said. "If we assume for the sake of argument that it's genuine, and that Harold bought it privately not long before he died, he had a good reason to hide it from May. In the last few years of his life, he was having a serious affair with a woman in Chicago—not just another casual fling with a student, of which he had several. I didn't know he'd asked May for a divorce, but I'm not surprised."

"That means whoever planted the fake must have been aware of his marital situation," said TJ, "but I wonder how he could have paid for a real one without his wife knowing. Even back in the seventies, they weren't cheap."

"Small paintings like that were not very expensive, especially in a private sale where the owner might be in need of funds for a specific purpose. I know of one instance where a Pollock was traded for a car. And given his estrangement from May, Harold could have had money squirreled away in Chicago, so it's not implausible for him to have acquired a real one. Unfortunately for May, that's not the case. I'm afraid she is going to be deeply disappointed."

"Let's talk about the last one on the list," said TJ. On his worktable was another manila envelope, containing the photograph and correspondence related to the fifth purported Pollock. TJ opened it and removed the picture labeled *Number 22, 1949.*

The accompanying letter from the owner, a Boston collector, said he bought it out of a fundraising exhibition at the Provincetown Art Association in 1985. A percentage of the sale price was a donation to the Art Association, so he was able to take a partial tax write-off. The documentation that went with it referenced the catalogue raisonné, but didn't give the name of the donor, who wished to remain anonymous.

"The entry for the genuine painting is on page seventy-seven," said Francis. "Not as large as the Stanleys' fake, but it must have sold for six figures. I'm sure the Art Association was delighted to get what looked like a very valuable piece, so they probably didn't ask too many questions."

TJ turned to the entry. "The book says a woman in Connecticut bought the real one from the Modern's art lending service, and it went missing around nineteen sixty."

"The owner had died when we inquired, and her daughter didn't know what had become of it. It was not in the estate. The presumption was that the mother had sold it or given it away sometime in the sixties. Unfortunately, even though it was well documented up to its sale, there was no photograph. Hence the blank space."

"I'll start with a call to the Art Association. Even though they didn't reveal the donor's name, they must have it in their records. And maybe they'll tell me the price."

"That would be interesting to know, but it's not important. What matters is where it came from."

"No, Francis, the price does matter. According to Massachusetts law, if the seller received two hundred and fifty dollars or more—which we assume they did—and they knew it was a fake, it's grand larceny. If the seller's a New York State resident, the threshold is a thousand dollars, but whichever jurisdiction prevails, it's a felony."

"Do you mean that exposing the culprit could lead, not just to debunking the fakes, but to criminal prosecution?"

"The current owners would have to press charges, because they're the ones who were defrauded. I doubt that Wagner would bother. He only paid twenty bucks for it, and it wasn't sold to him as a Pollock. Nor would May Rosenberg, since apparently neither she nor her husband bought it. But the Stanleys, the Fairfaxes, and this guy in Boston"—he checked the letter—"Bernard Rankin, paid serious money. Gloria Stanley wouldn't tell me how much, but Bea Fairfax said a hundred thousand, and the other two are certainly in that neighborhood or more. I'd be really surprised if they didn't want their money back and the forger behind bars."

"Don't be too sure of that," said Francis. "Art collectors are a pretentious lot, very proud of their judgment. In practice, most of them rely on dealers and advisors, but they want you to think they're sophisticated connoisseurs. To admit in open court that they were hoodwinked would tarnish that image, so they're far more likely to try for a quiet settlement, or just write it off and no one the wiser."

"Are you saying they could just go on letting people believe they have the real things, even after you've proven they're bogus?"

"You misunderstand the process," Francis explained. "Under the foundation's auspices, the authentication board's mandate is to identify and accept genuine works by Pollock for inclusion in the supplement. It is not in the business of declaring unacceptable works to be fakes. To do so would expose the foundation to lawsuits, so the procedure is simply to decline to include questionable works."

"Doesn't that make them fakes by implication?"

"Not necessarily. There are other reasons why we wouldn't approve them. A piece may just need further research or have been so heavily restored that it no longer qualifies. Or the board may not have reached a consensus."

From what Ellen had told him, TJ could imagine that happening fairly often.

* * *

Founded in 1914 by artists who had been frequenting the picturesque fishing village in growing numbers since Charles Hawthorne established a plein-air art school there fifteen years earlier, the Provincetown Art Association and Museum occupies 460 Commercial Street. Its collection, devoted exclusively to work by Cape Cod artists, runs the gamut from traditional to avant-garde. It boasts examples by some of the more famous abstract expressionist residents, including Robert Motherwell, Adolph Gottlieb, and Hans Hofmann, but nothing by Pollock, whose bibulous antics during a couple of summers on the Cape in the '40s were still being rehashed over drinks at the Atlantic House, Napi's, and other local hangouts.

TJ's Wednesday morning call was put through to the director, who listened attentively to his request for information about the fundraiser and his explanation of why he wanted it.

"I know about the supplement," she told him, "and I'll be glad to help. An agent named Roland Wilson, acting for a New York foundation called Art in Trust, brought the painting to us. He said the trust was selling off a substantial private collection in order to establish a fund to give grants to arts organizations. Proceeds from our fundraising exhibitions are split fifty-fifty between the donor and museum, so half of what we raised from the sale of their Pollock would go to them, and half to us."

"Wouldn't they have raised more by selling it at auction?"

"Possibly, but we're a non-profit, not a commercial enterprise. This way, our portion would be the equivalent of a grant, and the more interest we could drum up, the better we would do. Of course, I was thrilled. It was the star of the show and raised a bundle for us."

"Do you mind my asking how much?"

"Not at all. It's public knowledge, reported in the *Cape Cod Times*. It sold for two hundred and fifty thousand dollars, so we got a hundred and twenty-five. Quite a windfall."

"And you remitted the other half to Art in Trust?"

"That's right. I turned the check over to Mr. Wilson personally after the buyer's payment cleared. The painting went to one of our trustees, a real estate developer who lives in Boston and summers in P'town."

"Bernard Rankin. He submitted it to the authentication board."

"Bernie is a big booster of ours, and I'm hoping he'll eventually donate it to us, or leave it in his will. It would fill a major gap in the collection, and he knows it. Meanwhile, he says we can borrow it whenever we want."

Without implying that there was anything wrong with the painting, TJ eased into the question of its history before the fundraiser.

"Did Mr. Wilson share the provenance with you?"

"He had a copy of the Pollock catalogue raisonné entry, where it's documented, and a nineteen fifty-two bill of sale from the Museum of Modern Art, on behalf of the Betty Parsons Gallery, to a Mrs. Stanley Resor. She paid five hundred dollars for it—Bernie let out a hoot when he saw that. I have copies in the exhibition file if you need them."

"Is there anything from the period between Mrs. Resor's purchase and when it entered the Art in Trust collection? I need to trace it back to previous owners, if I can."

"You mean that missing section in the catalogue entry. Unfortunately, no, and Mr. Wilson wouldn't name the Art in Trust benefactor or discuss how or when he or she acquired it. He wouldn't even say if it's a man or a woman. He hinted that I'd recognize the name, but that his client insisted on remaining anonymous. I did check with the charities registry, and the foundation is real, though there's no list of trustees."

Like Loper's bank account, it's not hard to set up a charity, said TJ to himself. *It could look perfectly legit, and once the deal is done it could be liquidated just as easily.*

He had one more question. "What did this Mr. Wilson look like?"

"Like a businessman, I guess you'd say. Early forties, medium height, clean shaven, brown hair, a little gray at the temples. He wore a suit and tie, not like we're used to here, but that was no surprise. If you like, I can give you the Art in Trust address and phone number. Maybe he'll be more forthcoming with information when he knows it's for the catalogue."

"Yes, please, and I'd be grateful if you'd send me copies of what you have on file," he said, and gave her his home address. "I really appreciate your cooperation. I hope you do get a Pollock for your collection," he added, neglecting to mention that, if she did, it wouldn't be coming from Rankin, in his lifetime or after.

Nineteen

TJ called Francis and reported what he'd learned. "Well, that's the lot, unless you want me to go to Boston and interview Rankin. I doubt he can shed any more light, but I'll do it if you think it'll help."

"Not at this stage. I want you to call him and request a high-quality photograph of the back of the painting. And ask for close-ups of any labels. There should be one from Betty's gallery, and the Modern always put one on their art lending service works. Of course, they'll be counterfeit, but I want to know if the forger was that meticulous. As I've said before, the level of inside knowledge reinforces my suspicion."

"And your level of evasiveness reinforces my frustration! When are you going to share that suspicion? I don't see how I can make headway without a sense of direction."

After a reflective pause, Francis admitted, "You're right, I need to put you in the picture, if you'll forgive the pun. But first, get the photos from Rankin and ask Beatrice Fairfax to describe Loper. I believe he and Wilson and the office cleaner in Chicago will turn out to be the same man. Unfortunately, you can't ask one of the Stanleys to describe Meert's purported lawyer without arousing their suspicions."

"I could call Isaac Henry at the Salvation Army, give him the Wilson description, and see if it rings a bell. That's called leading the witness, but it might jog his memory."

"An excellent idea. Let me know when you have these last pieces of evidence. Then I'll explain my reasoning."

* * *

"Salvation Army Donation Center."

"Is Mr. Henry available?"

"Who's calling, please?"

"This is Tim Fitzgerald. I spoke to him last week regarding a donation."

"One moment, please."

When Henry came on the line, TJ reminded him of their conversation. "I'm just checking to see if you remembered anything about the donor of that abstract painting you sold to Mr. Wagner."

"I didn't forget about you, Mr. Fitzgerald. I have your card right here, and I would've called, but I'm afraid I got nothin' for you. It was too long ago."

"Well, I have a lead that maybe you can help me follow. I think it may have been a white man in his early forties, brown hair, clean shaven. Does that sound familiar?"

Henry chuckled. "Sure does. We get one of those every week. I'm sorry, Mr. Fitzgerald. I'd really like to help, and I'll keep your card in case the fog lifts."

"I appreciate that, Mr. Henry." TJ thanked him and hung up.

His next call was to the Boston number on Bernard Rankin's letterhead. His personal assistant answered the phone and screened the call before putting TJ on hold while the boss was queried. After a few moments, he was connected.

"Hello, Mr. Fitzgerald. Bernard Rankin here. I understand you're calling on behalf of the Pollock catalogue project. How may I help you?"

"In addition to the material you've already submitted, we'd like to get color photographs of the back of the painting, especially details of any marks, inscriptions, or labels. Would you be able to have them done, or should we send a photographer from New York?"

"No need for that. The same outfit that took the photo I sent can do the job. I should have thought of it myself. How soon do you need them?"

"It's not urgent, but at your earliest convenience," said TJ, repeating Francis' request for the best quality reproduction.

"The painting's at my home. I can get the photographer over there tomorrow, and you'll have them by the end of the week." Before TJ could give him Francis' home address, Rankin continued, "I'll overnight them to the foundation. I have the address. That's where I sent the original submission. I was delighted to learn that a supplement would be published, with the missing Pollock restored to its rightful place. Can you tell me when I may expect to see the book in print?"

He's pretty sure of himself, thought TJ, *but I guess he has every reason to believe the painting will be accepted.* To Rankin, he said, "I'm afraid not. They're still soliciting works for consideration and will be for some time. They want to be sure to find as many as possible before they publish. The foundation will keep you apprised of the process. At some point they may want to see the painting in person."

"Naturally. When the time comes, I'll be glad to take it to New York myself. It's not terribly large, but it's a beauty, a perfect example of his drip style. Not only did I get a small masterpiece, but the Art Association also benefited handsomely. A classic win-win situation."

If only that were true, said TJ to himself, *and if Francis is wrong, it is.*

* * *

"Rankin was cooperation itself," TJ told Francis. "He says he'll have the photos shot tomorrow and send them overnight to the foundation, so they'll arrive on Friday. No dice with the Salvation Army guy, though. He's still drawing a blank. Says the description is too vague, fits too many donors. I'll see what I can get from the others."

"I'm disappointed, but not surprised," said Francis. "The others should be more helpful. Call the curator at the Smart, see if he can remember what the cleaner looked like, though I think that's a long shot. Meanwhile, I'll study the photos and review all the evidence over the weekend. Will you be available to meet on Monday afternoon at your apartment? Say two p.m.? I should be able to lay it out for you then."

TJ couldn't hide his impatience. "Why not make it Monday morning,

Francis? I'll be on tenterhooks all weekend."

"Very well, I'll be there at eleven, assuming the photos get to me by Friday. Dickler's office is closed on weekends, so if I don't receive them until Monday, we'll have to re-schedule. I'll call you when I have them."

"Fair enough. If I'm not in the office on Friday, you can try me at home. Ellen will take a message if I'm out."

"You are fortunate in your marriage, TJ. Ellen is charming, intelligent, and obviously devoted to you. Although you and she pursue very different callings, you seem to be remarkably compatible. Even I, a confirmed bachelor, can appreciate the advantages of such a sympathetic union."

"I'm a lucky guy, all right," said TJ, pleased that Francis recognized what a loving couple they were, "and we have more in common than it seems. Did she tell you we met at the Art Students League? We were in Edward Laning's life class together, and I fell for her on day one. That was nearly twenty years ago, and she's still just as adorable."

"I didn't know you had studied art," said Francis, impressed. "Has that training come in handy in your investigative work?"

"Not really. I was pretty inept, and I dropped out after a year. It was Alfonso who encouraged me. He believed I had a creative streak, but it turns out whatever talent I have lies far outside the realm of art."

Francis' voice took on a wistful tone. "I, too, had artistic ambitions. The next time you visit me, I'll show you some of my youthful efforts. I keep them around to remind me that I'm much better at studying art than I was at making it."

Twenty

Friday, May 2

At 3 p.m., a call from Carla Evans in Gerry Dickler's office informed Francis that a Federal Express overnight package had arrived for him from Boston. He thanked her and told her he'd come down to pick it up.

Folding the latest issue of *The New Yorker* into his jacket pocket, he headed for the downtown entrance to the 68th Street Lexington Avenue IRT station. After a couple of interruptions on his walk, he entered the station, inserted his token in the turnstile, and descended to the platform, where he found a vacant space on a bench and settled in to wait for the train.

* * *

Although she should have been concentrating on the two-page layout for Lord & Taylor's fall catalogue, Ellen's mind was wandering. The view from her open window was only of the building across the street, yet she found herself gazing in that direction instead of at her work. She watched the spring breeze rustle the leaves on the sidewalk trees and felt restless.

She reached across the drawing table and switched on her portable radio, tuned to WNYC, the city's public broadcasting station. *Maybe some background music will help me focus,* she thought. What she got instead was the five o'clock news. She listened without paying attention until she heard:

"Service on the Lexington Avenue IRT was interrupted for an hour this afternoon after a fatality at the Sixty-Eighth Street station. A man identified as Francis O'Connor, a prominent art expert, fell onto the southbound tracks at about three twenty p.m. and was struck by the oncoming train. Witnesses are being interviewed to determine if his death was an accident or suicide, or if foul play was involved."

"Oh, my God!" said Ellen out loud. She jumped up, ran to the telephone, and dialed TJ's office. Sweeney answered.

"Pat, it's Ellen. Is my husband there?"

He could hear the anxiety in her voice. "Yeah, he's in his office. Something the matter?"

"I'll say there is. His client was just killed by a subway train."

"You mean O'Connor? What the hell happened?"

"I don't know, I just heard it on the radio. He fell, jumped, or was pushed off the platform, that's all they said."

"Hang on, I'll buzz yer old man." He put her on hold. When his partner picked up, he said, "Ellen's on the line with some bad news about O'Connor. He's dead."

"What?" TJ barked as he pressed the flashing button and connected to his wife. He was too shocked even to greet her. "Pat says you told him Francis is dead. How do you know?"

She repeated what she had told Sweeney. "They didn't give any details. They said the investigation is still in progress."

"Did they say where?"

"The Sixty-Eighth Street IRT station, the downtown side."

"That'll be the Nineteenth Precinct. I'll call over there and see what I can find out." He was about to hang up when he stopped himself. "Are you okay, honey? You must have been thrown for a loop, hearing it like that."

Grateful for his concern, Ellen let out a sigh. "I'd only just turned on the radio and was half listening, sort of daydreaming really. It felt like I was slapped awake. It's only now sinking in." She paused. "You don't think it could have been suicide, do you?"

"Absolutely not, no way," TJ insisted. "Francis was a man on a mission, and he was determined to see it through. Plus, he was ready to tell me who he suspected, so why would he kill himself before he let me in on it? Makes no sense."

"So it was either an accident, like somebody was fooling around and bumped into him, or they did it on purpose."

"Right. I need to get onto Samuelson, the chief of detectives at the Nineteenth, see if they've come up with any answers. I'll try reaching him now. I'll call you back if I find out anything."

* * *

TJ opened his desk drawer in search of the phone book. Next to it was his leather-bound pick set—inherited from his mother, now retired as an NYPD detective inspector—which he decided to use instead. He put the tools in his briefcase and went through to Sweeney's office.

"I'd better get up to O'Connor's place before the cops seal it," he told Sweeney. "Do me a favor, will you, Pat? Call Samuelson at the Nineteenth and find out what you can about the investigation. Especially whether they have good witness reports. I'll call in from O'Connor's."

"No problem," said Sweeney to TJ's back as he headed out.

A taxi took him up Eighth Avenue to Columbus Circle, through the park, and across East 72nd Street. He paid off the cab at the corner of Second Avenue and walked the last block to Francis' building. The doorman recognized him.

"Good afternoon, Mr. Fitzgerald. I'm afraid Dr. O'Connor is out, and I don't know when he'll be back."

Good, thought TJ. *The cops haven't been here yet.* He patted his briefcase. "I've got some papers for him. I'm supposed to take them up and wait for him. He gave me keys. I know the way, thanks," he said with an amiable smile as he moved off toward the elevator.

Louis returned his smile. "I'm going off as soon as the night man arrives, but I'll let him know you're here so he can alert Dr. O'Connor when he comes in."

107

The deadbolt on 11-C's door wasn't engaged, so TJ had to pick only one lock to gain entry. That took him no time at all, and he made a quick circuit of the apartment. He debated whether to slip on a pair of latex gloves, but in the unlikely event the police dusted the place for prints, he could explain why his were there, since he was known to have visited before.

One of the two bedrooms had been converted as an office, lined with filing cabinets and shelves filled with neatly labeled document cases and ring binders, evidence of the scholar's entire career. TJ's heart sank at the prospect of searching through such voluminous archives. He started with the drawers labeled JPCR, which contained files related to the original publication. He checked those on the missing works, but there was nothing new in them. As he scanned the labels on the remaining file drawers and boxes, he realized that none of the material was relevant to his inquiry.

On the shelves, sections were devoted to Francis' dissertation research, the New Deal art projects, the history of mural painting, spirituality, and psychology, as well as his financial records. An extensive series of binders containing his creative writing, arranged chronologically in orderly rows, indicated that he had been a serious poet since his youth.

One document case caught TJ's eye. The label on its spine read LAST WILL AND TESTAMENT. He pulled it out and flipped the lid. It contained not one will, but four. He wanted to look them over, but decided against it. Finding information about the art forger was his purpose, and who knew when the police might show up, so he reluctantly put the box back on the shelf.

TJ returned to the living room, where he and Francis had reviewed the forgeries on the long table that had been set up as a desk. This was apparently where Francis did most of his work. On it, in addition to office supplies and the telephone, was an IBM Selectric typewriter, a Xerox desktop copier, and an IBM Personal Computer, with a printer and a box of floppy discs. Unfamiliar with the machine, TJ hoped the information he needed wasn't on the discs. Fortunately, they were as carefully labeled as the archives, and he saw nothing related to the forgeries.

He turned his attention to the two-drawer file cabinet that sat under the worktable, where he found what he was after. The files on the five submissions were there. Another one, thinner than the others, was helpfully labeled SUSPECTS.

He collected all six folders, tucked them into his briefcase, and closed the drawer. Now, a quick call to Sweeney and then he'd go. He glanced at the clock and saw it was 6:00 p.m. He'd tell the doorman that he had another appointment and couldn't wait for Francis any longer.

Sweeney, it turned out, had nothing for him. Not wanting to tell Samuelson that his partner was working on a case for the victim, he said a friend (meaning Ellen) was a colleague of O'Connor's. She heard about it on the radio and was very upset, so she asked him to find out what happened. He wasn't sure Samuelson bought that half-truth, but he did say the incident was still under investigation. When Sweeney asked about witnesses, he was told that nothing definite had been learned. The platform was crowded, and everyone was looking at the incoming train—until a man took a header in front of it.

"The motorman's nightmare," as Samuelson had put it. "Some are suicides—what a way to go—but more often it's drunks or derelicts who fall onto the tracks, people who slip down between cars, nut jobs who go haywire, guys fighting, or kids trespassing in the tunnel. Can even be a careless maintenance man. They get dozens every year, and sometimes that's the end for the poor bastard who's driving the train."

* * *

Service on the Lex was back to normal. Standing on the downtown platform at 68th Street, now far less crowded than it had been in midafternoon, TJ tried to picture the scene at the time of Francis' death. As a regular subway rider, he'd seen plenty of dangerous situations, times when someone bumped into a moving car or got caught in the closing doors. He once saw a woman catch her heel in one of the sliding grates at the Union Square station, and another time he witnessed a deranged guy being restrained from jumping onto the tracks, but he'd never seen anyone fall in front of a train.

He rejected suicide outright, and he couldn't imagine Francis just losing his balance or tripping. Someone must have pushed him. Someone who knew about the forgery investigation and needed it to stop.

How close to the edge would you have to be for it to look like an accident? he wondered. *Probably less than a foot, about the width of the strip of yellow paint. Otherwise, he might just stagger and recover. And if it really was accidental, whoever jostled him would have come forward or been identified at the scene.*

His speculations were interrupted by the arrival of the downtown local. As the doors opened and the waiting passengers boarded, he was likely the only one who was aware of what had happened on that track three hours earlier.

* * *

Eager to examine the files, TJ bounded up the four flights to his apartment, where Ellen was in the kitchen working on dinner.

"Pay dirt!" he announced as he commandeered the dining table and spread out the contents of the briefcase.

Ellen joined him at the table. She put one hand on his shoulder and tilted his chin toward her with the other. "First things first," she said as she kissed him. "Let's keep our priorities straight." He chuckled and returned her embrace.

"Damn right," he said. "I wouldn't have known about Francis if you hadn't called, and I wouldn't have gotten this evidence. If that doesn't deserve a thank-you kiss, nothing does." And he threw in an extra hug.

"What is all this?" she asked.

"These five files have the information on the fakes. I've seen most, if not all of it already." He tapped the file marked SUSPECTS. "This is the one I really need. Notice anything interesting about the label?"

She studied it for a moment. "Oh, it's plural. More than one."

"Right. It seemed to me that he was focused on a single person, but apparently not. I had a quick look at the file on the ride downtown. He had three suspects."

He pulled up two chairs. They sat, and he opened the folder. Inside were three sheets of paper. Their headings read KLIGMAN, MATTER, and THAW.

Twenty-One

Ellen's eyes were fixed on the sheet marked THAW. Now she understood why Francis had held back the submissions from the board, and why he wanted to distance himself from the investigation. But how could he suspect one of the most highly respected art dealers in New York, whose advice was sought by major institutions and private collectors in the US and abroad? What would motivate a man like Eugene V. Thaw to risk his reputation by participating in a forgery scheme? She read Francis' notes:

> *Bitter over terms of LK will. Broke promise to leave JP Gothic to him—*
> *left it to MoMA.*
> *Significant financial loss.*
> *Has had access to JP materials since 72.*
> *WSL probably in on it too, needs him to go along.*
> *Q: Who painted them—MCW? Down on her luck, needs $$*
> *Q: Who planted them—NT?*

"It's incredible," said Ellen, as much to herself as to TJ. "I know they had a difficult relationship. Gerry Dickler said they argued tooth and nail about seemingly trivial details in the catalogue, and when Francis had one of his tantrums, Gene would usually have to give in just to keep things moving along. I bet they disagreed about leaving those blank spaces, so maybe Francis thought filling in the blanks was Gene's way of getting even."

"What's JP Gothic?" asked TJ.

"It's a big Pollock painting," she told him. "I'd say at least seven feet tall, way taller than Lee. She used to have it hanging in her bedroom. I often wondered why she chose that one to sleep with—it's kinda ominous, dark colors, contorted shapes—one of his transitional paintings. Here, I'll show you."

She went to the bookshelf, removed Frank O'Hara's 1959 monograph on Pollock, and opened it to the black and white illustration.

"Oh, yeah," said TJ, "I remember it. I've seen it at the Modern. It's mostly black, blue, and green, right?"

"That's it," said Ellen. "It's related to his mural for Peggy Guggenheim, but the forms are much denser. According to his contract with Peggy, he was allowed to keep one painting a year for himself, and *Gothic* was the one he kept in nineteen forty-four. Lee told me she didn't just inherit it when he died, he specifically gave it to her, and she held onto it for forty years, so it obviously had special meaning for her."

She pointed to the caption. "See here, it says 'Collection Lee Krasner Pollock.' And I was right, it's eighty-four inches tall. It really filled the bedroom wall."

"I think I'd have trouble sleeping with that thing looming over me," said TJ. "I wonder why she promised to leave it to Thaw, then reneged."

"I know the Modern was angling for it. Bill Rubin, the chief curator, used to come by regularly and discuss their Pollock holdings with her. He took over after Lieberman went to the Met. They'd be working out how to fill gaps in the collection by getting a collector to donate something or buy something for them at auction. He'd tell her what they wanted, and she'd put the pressure on."

"You think she said she'd leave *Gothic* to Thaw so he'd donate it to the Modern?"

"Maybe that was the original idea, but after she died, all bets would be off, and he could just sell it. He is an art dealer, after all. Gerry made a passing remark about Lee not fully trusting Gene, though he said she had no reason not to, but how could she be sure he'd honor her wishes once she was gone?"

Ellen also considered another factor. "Rubin wanted *Gothic* in particular because, according to Lee, it was inspired by the Modern's most important Picasso painting, *Les Demoiselles d'Avignon,* so it validated his theory that Abstract Expressionism evolved from Cubism. Plus, it bridged the gap from *The She-Wolf* to the all-over poured paintings like *Full Fathom Five.* And Rubin had an ace up his sleeve." She paused for emphasis.

"Lee had a major retrospective in the works. It was going to open at the Museum of Fine Arts in Houston and travel. She badly wanted it to go to the Modern—she'd dreamed of such a thing all her life—and Rubin could make it happen. That was the trade-off: leave *Gothic* to us, and we'll take your show. And that's how it went, quid pro quo."

"Well, she certainly deserved a show at the Modern, and *Gothic* wound up where she wanted it, so it all worked out in her favor. The whole New York art world turned out for the opening," said TJ, who'd been Ellen's escort on that memorable occasion. "A shame she didn't live to see it. At least she knew it was coming and she'd finally get the recognition she was entitled to."

"My guess is Gerry told Gene that she changed her will," said Ellen. "She probably didn't tell him herself. Or maybe she didn't leave it to him in the first place, and he found out about it when the will was read. Not that it makes a difference one way or the other."

"Sure, it makes a difference," said TJ. "If he knew well in advance that he'd been cut out it would give him plenty of time to plan the forgery scheme. It must have taken at least a couple of years to put together. I don't suppose Thaw painted the fakes himself, at least Francis didn't think so. So who's his 'MCW' suspect?"

Ellen shook her head. "Those initials mean nothing to me, but it must be someone Francis figured could paint convincing Pollock imitations. And there's someone else involved, this 'NT' person, presumably the phony lawyer, East Hampton carpenter, Salvation Army donor, Chicago cleaning man, and make-believe agent for the Art in Trust charity—ironic name for a swindle."

* * *

Dinner preparations forgotten, Ellen and TJ turned their attention to the file marked KLIGMAN. Francis' notes read:

> *Hated LK, wants to profit now she's out of the way.*
> *Hard up for cash, but primary motive = fool the experts, show us up.*
> *Especially me—wouldn't approve her bogus JP smear.*
> *Channels JP like a medium.*
> *Has had materials since 56.*
> *Q: Who planted them—latest boyfriend.*

"Now that makes perfect sense," said TJ. "Ruth has every reason to want to take advantage of the circumstances, both for profit and for revenge. And she's an artist, so she could have painted them herself. I had already considered her the top suspect, but I didn't want to say anything until I heard Francis' opinion."

Ruth Kligman was no stranger to TJ. Her liaison with Pollock had ended tragically on the night of August 11, 1956, when eight-year-old TJ and his parents, on vacation in East Hampton, witnessed Pollock's fatal car crash. The first time he saw Ruth, she was lying on Fireplace Road, badly injured after tumbling from the Oldsmobile convertible as it overturned.

After Pollock's death, Ruth embarked on a long amatory campaign, starting with his rival, Willem de Kooning, and worked her way through the roster of male New York School notables. In the years that followed, TJ occasionally saw her at gallery openings and art-world cocktail parties, where she would cling to her latest conquest and calculate who the next one would be. She cultivated the persona of a muse who inspired great artists, but her reputation was less flattering: star-fucker.

"I guess the bogus JP smear is a painting she claims is a Pollock," said Ellen. "She must have approached Francis to authenticate it, and he wouldn't."

"I seem to remember she said something in her memoir about having a Pollock. It's a while since I read it. Mom bought it when it came out, about ten years ago. You know Mom questioned her in the hospital, after the accident, right?"

Ellen nodded. "Yes, she told me all about how she and your dad helped the local police with the investigation, and how surprised and confused she was when she went to the hospital and saw a woman she thought was Ruth, only not injured. It turned out to be Ruth's identical twin, Iris. That was some experience."

"I need to get the book," said TJ. "Maybe Mom still has her copy. *Love Affair*, it's called. Wait, it's coming back to me. I think she wrote that Pollock gave her a painting, but she never got it because he was killed and she couldn't go back and claim it. Anyway, even if she had tried, you could hardly imagine Lee turning it over to her."

"If I know Lee," said Ellen, "she'd have burned it before she'd let Kligman get her hands on it. Maybe she told Francis he gave it to her earlier. It could have been any time during their affair."

"No, I'm pretty sure she said it was in the summer, when she was shacking up with him in Springs. I'll have to check. I remember thinking, boy, I bet she's bitter about that. It would be worth plenty now, and I don't mean sentimental value."

* * *

The third folder, marked MATTER, contained the following notes:

> *Feud with LK over 210, friendship on the rocks*
> *Lost 92 by mischance, LK not helpful*
> *HM & JP bonded*
> *Medical bills*
> *Q: Who painted them—HM? MM?*
> *Q: Who planted them—AM?*

"You know the Matters," said TJ. "Mercedes tried to woo you away from the League and recruit you for her art school."

"No one who ever met Mercedes could forget her. She must have been in her fifties then, but she was still a knockout. And that funny, high-pitched voice, like a schoolgirl's, so at odds with her forceful character."

"And Herbert just the opposite, with a deep baritone but always in the background, at least the few times I've seen them together. I think they lead separate lives. He teaches at Yale, and she's here at the Studio School. She has the carriage house behind it, a few doors down MacDougal Alley from Alfonso and Ted's old place."

"I think I know what those numbers mean," said Ellen. "They're catalogue raisonné numbers of Pollock paintings. Not long after I started working for Lee, Mercedes called up about number ninety-two. She told me a long story about how it had once belonged to her and Herbert, but it was stolen from them years ago. She wanted Lee to help her get it back, but Lee wouldn't speak to her. I thought they were best friends, from back in their WPA days, but by the early eighties, I guess they were, as Francis put it, on the rocks."

What had derailed the relationship was the other Pollock painting, *Number 7A, 1948*, catalogued as entry 210, a sizable canvas that Herbert claimed was a gift to him from Jackson in return for photographing his work. But when he put it on the market in the late '60s, Lee insisted that it wasn't a gift at all—it had simply been left behind in Herbert's studio after it was photographed and should be returned to her. The fact that he'd had it for some twenty years was immaterial, she said; it was part of Pollock's estate and therefore rightfully her property.

Needless to say, Herbert had challenged that assertion. He was deeply hurt by Lee's accusation that he was lying about the gift, and of course, Mercedes, equally offended, backed him up. And he had a more practical reason to claim ownership. He had been hired by Yale and wanted to buy a house in New Haven, so he needed the money from the sale. Even then, the painting was worth quite a bit, especially as there had just been a major Pollock retrospective at the Modern and the market for his work was enjoying a boost.

Lee took the complaint to Gerry Dickler, who informed her that the issue was moot, since the statute of limitations on reclaiming abandoned property had long since expired. Herbert's ownership was upheld, and the painting was sold. Lee neither forgave nor forgot.

"Herbert and Mercedes are both artists," said TJ, "so it looks like Francis was thinking either one of them could be the forger. But where would they get the materials?"

"The same places Pollock got them, just like Ruth," said Ellen. "Remember, they go back a long way. Lee was close with Mercedes even before she met Jackson, and the two couples were hanging out together in the city and out east for a couple of decades. I wouldn't be surprised if both Herbert and Mercedes tried their hands at drip painting back then. Especially Mercedes. She was tight with Hofmann, and he did it in the forties."

TJ was skeptical. "Okay, she and Lee fell out over the Pollocks, but I don't see that as enough of a motive for such an elaborate forgery scheme. One painting, maybe, if her school is in financial trouble. But five, and some of them giveaways? No, I don't buy it. My money is on Ruth."

Twenty-Two

The Manhattan telephone book informed TJ that Ruth Kligman lived at 242 West 14th Street. The address rang a bell, and as he walked across town, he tried to recall why. Once he got there, it clicked. The building next door, 240, was where, twenty years earlier, he had used his lock-picking skill to investigate Thomas Hart Benton's murder—his first sleuthing effort, and as it turned out, a successful one.

The two brownstones had originally been elegant town houses, long since converted to mixed commercial and residential use, with retail on the garden and parlor floors and apartments above. Built in 1853 for Gabriel Winter, a wealthy lawyer and real estate developer, 242 passed through several hands after Winter's death and by the 1890s had become a boarding house, with the lower two floors remodeled as a storefront. Several artists had lived there since the turn of the century, notably Pollock's drinking buddy, Franz Kline, whose former studio Kligman now occupied.

TJ scoped out the building from across the street. A tall stoop led to the entrance door over a ground-floor liquor store. On the floor above it, large, north-facing windows in the cast iron façade, installed in an 1897 renovation, were shrouded by translucent drapes that let in light while maintaining privacy. That was likely to be the studio, but to be certain, TJ crossed the street, climbed the stoop, and checked the doorbells. Sure enough, the second-floor bell was labeled KLIGMAN. At that preliminary stage, however, he had no intention of ringing it.

Satisfied that he'd located the suspect's residence, TJ walked home across 14th Street and formulated his plan.

The tactic most likely to produce immediate results would be to surveil the building, determine when Kligman was out, pick the lock, enter the studio, and search it. If she was the forger, the materials would almost certainly be there. If not, he could turn his attention elsewhere, always keeping in mind that she might have them squirreled away at another location. After all, there was an accomplice—the guy who planted the fakes—and he might be holding the evidence. So even an empty-handed search wouldn't eliminate Kligman entirely.

Another approach would be to question her and see what he could learn from her reactions. Thanks to his training at John Jay and his years of experience, TJ was a master at formulating leading questions and discerning the nuances of tone and gesture that unconsciously signaled evasion and deception, as well as honesty. A face-to-face visit would also give him an idea of the layout, making it easier to search later in her absence, and he might even spot something telling without having to break in.

If he went that route, what excuse could he use to call on her? Probably she had heard about Francis' death, which had been covered briefly in the morning papers, or if not, she soon would, given the art-world grapevine's efficiency. Her feud with him was common knowledge. Going on the assumption that whoever forged the Pollocks also killed Francis to keep him from exposing the scheme, TJ would have to distance himself from both cases.

What about the painting Francis had described as Ruth's "bogus JP smear?" Maybe he could follow up on that, tell her Francis had had second thoughts about it. He could say that they were friends, that Francis had said he might have been too hasty in dismissing the painting and had discussed hiring him to look into it further. Now that Francis was dead, he felt he owed it to him, and to her, to investigate her claim. That would explain his interest without implying that he was after her for either forgery or murder.

****

"I like plan B," said Ellen when he laid it out for her over lunch. "If she submitted the painting to the board, there might be something in their files. Would you like me to ask Charlie? Or maybe Gerry would be a better bet. Charlie's pretty new."

"Let's not involve the board unless we have to," said TJ. "They'll wonder why you're interested in Kligman's painting, and you won't have a good answer. You can't tell them the truth, and you're a lousy liar. Francis' note implies that he saw the painting, so he may have a file on it. Maybe I can get back into his apartment. It's worth a try. I also wouldn't mind having a closer look at his will, or rather wills. There could be a completely different motive for his murder lurking in those documents, nothing to do with the forgeries. There's no reason to assume they're linked. It could be a coincidence."

"You don't believe that, do you?"

"No, but I can't rule it out. At least not until I know who benefits from his death. All the more reason to revisit the apartment."

****

"I'm afraid you won't be seeing Dr. O'Connor today, or any other day, Mr. Fitzgerald," said Louis. "The poor fellow was killed yesterday afternoon, fell under a subway train. Happened not long before you got here."

"I know," replied TJ. "That's why I'm back. When I came yesterday, I left papers for him to sign, and I need to get them for his attorney to execute. May I go up? I have the keys."

"You won't need them," Louis told him. "His friend Miss Crowe is up there now. She can let you in." He cast his eyes down and shook his head. "Terrible, terrible. I was quite fond of the gentleman. I'll ring and let Miss Crowe know you're coming up."

TJ thanked him and headed to the elevator. At the end of the hall on the 11th floor, he knocked on the door of apartment C and was admitted by a small, compact woman in her early forties who introduced herself. She invited him in, offered him a seat, and took one herself.

"Francis mentioned you to me, Mr. Fitzgerald. I understand you were working for him, though he didn't say in what capacity. Is there something I can help you with?"

TJ decided to lay a foundation for plan B. "I don't know if Francis told you, but I'm a private investigator."

The brows over Crowe's hazel eyes went up, and she tucked her chin. "Well, well. No, he didn't. Why would he need to hire you?" TJ detected just a hint of concern mixed with her curiosity.

"He had been approached by Ruth Kligman, an artist who had an affair with Jackson Pollock. She was in Pollock's car on the night he died. She—"

Crowe interrupted him. "You don't have to tell me about Ruth. Everybody in the art world knows that tramp."

"Are you an artist?"

"No, I'm an art historian, like Francis. He was something of a mentor to me. I was a graduate student of his in the mid-sixties, before he turned his back on academe, or rather, academe turned its back on him. He'd have you believe he quit because he was too unorthodox, but the truth is he had to leave the university because he didn't get tenure. Not a team player. But he managed to carve out a remarkable career as an independent scholar, doing things his own way instead of bucking the administration and dealing with faculty infighting, so in the end he was better off."

She shrugged. "Anyway, you were saying about Ruth, and why Francis hired you."

"Did he tell you that Ruth asked him to authenticate a painting she owned that she said was a Pollock?"

Crowe made a sour face. "No sooner was Lee in the ground than this thing came out of the woodwork, like a cockroach. Ruth wanted him to go down to her place and examine it, but he didn't want anything to do with it, or with her."

"You mean he never saw the painting?"

"Not in person, but she sent him a color transparency. Not under her own name, mind you. I guess she figured he wouldn't even open the envelope if he knew it was from her, so she got one of her boyfriends to put his name and return address on it."

"Then how did he know it was Ruth's?"

"He wrote back to the purported owner to say he didn't like it, but that he'd take it to the board if he was authorized to proceed, and she called him to fess up. She said she didn't want the board's opinion, only his. I guess she doesn't trust Thaw and Lieberman, though why she'd rely on Francis alone I don't know. You'd have to ask Ruth."

"Yeah, especially since he didn't like it. She might have had better luck with the others. What was wrong with it?"

"I'll tell you," said Crowe, "but first you finish telling me what you were doing for Francis."

"Sorry, I didn't mean to get off track, but it has to do with Ruth's painting. I met Francis through my wife, Ellen Jamieson, who used to be Lee Krasner's personal assistant. As Francis may have told you, she's the newest member of the authentication board. She introduced me to him, and when he found out I was a private detective, he asked me to help him with the Kligman painting." Without missing a beat, TJ had switched smoothly from fact to fiction.

"He said he dismissed it at first, not knowing it was hers, and when he found out she'd tried to hoodwink him, he was even more adamant. But then he got to thinking that maybe he'd been hasty. So he hired me to look into it, kind of unofficially, and said that if her story was plausible, he might reconsider."

Crowe looked thoughtful. "That would be a first for Francis, who believed his eye was infallible, but then he hadn't seen the painting firsthand. Only the transparency."

This led TJ to his other objective: the room where the wills were kept. "Do you think it's in his files?"

"Probably," said Crowe. "Let's take a look, and if we find it, you'll see the problem."

Twenty-Three

Crowe led TJ to the bedroom-cum-office. It didn't take them long to locate what they were looking for. In the closet was a small filing cabinet TJ had missed on his first cursory search. One drawer, marked POLLOCK: FALSE ATTRIBUTIONS, was subdivided into two categories, Copies and Imitations, established by the first authentication committee. Copies were based on known works and therefore relatively easy to identify, while imitations might simply be in Pollock's typical style or deliberate fakes. There were a lot of files, some dating back to the 1960s, when the catalogue raisonné was in its infancy, but there was nothing on the Kligman painting.

The other drawer, labeled POLLOCK MISC, contained drafts of articles, correspondence with museums, auction houses, and fellow scholars, and a section labeled Problems for Study, which held files on works about which the committee had been indecisive. The material was arranged chronologically, the most recent at the front, where they found a manila envelope with a September 1984 postmark.

"This is it," said Crowe, pulling the envelope from the drawer. The return address had been roughly crossed out, and KLIGMAN FAKE was written across the envelope in bold caps. Those words were also crossed out, though less emphatically. Evidently, Francis had removed Kligman's submission from the false attributions and re-filed it among the study problems. It appeared that he really did have second thoughts about the painting, so TJ's fabricated story wasn't so fanciful after all.

Crowe opened the envelope and took out the contents, a large color transparency in a glassine sleeve and a cover letter, addressed to Francis, from a man who claimed to have received the painting directly from Pollock, in exchange for some repair work on the studio, shortly before the artist's death.

She glanced around the room. "There's a light table in here somewhere," she said, and started to look under piles of unfiled paperwork and art magazines. When she ducked behind a stack of banker's boxes, TJ moved over to the shelves and located the document case marked LAST WILL AND TESTAMENT. He'd have to find a way to get Crowe out of the room long enough for him to transfer the contents to his briefcase.

"Here it is. Can you give me a hand, Mr. Fitzgerald?" she called from the other side of the boxes. The portable light table was tucked under a desk.

"Sure thing," he said, moving a pile of books off the desk to clear a space. "By the way, you don't need to be so formal. I go by TJ, short for Timothy Juan."

She smiled and said, "Hi, TJ. You can call me Birdie."

"Robin. Crowe. Birdie. I get it," he said as he returned her smile and set the light table on the desk. "Glad to meet you, Birdie."

She found an outlet, plugged in the viewer, switched it on, removed the transparency from its sleeve, and placed it on the glowing surface. The image, on a mottled silver background, was a swirl of red surrounding a black blob.

"How familiar are you with Pollock's work?" asked Birdie. TJ said he had seen quite a lot of it in various exhibitions and in private collections, but that he wasn't by any means an expert.

"This doesn't look like any Pollock I've ever seen," he told her, "but it's the same technique as plenty I have seen."

"Yes," she said, "the technique is the same, but the marks are wrong, at least Francis thought so. He said that the forms don't flow. They look static, tentative. They lack the dynamic rhythms that he believed he could detect in all genuine poured Pollocks, even the inferior ones. My guess is he originally filed it as an imitation. Maybe not an outright fake, since it doesn't have a forged Pollock signature, but not the real thing."

"I agree that it's clumsy looking, but if Pollock did this at the end of his life, when he was a physical and emotional wreck, that might account for it," reasoned TJ. "He hadn't done any painting in over a year, so he would have been rusty, not to mention maybe with a skinful. Lee said he never painted when he was drunk, but this could have been the first, and last, time."

Birdie agreed. "That was probably Francis' reasoning when he decided to give Ruth the benefit of the doubt. I wonder if he told her he was reconsidering."

"I'm going to find out," said TJ, inserting the transparency back into its sleeve and returning it to the envelope. "Would you mind putting this on Francis' worktable in the living room? There's a Xerox in there, and I'd like to make a copy of the envelope and the letter."

"I can do those for you," she offered.

"Would you? Great, thanks. Meanwhile, I'll just check the files again in case there's something else that could be helpful. I don't want to take any originals."

He opened the POLLOCK MISC drawer and pretended to look for more documentation as Birdie left the room. It took only a moment for him to step over to the shelves, remove the wills and slip them into his briefcase. If Birdie noticed the label, opened the box and found it empty, she'd probably assume Francis had deposited the will with his lawyer. And there was no indication that there were four of them. It was important to determine which one was valid—possibly more than one, depending on the terms.

It would, he thought, *be just like Francis to make it complicated.*

* * *

After exchanging contact information with Birdie—she lived nearby on East 75th Street—TJ prepared to leave her to continue the sad chore of notifying Francis' family and friends.

"His parents live in Brooklyn," she said as she accompanied him to the door. "They've been informed. Francis was their only child. As you can imagine, his mother was heartbroken, too upset to speak to me, but his father gave me the okay to handle whatever needs to be done."

"How did you find out about it?"

"I heard it on the radio when I got home after work, the six o'clock news on WNYC. I called the precinct right away, explained who I was, and told them I had keys to his apartment. They asked me to come in with an officer, and I found his parents' address and phone number. The officer said it would be better if I told them."

Wow, they must have gotten here right after I left, said TJ to himself. *That was a near thing.*

"That phone call was the first time I ever spoke to his father," she continued. "Francis wasn't close to his parents, working-class Irish Catholics living in Flatbush. They're proud of their brilliant, scholarly son, so his father assured me, but they're remote from his world. He hardly ever mentioned them, and when he did, he was condescending. I've known him for twenty years and have probably been to every one of his lectures and exhibition openings, but they were never there. I assume he didn't invite them."

Unable to imagine excluding his parents from any professional or social occasion, TJ expressed his disapproval. "That's terrible. Even if I knew my folks would be bored to tears, I'd at least ask them as a courtesy. They could always say no thanks."

"Well, maybe he did. I shouldn't jump to conclusions. It's just that Francis was so judgmental, it's easy to imagine him closing the door on those he considered outsiders, even family."

With his forensic psychology training, TJ had already profiled Francis as a conflicted personality whose bluster masked deep-seated insecurity. What was it in his background that made him overcompensate? Was it a reaction against parental authority? Did they want the priesthood for him, or marriage and a slew of grandchildren? Maybe their pride was superficial, not sincere. Through their patronizing smiles, they might be saying yes, you have a doctorate, yes, you wrote books, yes, you eat lunch with millionaires, but we'd rather you were less high and mighty and more like your cousin Father Gregory, who tends to the poor and the sick. Or your cousin Dennis, with three kids and another on the way.

Birdie cut in on his train of thought. "I'm glad you came by. I've been on the phone for an hour, and I was getting depressed, telling the bad news over and over. Frankly, no one was exactly bereft. Shocked, of course, even incredulous, especially considering how he died, but grief-stricken, no. He wasn't what you'd call intimate with people. He kept a lot hidden from even those who considered him a dear friend, myself included."

* * *

Instead of heading home, TJ decided to take the wills to the office, where he could study them without distracting Ellen. Sweeney wasn't likely to be around on a Saturday, but if he were, TJ would be glad to have him look them over. His partner was good at seeing through the fog of legalese, a language that made TJ's eyes glaze over.

He arranged the four wills in date order on his desk. The earliest, dated February 14, 1968, drafted by an attorney TJ had never heard of, bequeathed his dissertation research files, and all documentation related to the 1967 Jackson Pollock retrospective exhibition, to the Museum of Modern Art, New York, which had organized the show. The will was duly signed and witnessed. Its terms seemed to be straightforward and limited in scope, though separating that material from the later, much more extensive archive might be a chore.

The second, dated February 14, 1978, drafted by Gerald Dickler, rescinded the 1968 will and left all of Francis' research files and his art books and catalogs, as well as his copious poetry output, to the New York Public Library Special Collections Division. Excepted from the bequest were the files related to the Pollock catalogue raisonné, which were to be retained by Hall, Dickler, et. al. on behalf of the Estate of Jackson Pollock. That will was also signed and witnessed.

The third, dated February 14, 1982, also drafted by Dickler, was a codicil to the second, separating Francis' New Deal art project research material as a bequest to the Archives of American Art, a branch of the Smithsonian Institution, founded in 1954 with the aim of collecting artists' personal papers, oral histories, and other primary resources. But, that will had not been executed. Perhaps there were ongoing negotiations; Birdie had suggested as much. Or maybe things were resolved in will number four.

That document, drafted by another attorney unknown to TJ, took him by surprise. Dated February 14, 1985, it dealt with matters absent from the other three. In addition to a $150,000 life insurance policy and substantial investments in mutual funds, New York State bonds, and Treasury bills, he owned Pollock's *Number 17A, 1948,* one of the paintings reproduced in the 1949 *Life* magazine article that had made the artist famous.

All those assets were left to his executrix, Robin Crowe.

Twenty-Four

After he copied all four wills on the office Xerox, TJ looked up *Number 17A, 1948* in the catalogue raisonné and found it on page 34 of the second volume. It wasn't large, about three by four feet, but it had all the earmarks of a classic Pollock. The vigor of its multilayered composition was apparent even in the black-and-white illustration. Three bold brushstrokes contrasted with thin tendrils of poured paint, creating a dynamic visual counterpoint to the loops and swirls that were the artist's trademark.

There was, however, a problem with the painting: it was listed as missing. The provenance entry noted that it had been sold to a collector in Paris, who sold it to someone in Brussels, and that, like the lost works that fit the catalogue's blank spaces, it could not be traced. But in this case, there was a photograph, as well as a significant exhibition and publication history—notably in *Life,* where it was reproduced in color. No question that if such a famous lost canvas were to reappear, it would fetch plenty at auction.

The bequest raised the possibility that Francis' killing was unrelated to the trove of fake Pollocks. If Birdie was in financial trouble or had some other reason for needing money, and she knew he'd left her a bundle—not to mention a major Pollock—she had a strong motive for doing him in.

And it wouldn't have been all that hard. They were old friends, and she lived in the neighborhood, so if he happened to see her in the subway station he wouldn't have been surprised. She could have stood right next to him without alarming him, even jostled him as they stood near the edge of the crowded platform and blamed it on someone behind her, then seized the opportunity and given him the final shove.

* * *

As this scenario was playing out in TJ's mind, he heard the door open and saw Sweeney standing in it. A welcome sight, because he was already second-guessing himself.

"What brings you in on a Saturday, Pat?" he asked, and was answered with a snort.

"Bills, sonny boy, bills and more bills. First of the month just rolled around, and I got a few checks to write." Without enthusiasm, he headed into his office, followed by TJ.

"I thought Saturday was when you play papa. Aren't the kids disappointed?"

"My wife's taking 'em to the movies."

"Why didn't you go along?"

"To see *Off Beat?* A flick about a dancin' cop? No fuckin' way!"

"Right. Well, I'm glad you're here, 'cause I need to bounce something off you."

Sweeney settled into his chair and lit a Chesterfield. "Bounce away."

TJ described the contents of the wills, reviewed his conversation with Birdie, and laid out his theory about how she could have done the deed. Then he started airing his doubts.

"First of all, Birdie would have to have known she was in for a big payday when Francis died. From what she said, it seemed to me that she didn't know about the will."

"You say she's his executrix? Then, sure, she knew. Francis would have asked her if she was willing to do it."

"Yeah, but maybe he didn't go into detail about the value of his assets. She might have assumed it was all about the research material. If she didn't know she was going to be the beneficiary of a big life insurance policy, plus inherit a ton of money and a valuable painting, she'd have no reason to hasten his demise."

"Suppose she did know and had been thinking about ways he might meet with a fatal accident. Her being a New Yorker, a subway mishap probably would have crossed her mind."

"That's hard to figure, Pat. How could she arrange to be in the station when he was there? He wasn't a regular commuter who turned up at the same time and place every day, so she could hardly plan it out in advance."

Sweeney had the answer. "It must have been a chance encounter. She was headed downtown herself, spotted him on the platform, knew his unwise habit of standing close to the incoming train, and impulsively took advantage of the situation. When everybody started screamin' and yellin', it would've been easy for her to slip away. I'm sure lots of people fled the scene before the cops arrived."

TJ agreed. "The token booth attendant is unlikely to remember her. And if she's a regular subway rider, she probably already had a token. She could have simply left the station, walked the few blocks home, and later heard the report on the radio, just like she told the police."

"From what Samuelson said," continued Sweeney, "since no one was seen deliberately push him, it'll be booked as an accident. The dumb cluck got too close to the edge, stumbled—maybe was bumped by someone inadvertently—and over he went. There's no evidence it was done on purpose."

"Frankly," said TJ, "unless a witness recognized her and her connection to Francis was established, Birdie would be an unlikely suspect. To look at her, you wouldn't think she had the moxie to pull it off. She's short, slightly built, pretty, but ordinary-looking. She would have blended into the crowd unnoticed. Francis probably didn't notice her, either. She could have come up behind him. If he had recognized her and addressed her by name, people near them would have been able to identify her, and she wouldn't have gone through with it."

Sweeney stubbed out his cigarette and leaned back. "So you're pretty convinced that this Birdie dame is the killer?" When TJ nodded, he held up a finger. "Don't jump the gun, pal. You believe she had a motive, but you can't be sure. You need to find out if she was aware of the will. The means are obvious, no weapon required. But did she have the opportunity? Was she there when he bought it? That's gonna be hard to establish without a witness ID. Birdie ain't gonna tell you herself."

"That's for sure, and anyway, I have no reason to ask her. That would be the same as accusing her of his murder. But before I do anything else, I've got to put the original wills back where I found them."

"Not so fast. Suppose she already opened the box and it's empty. Like I said, she knows she's his executrix, even if she don't know the terms, so after she's done makin' phone calls, why wouldn't she look for the will?"

"Damn, you're right. No point in returning to the scene of my crime." TJ thought for a few moments, then he had a question for Sweeney.

"What if I take them to the attorney, the guy who wrote the last one?" He retrieved the document from the table and read: "Raymond White, of Walker, Millburn and White, Four-oh-five Lexington Avenue. That's the Chrysler Building. I wonder if the office is open today." He reached for the phone book.

"How're you gonna explain where you got them?"

"I'll just have to tell him the truth, that I took them from the apartment while I was in there with Robin Crowe."

"Why would you do that?"

"Because I'm a private investigator, hired by Francis, and I don't believe his death was an accident. I was looking for a motive for murder. I don't have to tell him I found one. Besides, there are a few questions he may be able to answer."

"Like for instance?"

"Like why are all the wills dated February fourteenth? And where is the Pollock painting? It sure isn't in the apartment." He looked up the office number and dialed it.

Twenty-Five

"Good afternoon, Walker, Millburn, and White. How may I help you?" TJ had expected an answering service, but found himself talking to a receptionist, whose artificial courtesy was well practiced.

"May I please speak to Raymond White?" he asked.

"I'll see if he's available," said the amiable female voice. "Please let me have your name and the nature of your inquiry," TJ told her and was put on hold.

Presently, the line opened, and a male voice identified itself as belonging to Raymond White. "I understand you're calling about the late Francis O'Connor. I was shocked to read the report of his death in this morning's newspaper. What is your relationship to him?"

"I was working for him in a private capacity," said TJ rather vaguely, "and I have some documents I would prefer to discuss with you in person. I'm just across town and can be with you in fifteen or twenty minutes, if that would be convenient."

After a moment of hesitation, White's curiosity overrode his desire to head home to Larchmont. "Normally I'm not in the office on a Saturday afternoon," he told TJ, "but I had some loose ends to tie up, so I came in for a couple of hours. If you can come right over, I'll wait for you."

* * *

A short taxi ride from his Hell's Kitchen office took TJ to the landmark tower on 42nd Street and Lexington Avenue that housed the attorney's suite. Financed by Walter Chrysler, head of the car company, the Art Deco monument ran neck and neck with the Empire State Building to be the world's tallest when the two skyscrapers were under construction in 1930.

Although the Empire State Building won the height contest, the Chrysler Building's elegant styling and automobile-inspired decorations made it the popular favorite. TJ often walked through the lobby when he was in the neighborhood, just to admire the intricately patterned African red granite walls, gleaming travertine floors, elevator doors with their elaborate fan-shaped inlays, and the ceiling mural, *Transport and Human Endeavor,* by Edward Trumbull, who also painted the Graybar Passage ceiling in nearby Grand Central Terminal.

Taking one of the elevators to the 23rd floor, TJ entered the Walker, Millburn, and White suite and met the amiable female voice in person. She buzzed White's office, received his okay, and led TJ down the corridor to the corner office, where the attorney greeted him with cool cordiality and offered him a seat in front of his splendid mahogany desk.

White got directly to the point. "How do you know that the late Dr. O'Connor was a client of ours?"

TJ was equally direct. "Because I have a copy of his will, drafted by you." He removed the document from his briefcase and handed it to White, together with his business card.

"I am a private investigator. Francis hired me to look into the provenance of some artworks he was researching. When he was killed, I went to his apartment to collect material related to the inquiry and found the will."

White regarded him shrewdly. "Why did you take it? Does it have some bearing on your investigation?"

"In a manner of speaking," said TJ. "I don't mean to be evasive, and the will has nothing to do with what I was working on, but when I learned how Francis died, I couldn't believe it was an accident or suicide. I believe he was murdered, and I thought the will might suggest a motive."

"And did it?"

Now, TJ did intend evasion. "It says nothing about the likely reason he was killed, which relates to the confidential matter I'm working on, and will continue pursuing until I get to the bottom of it, even though my client is dead. I didn't know Francis long, but I liked and respected him and want to bring his killer to justice."

"That is admirable," said White, "but if the will is unrelated to that aim, I don't see why you took it." His tone betrayed a hint of disapproval.

"Well, I shouldn't have removed it from his apartment, but it does raise a couple of questions I'm hoping you can answer." TJ reached into his briefcase, took out the other three wills, and laid them on White's desk. He sat quietly as the attorney looked over each one in turn. When he finished, he uttered a single word.

"Interesting."

"I'll say," replied TJ. "I know some people have multiple wills, and I can see why Francis would want to leave his papers to the museum or the library, but why don't the earlier wills say anything about his other assets? Isn't it unusual for a will not to cover an entire estate?"

"Unusual, yes, but not unheard of. The first will, which is no longer valid, was made in 1968. Dr. O'Connor was only thirty-one at the time, and it's likely he had few other assets, which in any case would have gone to his next of kin, presumably his parents, on his death. He appears to have been interested only in separating what he considered important archival material from whatever they would automatically inherit.

"The same is true for the 1978 will, though by that time, he must have had investments and other financial resources. As he was unmarried and didn't name a beneficiary, those assets would go to his parents. It's odd that he didn't include a monetary sum in his bequest to the library. Organizations often want some sort of endowment to maintain such a collection, though perhaps the New York Public Library is less restrictive than a university or museum. That may be why the 1982 codicil was never finalized. The Archives of American Art might require money to go with the papers."

"That makes sense," agreed TJ, "and maybe it got him thinking about just where his money should go. Not to the Archives, apparently. The 1985 will leaves it all to his friend Robin Crowe. I wonder why."

"I'm not at liberty to discuss my dealings with Dr. O'Connor," said White, "but I can tell you that he was very insistent on the terms. The 1978 will is still valid, though the library could decline the bequest. If they do, the material will revert to his heir, Miss Crowe, to dispose of as she sees fit."

"What about the Pollock painting? I guess she can dispose of that, too."

"Naturally. She will inherit it along with everything else. If she sells it, I expect it will pay off handsomely."

"It's not in Francis' apartment. Do you know where it is?"

"I believe it's in storage at Morgan and Brother, unless he moved it since the will was signed, which was only last year. He deposited a copy of the storage contract with me, as well as his insurance policy and other documents related to his estate."

"That reminds me," said TJ, "All four wills were signed on February fourteenth. Do you know why?"

White chuckled. "When he made the appointment to have the will executed, he said it had to be on that day, and I asked him why. He told me it was a superstition of his. It was a charm to ward off his death, to symbolically obviate the will. He was born on Saint Valentine's Day, February fourteenth, nineteen thirty-seven."

Twenty-Six

Having entrusted the originals of the wills to Raymond White, TJ headed home to hash out his theories with Ellen. Now he had two crimes to solve—who's the forger, and who's the killer. At first, he'd assumed they were one and the same, but the 1985 will had made him think again.

"Robin Crowe, hmm," said Ellen as they sat together on the couch, with TJ's copies of the four wills spread out on the coffee table. "The name rings a bell, but I can't place her."

"You, my beautiful wife, are memorable," said TJ, "but Robin Crowe, alias Birdie, is not. Nothing distinctive about her, sort of like Sweeney in that way, though one on one she does have plenty of personality—also like Sweeney, come to that."

"She must have visited Lee with Francis and been introduced to me. It'll come back to me. But it doesn't really matter. What's important is whether she pushed him in front of the train. How are you going to handle it?"

"I need to find out about her finances. Is she hard up for cash, so broke that she's willing to kill for the inheritance? And did she know how much was at stake? I asked White to hold off notifying her until Monday. I could go up to her place, tell her myself, and see how she reacts. Maybe I could also find out why Francis left her all his money and the painting."

Ellen shook her head. "I know how good you are at spotting the little things that give people away, but she's not likely to leave her bank statement or a pile of unpaid bills lying around where you'd see them."

"No, but I could tell if the bequest was a surprise or if she already knew.

And if I ask the right questions, she might let something slip. I'm especially curious about the painting. Maybe she knows how Francis got it. According to the catalogue raisonné, it's been AWOL for over twenty years."

He reached into his briefcase, took out a Xerox of the catalogue entry, and showed it to Ellen. The provenance listing ended in 1964, when it was exhibited at Marlborough-Gerson Gallery in New York City, which was then representing the Pollock estate on Lee's behalf. Presumably, it was sold from that show.

"I wonder who bought it, and why Francis couldn't trace the new owner. Guess I'd have to go back into his files to find out. I really should do that, because there's likely to be evidence of where he got it, hopefully a bill of sale."

"The doorman will wonder why you're showing up again," cautioned Ellen. "What's your excuse this time?"

"Like with the lawyer, I'll tell him the truth. I don't think Francis' death was an accident, and I'm trying to find out who killed him."

Ellen's head shook more vigorously. "Very bad idea. Attorneys keep their mouths shut. Doormen do not. It'd be all over the building, then all over the neighborhood, in no time. It could even get to Birdie before you do, and how would that work out?"

"Good point. I'm sure Louis has Birdie's phone number. I'll have to think up another reason."

"What did you tell him last time?"

"That I had to pick up some papers to take to the lawyer. Francis was supposed to have signed them."

"Okay then, tell him the lawyer needs more stuff, and he sent you to get it. Did he give you his card? Good. Show it to Louis if you think he's not buying it. Go tomorrow morning. The office will be closed, so he won't be able to call and verify until Monday. By then, you'll be long gone."

TJ gave her a smile and a hug. "When I tell people I married you for your brains, they don't believe me, but it's true."

She gave him a playful punch. "Of course, they don't believe you. Everyone knows it was my gorgeous body, and the family fortune, that hooked you."

* * *

Sunday, May 4

Following Ellen's advice, TJ arrived at Francis' building at nine a.m. and had no problem convincing Louis that he was there on behalf of Raymond White, whose card he handed over, to search for various documents related to the estate. His visit the day before had set it up rather nicely. He had made an appointment to visit Birdie at ten, which he felt gave him plenty of time to go through the relevant files and do a more thorough search for anything else that might be useful, then get to her place a couple of blocks away.

Once inside the apartment, he made straight for the office and the file cabinets marked JPCR. The files were organized by category—paintings, drawings, ceramics, mixed media, collage, sculpture, and prints—then chronologically within each group. But the numbering system was continuous, starting with a landscape on a cigar box lid, presumably Pollock's earliest painting, and ending with a poster for his 1950 solo show at the Betty Parsons Gallery, for a total of 1090 entries.

TJ's objective was entry 211. He removed the file and opened it on the desk. Considerably thicker than most, it contained a couple of 8 x 10 glossy photographs of the painting, copies of the brochure for a 1952 show in Paris, the checklist of a 1961 show in Basel, Switzerland, and the catalogue of the 1964 Marlborough-Gerson Gallery show in which it had made its final appearance before dropping from sight. There were also clippings of the reviews and articles listed in the catalogue, including the 1949 *Life* piece, rhetorically headlined "Is he the greatest living painter in the United States?" (Readers had overwhelming answered "No.").

More important, however, was Francis' correspondence with the galleries and former owners he had contacted in the 1970s in an effort to trace the painting, including carbon copies of his queries and the replies. TJ realized that his meticulous record keeping would be a valuable resource for future scholars, but right now he was hoping it would solve the mystery of the missing painting.

Nine years after the 1964 show, the Marlborough registrar had written to say that no sales record could be found, prompting a scathing reply from Francis, who demanded personal access to the gallery's files. The answer was a terse letter from Frank Lloyd, the gallery owner, agreeing to let him look for himself. Apparently, he did, and found nothing. A handwritten note from Gene Thaw to Francis said he'd spoken to Lloyd and got the same result. Even a fellow art dealer with Thaw's considerable clout couldn't get past the Marlborough roadblock.

That such a well-known and widely reproduced painting had gone missing was surprising, but that Marlborough had lost track of it was unbelievable. The assumption was that whoever bought it wanted to remain anonymous, and for some reason, Marlborough was willing to shield his or her identity. But the work's bona fides were established, and there was a copious paper trail, duly recorded in the catalogue entry, which noted dryly, "It cannot now be traced."

TJ closed the file with disappointment. It told him nothing he didn't already know, though it did fill in the details of Francis' unsuccessful location efforts. But as he replaced the file, he saw a small manila envelope that had been tucked in behind it. It was addressed to Francis and postmarked in Greenwich, Connecticut, on January 8, 1979. There was no return address.

He took it out of the drawer, sat down at the desk, and removed the contents. Inside was a plastic sleeve holding a 35-millimeter slide labeled "Pollock painting." He switched on the light table, placed the slide on it, and saw a color photo of *Number 17A, 1948*. A typewritten letter explained that the writer's father had purchased the painting years ago and now wanted to dispose of it. Could Dr. O'Connor advise him, in confidence, how best to go about it? There was a Connecticut telephone number, but no signature.

Wonder why the secrecy, thought TJ. *Why not just take the thing back to Marlborough?* Then he remembered how the gallery's reputation had been tarnished in 1972 by the Rothko scandal, and how Frank Lloyd had fled the country to avoid prosecution for grossly undervaluing Mark Rothko's estate. In light of the recently published Pollock catalogue raisonné, it would make sense to contact one of the editors for advice. But why O'Connor, the art historian, rather than Thaw, the art dealer? Maybe the Marlborough shenanigans had made him distrustful of dealers, and who could blame him? And there might be other complications, like why the owner still wanted to remain unknown. What was keeping him from sending it to auction? Pollocks of that vintage and size were fetching upwards of $150,000 in the late '70s, plenty more than it had cost him fifteen years earlier. Even after paying the seller's premium, he would have come out way ahead. An auction house would agree to an anonymous sale, but clear title would be required, and that could lead to exposure.

A private sale would be the best option, and Francis would know who was on the lookout for one. Turns out it was Francis himself.

* * *

Looking back over the letter, TJ noticed that the writer had used the word "dispose" rather than "sell," suggesting that the owner might be considering donating it to a museum or charity for a tax write-off. Arranging that anonymously could be a problem, also because of the need to establish title. But obviously, the painting had changed hands, so there must be some paperwork beyond the initial query.

TJ rose from the desk and began to check the other file cabinets and document boxes on the shelves. Once again, he silently complimented Francis on his well-organized system, with each drawer, ring binder, and box carefully labeled. Sure enough, a few boxes to the left of LAST WILL AND TESTAMENT was one labeled JP RECEIPTS. He took it down, returned to the desk, and opened it.

Inside was a bill of sale for two Pollock screen prints, a crayon sketch, and a watercolor, all of them small works that Francis had bought from Wally Strautin, the widow of Ed Strautin, in 1969 for $400. They had been sent as holiday cards to the Strautins, who were old friends of the artist from the 1930s. There was a separate bill of sale for a hammered copper plaque

Wally Strautin sold him a couple of years later. Pollock made two such plaques in 1938 as a kind of art therapy project when he was in treatment for alcoholism at a clinic in Westchester. The piece was anomalous and not especially valuable, at least not at the time. Francis had paid only $500 for it. These minor works were duly recorded in the catalogue provenances as gifts from Pollock to the Strautins, purchased from them by Francis, and now in his collection.

Also in the box was a folder labeled "Warranty Deed." TJ opened it and saw that it was what he was after.

The deed, executed on February 14, 1979—that auspicious date again—conveyed the painting from a Greenwich holding company to Raphael Research, a nonprofit corporation chartered in Delaware, of which the president was Francis V. O'Connor. The warranty promised that the conveyor held good title to the property described in Addendum A, which was a copy of the catalogue raisonné entry for *Number 17A, 1948*. Addendum B, the 1964 bill of sale for $20,000 from Marlborough-Gerson Gallery to the original buyer, a prominent businessman and officer of the holding company, established proof of title. Francis must have insisted on verifying the purchase before agreeing to the deal.

But what was the deal? The deed said only "due and proper consideration," nothing about a selling price. There must be another document dealing with the sale itself.

TJ glanced at his watch and saw that he'd already been there for over half an hour. Birdie's apartment was just a few minutes' walk away, but he only had another 15 minutes or so before he'd have to head out.

He returned to the shelves, but none of the boxes seemed relevant. Checking the file cabinets, he saw one with drawers marked RAPHAEL RESEARCH. Inside, the files were organized chronologically, starting in the mid-1960s, and dealt with various projects. It seemed that Francis had created a nonprofit entity to enable him to get government and foundation grants for his scholarly work. It also allowed his private clients to make their payments as donations that could be written off their taxes.

TJ flipped through the files to 1979 and found one labeled "JPCR 2:

211.". It contained a letter from the holding company's attorney stating that the painting was a charitable gift to Raphael Research in support of its educational mission and requesting Dr. O'Connor to arrange for its collection at a mutually convenient time. A carbon copy of Francis' reply acknowledged the donation with gratitude, noted that his tax-exempt certificate was enclosed, and said he would make arrangements with the moving company to pick up the painting as soon as it could be scheduled. There was also a receipt from the shipper and a bill of lading for delivery to the Morgan and Brother warehouse.

With little time left to spare, TJ turned on the Xerox and copied the manila envelope and its contents, the deed, the Marlborough bill of sale, and the documents in the Raphael Research file. After replacing the originals, he left the apartment and returned to the lobby.

"Find what you were looking for, Mr. Fitzgerald?" asked Louis.

"Yes," said TJ aloud, and to himself said, *I sure did*. "At least I got what Mr. White asked for. If he needs anything else, I'll be back. Oh, one other thing. Please let me have the name and number of the rental agent. Mr. White will arrange for the rent to be paid while the estate is settled." This was simply a tactic designed to make his relationship to the attorney appear official.

Louis jotted down the information on the back of Raymond White's card and returned it to TJ. Apparently, he wasn't going to call and confirm. "Here you are, sir. If you don't mind, I'd like to be informed of the funeral arrangements. As I said, I was fond of the gentleman and want to pay my respects when the time comes."

Twenty-Seven

Robin Crowe's apartment was in a modest walk-up building at 240 East 75th Street, not unlike the converted townhouse on 14th Street where Ruth Kligman lived, with commercial space on the street level and residential units above. Also like Ruth, Birdie was on the second floor, front. Just shy of ten a.m., TJ rang the bell and was buzzed in.

"Would you like some coffee or tea?" she asked as she led him inside. When he declined, she said, "Come into the living room and tell me why you're here. You were very cryptic on the phone."

It was a pleasant, book-lined room, more library and study than parlor, with a long desk under the north-facing windows. Bookshelves occupied the interior walls, and a handsome Oriental rug covered most of the wood floor. A couple of small armchairs with a coffee table between them were the only other furnishings, and they each took one of the chairs.

"I have a confession to make," he said, disarmingly, and got the expected quizzical look in reply. "The Kligman copies you made for me weren't the only documents I took from Francis' apartment yesterday."

He paused. Although he had worked out in advance how he was going to frame it, he wanted to be sure his tone was right, so he gave himself a moment, just a couple of beats, before he broke it to her.

"I found his will, and I removed it."

She frowned. "So that's why it wasn't in the box. I looked for it after you left. He asked me to be his executrix, and I said I would. Why on earth did you take it?" She seemed annoyed, not anxious or fearful.

"Just an impulse," he said, his tone neutral. "Have you seen it?"

"No. I was under the impression that it was a work in progress, that his on-again, off-again deal with the Archives was holding things up. He said I didn't have to be a witness, and he'd let me know when it was done."

As far as TJ could tell, she was being truthful. She must realize that he'd read the will and was aware of her role, which didn't seem to bother her.

"The will was fully executed in February 1985," he told her, "and you are named as executrix." Again, he paused. "Also, his primary beneficiary. Apart from the catalogue raisonné and authentication files, which go to the Pollock-Krasner Foundation, and a bequest to the New York Public Library, he has left his entire estate to you."

* * *

Birdie stared at him in what looked like genuine astonishment. He was an expert at detecting the small, often unconscious changes of expression that expose deception, but all he could see in her face was shock.

When she found her voice, she asked the obvious question. "Nothing to the Archives?" The question was only obvious if she assumed that Francis' papers were the entire estate. Did she really not know that it comprised money and art as well?

"The library will get all his papers. There's a separate will covering that."

"You mean he had two wills?"

"Two valid ones, yes. One, written in 1978, deals with the papers, and Gerry Dickler is the executor. The one that names you, written last year, deals with his other assets." He opened his briefcase, took out the copy, and handed it to her. He watched her closely for any sign that she already knew what it said.

She read it in silence, then surprised TJ with her reaction.

She laughed.

Not a giggle or a chuckle, but a startled laugh, like a response to unexpected humor. Then she took a deep breath.

"I'm sorry, I just can't believe it. What in God's name was he thinking?" She sighed and sank back in the chair.

TJ had no answer to that, but perhaps Birdie did if she thought about it. "Didn't he discuss it with you?"

She looked indignant. "If he had, I wouldn't have accepted. This isn't right. Nothing to his parents, nothing to the Archives, not even funds to the library to support the collection, or is that in the other will?"

"No, there's no money in that bequest. It all goes to you. And the Pollock painting."

She put the will on the coffee table and stood, a bit unsteadily. TJ wondered if it was an act, but decided no, she really was shaken.

"Excuse me, I need a drink of water," she said, and headed for the kitchen. When she returned, she had composed herself, and brought a glass for TJ as well. "I hate to drink alone," she quipped.

He took the water and thanked her. "I wouldn't blame you if you needed something stronger. You really had no idea about this?" Although he was now reasonably sure that Birdie was telling the truth, he wanted to press her until he was certain.

"Not a clue. I'm trying to think back to our conversation. It was in late eighty-four, November, I think. He invited me out to lunch. We went to JG Melon, around the corner on Third Avenue. I remember because I was a bit surprised that he wanted to go out. He usually enjoyed preparing lunch or dinner at home—he was quite a good cook, you know—but he said it was a special occasion. It wasn't his birthday, that's in February, so I asked what it was, and he was his usual secretive self, said he'd tell me over a glass of wine at lunch.

"When the moment came, he got quite serious. He said he'd made a decision about his estate. Then he surprised me by taking my hand. You remember I told you he wasn't really intimate with people. I never saw him embrace anyone, and he very seldom touched other people, at least in public. Anyway, he took my hand and said, 'I trust you, Birdie. You're the only one I trust. Will you be my executrix?'

"I was flattered, and touched, so of course I said yes, again assuming it was to do with handling the disposition of his papers. That'll be a big job, but now it seems it won't be my job, because that's not what it was about."

"Didn't you wonder why he was anxious to get his affairs in order?" asked TJ.

"Not really," she replied. "He was always talking about his legacy, how to perpetuate his contribution to scholarship. He had no intention of leaving his papers to his alma mater, which had discouraged his interest in modern art, so he kept considering alternatives. The Archives seemed the natural place, but there were complications."

"Like what?"

"They only wanted the papers related to his art research. They wouldn't take his books, and they weren't interested in his poetry collection. You probably don't know, but he was a serious poet since his youth, though none of his poems were ever published."

"I saw those ring binders on the shelf in his office. I guess that's why he wound up choosing the New York Public Library. They must have agreed to take the lot."

"Yes," said Birdie, "but from what you tell me, he'd already dealt with that years ago, in the previous will. I thought he was still negotiating with the Archives."

"Evidently, he was. There's a third, more recent will naming them, but it was never finalized. And neither the library nor the Archives bequest includes any money to go with the papers. It all goes to you."

Birdie considered this information as she finished her glass of water. "I still can't take it in. I cared deeply for Francis, and clearly he cared for me, but we weren't lovers. I always assumed he was gay, though he never had a boyfriend in evidence. Maybe he was asexual, I don't know. I'm very confused."

* * *

Suddenly, she went still, and TJ sensed that she'd realized the implication. She looked at him, and for the first time, he saw fear in her eyes.

"You do believe I had no idea what he left me, don't you?" She didn't have to elaborate.

"I'm inclined to, yes," he said. Not exactly wholehearted acceptance, but he went on. "You and I both know that someone pushed him in front of the train. Not accidentally. He was murdered, and inheritance is a common motive for murder."

She started to interrupt him, and began stammering a denial, but he held up his hand.

"Wait, hear me out. I lied to you when I said Francis hired me to look into the Kligman matter. It had nothing to do with her so-called Pollock painting. It was something else entirely, and while I can't tell you what it was, I figured it was what got him killed. But once I read the wills—and there are four of them, including an early one that's no longer valid—and I saw what you inherit, I had to reconsider."

"But I *didn't know*," she protested. "I knew he had investments. He sometimes talked about a nest egg that made it possible for him to work independently. What's listed in the will is far more than I would have guessed, but I just assumed the nest egg would go with his papers.

"And the painting. Where on earth did he get it? I've seen a few small things he bought years ago, and you probably saw the round copper plaque, it was on the bookshelf in the living room. He got them from a friend of Jackson's. They're only minor works, not worth a lot, though I'm sure they'd sell for much more than he paid for them. But I don't know anything about the painting, so I have no idea how valuable it is."

"You mean he never told you about it, or showed it to you? Not even a photograph?"

"I swear to you, TJ, the first I learned about it was reading the will just now."

"Do you have a copy of the catalogue raisonné?"

She did, and he asked her to get volume two. She brought it to the coffee table, and he opened it to page 34. Her eyes widened as she studied the entry.

When she looked up at TJ, all she could say was, "Oh, my God."

Twenty-Eight

"Do you believe her?" Ellen asked, after TJ had given her a rundown of his meeting with Birdie.

"Like I told her, I'm inclined to," he said. "I pumped her pretty hard, and watched her very closely, and as far as I could tell, she knew nothing about the contents of the will until I showed it to her. The only thing that was a bit off was her initial reaction. She laughed out loud, but that's the way some people react to a shock. My instinct is that she's innocent, but Mom and Dad, not to mention Sweeney, would tell me not to go on instinct alone, and right now that's all I've got."

"Don't forget the other motive," she reminded him. "Getting Francis out of the way so he couldn't expose the forger. We know he had three suspects. He was ready to tell you who it was and how he knew. That person must have got wind of it. Francis must have done something to give himself away."

"I don't see it that way," he said. "He was being super careful, and the whole reason he hired me was so he could stay out of it. I can't imagine him slipping up when he'd gone to such lengths to shield himself."

"Well, let's think more about it over lunch," said Ellen. "There's some ham and cheese in the fridge. How about a sandwich?"

"If it comes with a beer, I'm all for it." He followed her into the kitchen. "Speaking of Mom and Dad, I wonder if I should hash it out with them." His parents, both retired New York City police officers, lived nearby in Stuyvesant Town.

Ellen turned, tilted her head, and gave him a gimlet eye. "Timothy Juan Fitzgerald, you are a thirty-eight-year-old man with a master's degree in forensic psychology, a private investigator's license, and thirteen years of solving cases under your belt. As much as I love and respect your parents, I really don't think you need their advice on how to solve this one."

"Yeah, I get your point, but Juanita Diaz, alias Mom, is the best sleuth I ever knew, and she never steered me wrong in the past." After 38 years on the force, having risen from beat cop in the 1940s to chief of detectives at the Twenty-third Precinct in Spanish Harlem, TJ's mother was now teaching at his former school, John Jay College of Criminal Justice. His father, Brian Fitzgerald, a 40-year veteran, had retired as a deputy commissioner and was now serving as a security consultant to the United Nations.

"Why don't you hold Nita in reserve for now, at least until you have more to go on," said Ellen as she carried the sandwiches to the dining table. "Maybe you can eliminate one or two of the three without too much trouble. I'd say the least likely is Thaw. He has the most to lose if he's exposed. And he's got plenty of money, so why risk it?"

TJ followed her with the beers. "In my experience, baby, people with money always want more. If that sounds cynical, I'd argue it's realistic. Thaw places the fakes, authenticates them, waits a while, then approaches the owners and offers to find them buyers at a substantial gain. Not all of them would go for it, but even if only one or two did, he'd stand to make a pretty penny on his cut. That would compensate him for losing out on *Gothic*. He'd get even with Lee and turn a profit doing it."

"Let's look at Francis' notes again," said Ellen. She went to the file cabinet where she kept her paperwork, pulled the SUSPECTS file from the drawer marked PENDING, and took it to the dining table.

"Okay, I grant you the motive," she said as they reviewed his comments on Thaw, "but what about the means? Francis thought they were painted by MCW, but who is that?"

"I have no idea."

"Well, I do have an idea, at least how to find out. I'm going to ask the registrar at the Art Students League if he knows an artist with those initials. He's been there forever, and he knows everybody."

"I like it," said TJ. "So who's WSL?"

"That must be William S. Lieberman, the other board member. All the more reason why Francis wanted to stay in the background. He couldn't possibly accuse Thaw and Lieberman unless he had proof, especially if he thinks they're in cahoots. But I don't buy it. From what I saw at the meeting, if Thaw made a strong case for the paintings, I think Bill would go along with it. After all, they fill the missing slots. Having another person in on it would not only increase the risk, it would also cut into the profits."

"As far as opportunity goes, let's assume this NT person planted all of them. Why the hell did Francis have to use just initials? He could have written out the guy's name, for Pete's sake."

Ellen sat up. "Wait a minute, let me think back. Once, when Thaw came to visit Lee, he brought his son, and I was introduced to him. Damn, what was his name. Rick, Dick—no, Nick! Nick Thaw. NT!"

TJ leaned over and kissed her. "I love to watch you work."

"One little problem. Nick Thaw was about fifteen years old. Even a few years later, I think he'd have a hard time impersonating a middle-aged man."

TJ tapped the page. "When Francis made these notes, he didn't know that the paintings were planted by a grown man, not a teenager. That's what I found out. But knowing what we know now, we can cross NT off the accomplice list."

"Couldn't the same person who painted them, the mysterious MCW, also have planted them?"

"Sure could. The fewer people involved, the less risk of exposure."

"All right, then. On Monday, I'll hit the League and see if I can track down MCW. After that, I'll go to the Studio School and look up Mercedes Matter. She and Herbert seem more likely to me than Thaw."

"Hey, hey, hold on," said TJ. "I'm the detective, remember? Francis hired me, not you, to get to the bottom of this. Not that I don't appreciate your help, but—"

"But, what? Mercedes knows me. She once tried to recruit me for the school, remember? I could say I'm reconsidering, maybe wangle an invitation to see her studio. That would be where the materials are."

TJ decided to put his foot down. "Listen, Ellen, you don't understand.

I don't want you to confront anyone. It could be dangerous. I'm not just looking for an art forger, I'm looking for a killer. Getting information from the League is one thing—you can say you bought a painting signed MCW and want to identify the artist, or some such bullshit story—but that's it."

She started to protest, but he cut her off. "If I want to find out whether Mercedes or Herbert has the materials, I'll let myself into their studios when they're not around. You know I can do that as easily as I open our apartment door, with or without a key. I mean it, Ellen. Don't go near them."

He was really angry, and while she realized it was out of concern for her safety, her stubborn streak was threatening to outweigh her common sense. She knew he was right, but she didn't like being bossed around. She took orders from Lee Krasner because she was paid to, but this was different.

Grudgingly, for the sake of peace, she decided to concede. "Okay, I read you loud and clear. You're the detective. I'll just watch from the wings."

He got up from the table, lifted her out of her chair, and hugged her tight. "Promise me, baby. If anything happened to you, I don't know what I'd do."

Twenty-Nine

Monday, May 5

Ellen had decided to use TJ's excuse to try to track down MCW at the Art Students League. But before she headed uptown, she wanted to be prepared in case the registrar asked what the painting looked like. She leafed through Michel Seuphor's book, *Abstract Painting,* until she found a full-page reproduction of a work with no visible signature. It was by Erich Buchholz, a German artist whom she was sure had never attended the League. With white tempera and a fine-tipped brush, she added the initials MCW in the lower right corner. She took the book to the Federal Express office on Union Square and had a copy made of the page, without the identifying caption. As it turned out, her preparation was unnecessary.

She was well known at the League, where she was a life member. The registrar greeted her warmly and asked if she was thinking of joining the faculty, since her former instructor, Dagmar Freuchen, had retired and returned to her native Denmark. Joking that she could never fill Dagmar's very classy shoes, she got down to business.

"I'm thinking of buying a painting I spotted in a gallery in the Village, but I don't know the artist's name. It's signed with three initials, MCW, and there's no other identification on it. I'd like to find out who the artist is before I decide. I'm hoping it's someone who went to the League, so he or she will be in your records."

"It's a very long list," said the registrar, "but at least you only have to search for someone whose last name begins with W." He opened the office door and escorted her to the bank of card files dating back to the League's founding in 1875. He pointed out the drawer marked W-Z and said, "Happy hunting."

Remembering that artists sometimes drop their first names (Paul Jackson Pollock came to mind), she decided to look for anyone with a first name starting with either M or C. She found Max Weber, a distinguished early 20th-century cubist painter, but he'd been dead for years. Then she came to Corinne M. West, who attended from 1932-35. Right initials, wrong order, but she jotted down the name and continued working her way through the drawer. Eventually, she got to the end of the W's—Russel Wright, the famous industrial designer—without having found any other candidates.

She went back to the registrar's desk and asked, "Ever heard of Corinne West?"

"Sure," he answered. "She was Arshile Gorky's girlfriend. They were a hot item back in the thirties when she was a student. She was a real dish, or so the old-timers tell me, not so much anymore. I haven't seen her in a while, though. She used to submit paintings to the members' shows, only she let her membership lapse a few years ago. But she doesn't go by Corinne. Calls herself Michael C. West."

"She's not the only woman to use a man's name professionally," said Ellen. "I used to work for Lee Krasner, and while I don't think she deliberately tried to hide the fact that she was female, having an androgynous first name probably was an advantage."

"Yeah, that and having a last name that wasn't Pollock."

"Frankly, Lee could never get away from the association with her notorious husband. It caused her a lot of grief, but it also gave her plenty of clout in the art world. I doubt she would have gotten a retrospective at the Modern if she hadn't been Mrs. Jackson Pollock. Meanwhile, back to Michael C. West. What's her work like?"

"Real gestural, splashy, lots of energy. Out of fashion now, but she came up with the abstract expressionists and stuck with it. I kind of admire that."

"You know, I think I could be on the right track," said Ellen, improvising. "What you described is just like the picture I'm interested in. Do you have a current address for her? I'd like to show her a photo of it and see if she recognizes it."

"Let me check the members' files," he said. "Like I said, her membership lapsed a while back, so I don't know how current it is. Still, worth a try."

The address on file was 89 East Broadway, on the eastern fringe of Chinatown. There was a telephone number as well.

He copied the information and handed it to Ellen. "Hope it pans out. Good luck." She thanked him for his help and left with a feeling of satisfaction. Also with the determination to take one more step before turning over her information to TJ.

The Sixth Avenue local F train from 57th Street took her directly to East Broadway. What had once been a Jewish and Eastern European immigrant enclave was now largely Asian, with signs in Korean and Vietnamese as well as Chinese. She found the building in a row of dingy commercial structures a block and a half south of the subway station, almost directly under the Manhattan Bridge, which had plowed through the neighborhood in 1908.

There was a Vietnamese restaurant and deli on the ground floor, with lofts above that had been sweatshops when the building was new. The door that led to the upper floors had only four bells, one for each floor. The bell for the third floor was labeled WEST.

* * *

"I swear I didn't ring the bell," said Ellen when she finished telling TJ what she'd found out. "All I did was verify that she's still at that address. I don't know if she's our MCW or not, or even what she looks like, except that the registrar said she used to be a dish, whatever that means. But if she does turn out to be Francis' suspect, she's not the same person who planted the fakes, 'cause that was a man."

She had phoned him at the office, where he was checking on the whereabouts of the Matters. He had spoken to Ted Dragon, his reliable source for art-world gossip, and learned that, a few years after Herbert retired from Yale, he and Mercedes built a house in East Hampton, not far up the road from their estranged friend Lee Krasner. Ted thought that was odd, though maybe they were patching up their differences and planning to reconcile. But in 1984, when the house was just about finished, Herbert died, only a month before Lee.

TJ knocked on Sweeney's office door and heard the familiar rumbling sound that meant, "come in."

"I'm headed out, Pat. Gotta follow up a couple of leads on the O'Connor case. Is it okay if I'm off the clock for a while?"

"Well, this month's bills are paid, so I guess we can afford one charity case, if it don't take too long. You got that bribery matter to look into, remember. How good are them leads?"

"One is a long shot, a painter whose initials match one of Francis' suspects. She lives in Chinatown, so I'm gonna go pay her a visit, see if I can get a look at her work. The other's an artist who has a studio in MacDougal Alley. She and her husband were old friends of Jackson and Lee. Ellen and I know them slightly. The husband's been dead for a couple of years, but he could have painted the fakes any time after the catalogue was published. Or the wife could have done it."

"You don't sound enthusiastic," observed Sweeney.

"No, I'm not. The first one would have been working for the guy who dreamed up the scheme, and the more I think about it, the less likely he seems. The other two are more likely, because their motive is stronger. But there's someone else with an even stronger motive, and I'm leaving her for last."

"Why not start there?" said Sweeney. "You told me you're pretty sure the gal who inherits didn't kill him, so it must've been the forger after all, or somebody in cahoots with him. Or with her, since you say suspect numero uno is of the female persuasion. Why waste time eliminating the possibles when you got a probable?"

"Yeah, maybe you're right. As a matter of fact, I know her slightly, too. She won't remember me, but I do have a way in with her, a painting she owns that she wanted Francis to look at. I'm sure she knows he's dead, but I could still use it as an excuse for a meeting. I need to check out her studio."

"You got her number? Why not give her a call and make a date?"

Thirty

The phone rang and rang. TJ was on the verge of hanging up when a breathless voice answered. "Hello. Sorry, I just got in. Who's calling?"

"This is Timothy Fitzgerald. Am I speaking to Miss Kligman?"

A little sigh was followed by, "Yes, this is she. Mr. Fitzgerald, you say?" Clearly, the name meant nothing to her.

"I'm calling on behalf of Francis O'Connor."

"Oh, God, what an awful thing! He and I didn't get along, but I wouldn't wish that to happen to my worst enemy, and he certainly wasn't that!"

Her tone betrayed her tendency to overdramatize, also a characteristic of her memoir, *Love Affair*. TJ had borrowed his mother's copy and re-read it before making his call. In addition to chronicling her dalliance with Jackson Pollock, it vividly replayed the events of August 11, 1956—Pollock's fatal car crash, the death of her friend, Edith Metzger, and her own injuries. In the Afterword, she swore eternal love to Pollock's spirit. Yet, less than a year after his death, she was torridly involved with his archrival, Willem de Kooning, which made her words ring a bit hollow.

"Of course not," said TJ, encouragingly. "Francis' death was a tragic accident. The reason I'm calling is to follow up on your inquiry to him about your painting."

There was a moment of silence on the other end of the phone, then

Kligman's tone changed to one of curiosity mixed with suspicion.

"Really? Who are you?"

TJ told her that Francis had had second thoughts about her claim, which appeared to be true, then handed her his phony line about Francis hiring him to check out her story. He explained that Francis wanted to distance himself until more evidence was available, so he decided to use a private investigator.

"I want to see it through," he told her, "even though Francis is dead. I feel like he would rest more peacefully if it was settled, one way or the other."

She seemed to approve of that sentiment, especially as it implied that her claim might be substantiated. In which case, she'd be the owner of a very valuable painting.

"Why don't you come to my studio, and I'll show you the picture?" she suggested, as he knew she would. "Now, if you're free. I'll tell you the whole story, and you'll understand everything."

The hint of mystery was deliberate; she wanted to intrigue him, not knowing that his motive for visiting her had nothing to do with the painting in question.

He accepted her invitation.

* * *

It was a little over a mile from his office to Kligman's place, and it was a fine spring afternoon, so TJ decided to walk down 8th Avenue instead of taking a taxi or the subway. That gave him time to consider how to approach her, and also to ask himself why he'd been reluctant to tackle her first. After all, as Sweeney had pointed out, she was the prime suspect.

It had to do, he decided, with a deep-seated feeling of sympathy for her. He had first laid eyes on her thirty years earlier at the accident scene, lying half-conscious on Fireplace Road next to the overturned convertible and the bodies of her lover and her friend. His father had tried to shield him from the sight, had sent him across the street to ask the neighbors to call an ambulance, but he had seen his mother roll up her sweater and tuck it under Kligman's head.

As the accident investigation progressed, he'd heard his parents talk about her injuries and her treatment in Southampton Hospital. It was a miracle that she'd survived without any broken bones, though her whole body was bruised, and she had a concussion. It took months for her to recover fully, and when she did, she fashioned herself as an inspirational force to which great artists gravitated. Her memoir chronicled her affair with Pollock and ended with his death, but that was far from the end of her erotic adventures.

Psychologically speaking, as far as TJ was concerned, Kligman was not the muse; her lovers were *her* muses. She was using them to fill a void in herself. In the memoir, she described a revealing incident during the few weeks when she and Pollock were living together in the Springs house, while Krasner was in Europe. She was painting in Krasner's upstairs studio and asked Pollock for a critique. He said her painting was lousy and tried to dissuade her from becoming an artist.

Did that rejection haunt her? Did it make her doubt her talent? If so, she might imagine that, by sleeping with art stars, some of their creative genius would migrate to her. If it didn't work with one, it might with the next. She didn't have enough time with Pollock, but the long list of his successors seemed to bear out TJ's theory.

He also considered the fact that she had approached Francis to authenticate her purported Pollock. Why would she kill him when she needed his approval? And why muddy the waters by introducing a bunch of fakes that he was bound to suspect her of producing? If the forger and the killer were one and the same, it was unlikely to be Kligman.

On the other hand, Francis had rejected her initial approach, and she wasn't aware that he was reconsidering. If she thought she'd have better luck with the other board members, she'd have to get Francis out of the way. Likewise, if she made the bogus Pollocks. She could have painted them years ago, when the catalogue was published, and waited until Krasner died to get her own back for losing the undisputed Pollock she claimed he gave her.

But how would she know Francis wasn't fooled by the fakes? Only one had gone to the board and, having passed the forensic analysis, was still under consideration. Francis had hired TJ to cover for him, and as far as anyone knew, his inquiries were for himself as an art collector or on the board's behalf. Still, someone must have figured it out, or Francis wouldn't be dead.

Thirty-One

He climbed the stoop at 242 West 14th Street and rang the parlor floor bell, then stood back as she'd asked him to. She'd also asked him to describe himself.

The drape on the front window moved aside slightly and dropped back in place. Then the latch buzzer sounded, and he was admitted.

He hung his jacket on an old-fashioned coat rack in the entrance hall. A door on the right stood ajar. He entered a large, loft-like space that doubled as a painter's studio and a sparsely furnished living room. He stepped into the work area, with a palette table, easel, shelves for materials, flat files, and a tall stool, which occupied the front. A few canvases leaned against the wall, face in. There was also a metal storage cabinet and a couple of lockers that probably held paints and other supplies.

At the back, where painting storage racks lined the rear wall, floor to ceiling, were a Victorian récamier settee and an ornate armchair with a high back. A couple of gossamer banners, loosely painted on translucent material similar to the window drapes, hung from the high ceiling.

The back of the room was in shadow, so he didn't see her at first. She was lounging on the récamier, propped on one elbow like the David portrait of the sofa's namesake, only turned frontally and wearing an elaborately embroidered silk kimono fetchingly draped to reveal her bare legs and a liberal helping of cleavage. Her hair fell in loose waves to her shoulders. No longer lustrous dark brown, it was now a rusty red that hid its natural gray.

"Hello, Timothy Fitzgerald. Come and sit by me."

Her voice was soft and inviting, with just a hint of sultry. As he approached, she smiled and held out her left hand—such a theatrical gesture that he wasn't sure whether he was expected to shake it or kiss it. He opted for the former.

She swung her bare feet to the floor, which suggested that she expected him to sit next to her, but he took the armchair instead. Besides wanting to address her face-to-face, he was disconcerted by her louche, informal attire. It was a pose, he knew, deliberately designed to unsettle him, so he needed to deflect her aim.

"It's a pleasure to meet you, Miss Kligman. Thank you for seeing me at such short notice," he began, aware of her intent focus. It's a ploy women believe makes them more attractive to men, who like to think they're fascinating conversationalists, while their audience is probably bored stiff.

"Please, it's Ruth. May I call you Tim?" she asked politely, with a charming tilt of her head that he was sure she had deployed countless times in her 56 years on earth. TJ had seen other women use it often during his own 38 years.

"Of course, Ruth. Let me explain my mission. As I told you when we spoke, it's kind of a posthumous favor to Francis." He then embarked on his fabrication about Francis' hiring him to investigate the painting's backstory.

"I'm sure you know how stubborn he was, but he was also a man of integrity, and once he had doubts, he wouldn't rest until he got to the bottom of it. But he also didn't want to be seen second-guessing his own judgment. How would it look if the foremost Pollock expert wasn't sure of himself? He needed some solid evidence before he'd go on the record. If it exists, he thought I could find it."

"Oh, it exists. It was thirty years ago, but it's like yesterday to me." She leaned forward, revealing a bit more cleavage, as her gaze shifted from his face to somewhere near the front windows, as if their light was illuminating her memories. He had to admire her performance.

"I'm sure you've read my book, so you know how deeply and passionately I loved Jackson. And that love was returned equally. He was going to divorce Lee and marry me. But it had to be handled carefully. Even though he didn't love her anymore, he depended on her for so many things. Sidney Janis was his dealer, but she controlled his career, and it was paying off. It wasn't going to be easy to get away from her, so I understood why we had to wait."

Well, well, said TJ to himself, *so she fell for that old line. I want to marry you, but my wife won't agree to a divorce. She'll come around eventually, so just be patient and let me keep screwing you.*

"The only way he could prove his commitment to me was with his paintings. Giving me one was like giving a piece of himself. As soon as I moved in with him, he took me into the studio and told me to choose one of his major canvases. I couldn't believe it! The room was absolutely lined with masterpieces, and he let me pick any one I wanted!" Her voice swelled with emotion, as if she were still in the studio filled with Pollock's work.

"It was far too big for me to take back to my apartment in the city, and if it was missing, Lee would know, and demand that he get it back, so we decided to leave it there until he was free and I could claim it. He sealed the promise with a kiss, and suddenly we were making love in the studio, right in front of the painting. It was magnificent!"

"In the book, you say you never got the painting, so that's not the one you contacted Francis about."

"No, that's a much smaller painting, on one of my canvas boards I'd brought from the city. I wanted to paint in the country, to get a new perspective on things, and I thought being around Jackson would stimulate me. In a way, it did, but I wasn't getting anywhere. I did a landscape, but it didn't work. That was Jackson's word to describe a successful painting, it worked. Mine didn't. He said it was too tight. He wanted me to loosen up, to paint freely, without preconceptions. 'Don't copy the scenery,' he said, 'paint how it makes you feel.' Then he said, 'I'll show you what I mean.'

"He grabbed a still life I'd been working on in town and brought it out to finish in Springs. He took it outside and laid it down on the lawn, then he went into his studio and came back with a few cans of paint, a brush, and a couple of basting syringes. You know, the kind you baste turkey with, Pyrex, with a rubber bulb. He used them to get long lines of liquid paint.

"He dipped the brush in a can of aluminum radiator paint, completely covered my still life with silver, and put it in the sun to dry. While it was drying, he talked to me about getting back to work. He said that my being there was inspiring him, and even though it was only a demonstration, this painting would help him find the way back. I was ecstatic! This was what I'd dreamed of. I would be the one to save him!"

She was getting agitated again, and TJ could feel her verve animating the story. She really knew how to put it over. What she didn't mention, and what he assumed, was that Pollock was as tight as Ruth's landscape. According to his friends, he'd been on a bender for months.

"It didn't take long for the silver paint to dry enough that he could work over it," she continued. "It was one of his favorite colors, but he usually used it as a kind of highlight to contrast with flatter colors. I asked him why he made it the background, and he said so the next layer would stand out against it. That would make it more dynamic. He wanted it to be overflowing with energy. Even though it's small, the size doesn't matter as long as it has energy, and it does. You'll see."

TJ has already seen the transparency, so he knew what the composition looked like, though he didn't tell her that. And while he agreed that there was plenty of energy on the canvas, it seemed to him unfocused, not on a par with Pollock's other, small poured works.

Ruth continued her narrative. "Next, he took a baster and dipped it in a can of black enamel. He would often lay down a framework of black lines and then elaborate on the design with other colors, but he surprised me by making just one black shape, letting the paint run out rather than squirting it or making lines. I said, 'Is that it?' and he said, 'I don't know. I have to study it a while.' So we sat on the rocks and smoked while he looked at it, then he said he needed to clear his head and he went in the house."

Probably to get a drink, said TJ to himself.

"When he came back out, he went straight to the painting, picked up a can of red paint, sucked up a lot of it in the other baster and started swirling it around on the canvas. His movements were so graceful. He seemed so sure of himself, like a great dancer. I just watched spellbound. It was only a few moments, and then he stepped back and said, 'It works. Do you see what I mean about freedom, letting the process take over?'

"I asked him where the image had come from. I always needed to start with something, like a still life or a landscape, but his image seemed completely intuitive. He said, 'Look around. Nature generates my imagery, but from the inside out.' Of course! How could I not have realized? It was inside him, struggling to come out, and now there it was, his beautiful life force liberated. I cried with joy."

Her story was captivating, but TJ realized that it contradicted what she had written in the memoir. She'd said that, during the time she was living with him, he wasn't painting at all. So he had to ask the question it raised.

"Why didn't you mention this in your book? You talked about the other one, the painting you didn't get."

She had the answer. "But that's the point. That one had already been shown, and I wanted to lay claim to it. One of Jackson's friends said he'd help me get it, but he never did. I'm sure Lee saw to that. But the other one was painted just for me, while I watched, and it was small enough for me to carry back to the city when I went in to, ah, take a little break."

As gushingly romantic as much of her memoir was, she had also confessed to misgivings about the long-term prospects of her relationship with Pollock. At one point, she had felt an overwhelming need to consult her psychiatrist—it seemed everyone was in analysis in the 1950s—to confide in her friend Edith, who was also having an affair with a married man, and even to date someone else.

"I'll be honest with you, Tim." Her tone was earnest, as if she was about to reveal a deep secret. *Hasn't she been honest all along?* he thought.

"I didn't mention it because I was afraid Lee would sue me to get it. She controlled his estate totally, and her minions were beating the bushes for the catalogue raisonné. That's when I first contacted Francis, in the early seventies. I wanted to find out if he knew the whereabouts of the big painting Jackson gave me. Of course, he did—Lee still had it—but he wasn't going to help me, so I considered suing her for it. But I had no proof, and I got to thinking that if I took her to court and got mixed up with her lawyers, she might find out about the other painting. So I dropped the whole thing and didn't show it to Francis and didn't write about it. Maybe that was a mistake, but I was afraid I'd lose the only piece of Jackson I had."

Thirty-Two

"You've put your finger on the problem," TJ told her, "not only with the big painting, but with the small one as well. The lack of proof. In both cases, it's only your word for it."

"I told a couple of friends about it at the time," she said. "They'll back me up."

"You could have made up a story, and they'd have no reason to doubt you. A lawyer would argue that they're unreliable precisely because they're your friends. It's all hearsay anyway."

Ruth rose from the sofa and adjusted her kimono in a carefully executed, unsuccessful effort to minimize her décolletage. "The painting speaks for itself," she said. "Come with me and I'll show you."

TJ glanced at the storage racks as he stood up. "Isn't it here?"

"Those are all my things. I keep it in a special place." She treated him to a conspiratorial smile, looped her arm in his, and gave it a little squeeze as she led him across the studio toward the hall.

Her provocative behavior was making him uneasy. He was well aware of her reputation. It crossed his mind that that was another reason he'd been reluctant to deal with her, but what choice did he have? She was undoubtedly his most promising suspect for both crimes. He wanted to search the racks to see if there were any imitation Pollock practice efforts, and to check the storage locker for vintage enamel paints, rolls of old canvas, and Masonite baseball game boards. He'd have to make a tour of inspection when she was absent. At least he now knew where to look.

They walked down a hallway lined with photographs of Ruth, a couple of dozen in all, some of her alone, others of her with friends and lovers. She had been beautiful in her youth and well into middle age, and the camera was kind to her. In the early days, it captured a mane of dark curls framing a face that some had compared to Elizabeth Taylor's, and a body that Pollock had described to a friend as "loaded with extras," like a high-end car. Later, after the hair turned from deep brown to artificial red, she was still alluring. Even in candid shots, she oozed sensuality, though most of them were designed to maximize the effect.

"How do you like my photo album?" she asked. Without waiting for an answer, she toured him through the display.

"There's me with Bill, on the beach in East Hampton. He taught me so much about art, and about life. Here I am with Franz. This was his studio, you know. He died so young—not as young as Jackson, but he had a bad heart. Ironic for a man everyone said was good-hearted. I love this one of me by Bob Mapplethorpe. He took another one of just my hands, like Stieglitz did of O'Keeffe's. We weren't lovers, but he treated me tenderly, as if we were."

What was missing was the well-known snapshot of Ruth in a bathing suit, sitting on Pollock's lap in the back yard in Springs: he, bearded and bloated, clutching her bare leg and leering at the camera; she, pressing his arm to her chest and grinning ear to ear. Edith had taken the picture in the afternoon before the fatal accident, and Ruth had used it as the frontispiece of her book. But it wasn't in her ego gallery.

TJ found out why when they got to the end of the hall and entered her bedroom. The picture, elaborately framed in silver filigree, had a place of honor on the wall opposite the double bed.

She stopped in the doorway, so TJ could get the full impression. "We were so happy, so full of love for each other," she gushed. "He's with me always. He greets me every morning when I wake up, and I kiss him good night every night."

Apart from being a bit morbid, this ritual struck TJ as disingenuous, if not downright hypocritical. He wondered how often she had turned the picture to the wall when entertaining another man in her bed. How many had there been? Who was the current one?

She was still attractive and making an effort to show it. There must be plenty of guys who would want to sleep with her, even if only so they could brag about having plowed the same field as Pollock and de Kooning. Maybe she was between lovers, which is why the photo was prominently on view.

* * *

"Sit here," said Ruth, patting the bed. Not much choice, since there was no chair in the room. He did as she asked. Opposite him was a chest of drawers, with a wardrobe to the left.

Ruth put a hand on his shoulder and gave it a little caress. "Stay right where you are and you'll see why I brought you in here," she said, and he wondered if that was a double entendre. She crossed to the wardrobe and opened the door to reveal a full-length mirror, in which he was reflected. It startled him to see how awkward he looked, perched stiffly on the edge of the bed, as if ready to bolt from the room.

She picked up on his discomfort and chuckled. "Don't be nervous. I don't bite. At least not unless I'm asked to." That remark made him even more edgy. Suddenly, a line from "The Graduate" flashed into his head. *"Mrs. Robinson, you're trying to seduce me."* He tried to bury that thought. Ruth was almost old enough to be his mother. Which, he realized, was the age difference between Anne Bancroft's Mrs. Robinson and Dustin Hoffman's Benjamin Braddock.

Ruth reached into the wardrobe, removed a rectangular object covered in cloth, and propped it up on the chest of drawers, so TJ faced it directly. "Close your eyes," she said, and he did. He heard the cloth being removed, and then felt Ruth sit down next to him, just close enough for him to feel the warmth of her body without her actually touching him. "Now open them," she whispered.

On a standard-size canvas board, 24 by 20 inches, was the painting Ruth had described in her narrative. On the silver background, through which traces of her underpainting could be detected, a single ovoid shape in dense black enamel was surrounded by swirls of bright red paint.

As they studied the picture in silence, TJ became aware that Ruth's breathing had quickened. He groped for something to say to dispel his anxiety. He felt his throat tighten, and he cleared it.

"Too bad he didn't sign it." Kind of lame, but his thinking was a bit foggy.

"He didn't need to. His essence is in every stroke." Her voice was husky, and her hand made its way to his thigh. "Every movement, every touch. His power, it's so strong. I feel it deeply. You feel it too, don't you?"

No, that's not what he felt. What he did feel, in spite of himself, was arousal. The pulse beating in his ears was echoed by the throb in his crotch.

With well-practiced movements, Ruth shrugged the kimono off her shoulders. As he'd suspected, she had nothing on underneath. For a woman in her mid-fifties, her breasts were remarkably round and firm, and the nipples were erect.

TJ had lost his virginity with Ellen when they were both 19, and he'd been faithful to her ever since. Naturally, there were opportunities to cheat, especially in his line of work. Occasionally, a female client would hit on him, but he'd always resisted temptation. A couple of male clients had tried it on, but he had no interest in working that side of the street. His standard response was either to ignore the come-on or, if it were too blatant, to deflect it with the "I'm flattered but happily married" gambit.

Why wasn't he doing that now? What was stopping him from standing up and walking out? Well, standing up might be awkward, but not impossible. Yet he just sat there as Ruth nuzzled his neck and ran her hand up his thigh until it reached the bulge between his legs. Then his hand was on her breast, and she moaned with pleasure as she gently pushed him down on the bed, unbuttoned his trousers, and unzipped his fly.

Thirty-Three

The moment it was over, he was flooded with remorse. Mindless fucking, almost automatic—it disgusted him to realize how gullible he'd been. He should have jammed on the brakes the moment he knew what she was up to.

He rolled over and sat up. God, this was so sordid. He wasn't even fully undressed. His shirt was bunched up, and his trousers and briefs were around his ankles. She had taken charge, using her lips and tongue to ensure his readiness, then pounced on him like a predator. Now she lay beside him, wearing only a satisfied smile. He closed his eyes, turned away, and struggled to get his clothes back in order and retrieve his shoes.

When he stood to zip up, she slipped back into her kimono. Realizing that he was conflicted, she used an excuse calculated to reassure him while reinforcing her claim. She spoke with what she intended to sound like heartfelt sincerity.

"Now you understand the incredible force of Jackson's art. His genius engulfed us, overwhelmed us, carried us away. Only Jackson could have created something with the power to transport us like that. Now you know that what I told you about the painting is true."

He looked at her in disbelief. "Are you trying to tell me that that thing"—he gestured dismissively at the canvas—"made me have sex with you? It's ridiculous."

"It wasn't just sex, Tim," she said softly. "It was a beautiful, spiritual experience. Jackson's spirit flowed from his creation and entered me through you." She reached out to touch him, but he pulled away.

"You're crazy if you think I'd swallow that! I made one mistake, and it was a whopper, but I'm not going to make another, even bigger one."

Fueled by regret and shame, his anger propelled him out the door and down the hall. Still somewhat disheveled, he grabbed his jacket off the rack, left the building, and put the painting, Ruth, and her absurd fantasy behind him.

* * *

He walked up to 23rd Street and spent half an hour in the McBurney YMCA steam room. But even after sweating and showering, he didn't feel clean, especially after he dressed in the same clothes. The pants were okay, but the shirt still carried Ruth's scent.

He detoured over to Macy's and bought a new shirt, as close to the old one as he could find, but it wasn't an exact match. At a street vendor's cart, he bought a chili dog and spilled most of it down his shirt front; the rest he threw in a corner trash bin. He could change when he got to the office and try to wash out the chili stain in the sink. That would be his excuse to Ellen, who couldn't fail to notice the new shirt.

Ellen. He would have to tell her that he'd visited Kligman and seen the painting—they had discussed his plan to do just that. She had no reason to suspect that it was anything more than a routine part of the investigation. After all, that's what it was, until Ruth turned him into another of her conquests, with the deeper aim of convincing him that her painting was authentic. But Ellen was so observant. Would something in his eyes or his voice or his manner give him away? He was sure that, if the shoe were on the other foot, he'd know she was lying to him.

The walk north to West 49th Street was the longest of his life. The afternoon sun was warm, but he felt clammy inside his jacket, and he realized what it meant to be wracked with guilt.

Even more troubling was the realization that he'd have to go back. He had seen no physical evidence of the materials used to produce the forgeries, but he was more convinced than ever that Ruth was the forger. What was it Francis that had written in his suspects file? That she channels Pollock like a medium? That was exactly how it felt to TJ while she was drawing him into her psychosexual orbit. If she was capable of mesmerizing him—and here he began to imagine a way to lay the blame for his transgression exclusively at her feet—then surely she could self-induce a trance in which Pollock's ectoplasm would guide her as she made paintings in his style with his materials. For all TJ knew, she'd been doing it ever since he died. Her storage racks might be filled with them.

Yes, he would return. But she wouldn't be there.

Thirty-Four

When TJ got back to the office, Sweeney was out. He found a note on his desk reminding him that the bribery case (for a paying customer) needed his attention. He read it and thought, *Thanks a lot, Pat. As if I don't feel guilty enough already.*

He changed into the new shirt, dumped the soiled one in the restroom sink, and let it soak in cold water. He pulled the case file and opened it on his desk, but couldn't focus on it. Besides, it was after five. Today was his turn to cook dinner, so he'd have to head home soon. And face Ellen.

How about if he called her, told her he had to work late on the bribery case, and asked if she'd be okay with takeout? It wouldn't be the first time he'd stayed after hours. Then he could give her an expurgated account of the Kligman visit over the phone. That might relieve some of the emotional pressure.

He waited half an hour before making the call. Another stab at the case file had done nothing to help get his mind off Kligman. What did help was changing his shirt. Now he couldn't smell her anymore. And he'd been able to relax a little and rehearse his story, which would all be true, as far as it went.

It was just before six when he dialed his home number.

"So there you are," said Ellen, with a hint of teasing reproach in her voice. "It's Tuesday night, remember, and I'm getting hungry."

"I know, I know, and I'm sorry for being late. Sweeney is on my ass about a job I've been neglecting in favor of the Francis freebie, so I was trying to catch up. I'll head out in a few and pick up some Chinese on the way. Or would you rather have Italian?"

"I'd rather have your chicken cacciatore, but by the time you get here, I'll be ready to eat whatever you bring. And screw the other job. How is the Francis freebie going?" Her choice of slang gave him a twinge.

"I visited Kligman's studio this afternoon," he told her, keeping it conversational. He was glad he'd decided to get it over with on the phone, much easier than being evasive face to face. "I fed her the line about Francis rethinking her claim. She showed me the painting, but she didn't have any tangible proof that it's real. She tells a good story, only there's nothing to back it up. But that's not really why I was there, so I listened politely and tried to spot any evidence that she painted the forgeries."

"And did you?"

"Afraid not. The only paintings I could see in the studio were her own things, kind of like banners, hanging from the rafters. There were a few canvases stacked against the wall, but the stretchers looked pretty new, not like the ones on the fakes. There are a lot of paintings in storage racks, and cabinets and lockers where old materials could be stored, but I couldn't get a look at them. Not with her there, anyway."

Ellen chuckled. "I think I detect an urge to dust off the pick set. Am I right?"

"Hmm. Could be. But I'll have to find a time when she'll be out or get her to leave at a certain time. Gotta work on that."

"Right now, could you work on locking up the office and bringing home some food?"

"You bet, baby. I'm heading out this minute." He hung up with a sense of relief, though she'd be bound to have more questions, want more details. What's her place like? What's *she* like? That one was going to be tricky, but at least he'd done the groundwork.

* * *

Emerging from the Union Square IRT station, TJ headed to Paul & Jimmy's Ristorante on East 18th Street and picked up a double order of lasagna and a spinach salad. Home was just three blocks south and four flights up.

Ellen had already uncorked a bottle of Chianti and poured a glass for herself. When she heard TJ's key in the lock, she poured one for him.

"Perfect to go with P and J's lasagna," he said, as he set the takeout on the dining table and, as nonchalantly as possible, hugged and kissed his wife. Perfectly normal, just routine, really, so why did it make him feel like a phony?

He needed a distraction, so he picked up his wine glass and toasted the lasagna, the restaurant's signature dish since 1950.

Seconding the motion, Ellen raised her glass and touched his. "Here's to perfect pasta. Cin cin! It smells delicious. Open it up while I get some plates."

"I got salad, too," he told her. "Spinach, your favorite."

While she was in the kitchen, he took off his jacket and hung it up. When she came back, she spotted the difference. "Where'd you get that shirt?" she asked.

He told the lie he'd worked out: he stopped at a street vendor to grab lunch on his way downtown; was jostled by a guy reaching for the mustard just as he got the chili dog to his mouth; made a mess on his shirt; couldn't go to the interview looking like that, so ran over to Macy's and bought a replacement. It sounded quite reasonable.

"Where's the dirty one?"

"I left it to soak at the office. Cold water, was that right?"

She nodded. "Uh, huh. Bring it home tomorrow and I'll put it in the wash." Grinning, she added, "Better tuck a napkin under your chin, or history might repeat itself with the lasagna. Wouldn't want to spoil a brand-new shirt." He returned her grin and looked suitably contrite.

"By the way," she said, as she served up the dinner, "I remembered where I met Robin Crowe. It wasn't at Lee's. She's the art librarian at Hunter College. She started the semester I left, so I didn't see much of her. She was just Miss Crowe to me, but now that I think about it, I'm sure it's the same person."

"That makes sense," he said, glad to be talking about someone other than Kligman. "She lives just a few blocks from Hunter, and her living room looks like a library. She told me she's an art historian, but she didn't mention where she works."

"I think she teaches there as well, though I didn't take a class with her, or I would have remembered her sooner. As you said, she's not a standout. Very soft spoken and reserved, sort of a librarian stereotype."

"I need to call her, find out about the funeral arrangements. The body has probably been released to the family, no point keeping it in the morgue. I doubt the cops would bother with an autopsy. The cause of death is obvious."

* * *

To TJ's relief, Ellen wasn't curious to learn more about his interview with Kligman. He had given her enough over the phone. She was more interested in pursuing the line of inquiry she had opened by identifying MCW.

"Are you going to follow up on Corinne West, known professionally as Michael? I checked the phone book, and the number I got is still valid. Why don't you give her a ring?"

"You mean now?"

"Well, after we finish dinner. She's likely to be home in the evening." She took a sip of wine and offered her theory. "I've been thinking—"

"Always dangerous," he interrupted.

"Now stop! I know you're not sold on Gene Thaw as a suspect. Too much to lose if it blows up. But just because Francis thought MCW painted the fakes for Thaw doesn't mean she did. What if she painted them on her own? We know Nick Thaw didn't plant them—he's too young—so maybe West did them and had a male accomplice do the planting, someone we haven't identified yet, a relative or—"

TJ interrupted again. "Hold on, what's all this 'we' stuff? I asked you, no, I told you not to get involved. I appreciate what you did to track down West, but that's the end of it as far as you're concerned. You promised, remember?"

Ellen frowned and stabbed at her spinach salad. "Oh, all right, but I don't see why I can't be helpful."

"You are helpful," he said sympathetically, "and I hope you'll go on helping me work through the possibilities. What you just suggested hadn't occurred to me, but now that you say it, I can see how it could have gone down. It seems like Francis believed West had the talent to turn out credible fakes, and if she did do them, she used a man to plant them for her. But if Thaw didn't commission her, what's her motive?"

"Francis' notes said she needs money. She let her League membership lapse, and that place she's living in isn't exactly the Ritz."

"Yeah, that would explain her selling them, but what about the two she gave away to Chicago and the Salvation Army?"

Ellen considered that. "She knew she'd get a good chunk of change from Stanley, Fairfax, and Provincetown, so maybe the others were thrown in to make the scheme look more plausible. Having a couple turn up over the transom, so to speak, would deflect attention from the money makers."

With the table cleared, dishes washed, and the leftovers stashed in the fridge, TJ got West's number from Ellen and dialed it. After a few rings, the call was answered by a husky voice, slightly slurred, which asked abruptly, "Hello, who's this?"

Uh, oh, said TJ to himself, *she's had a couple of snorts. I hope she remembers this conversation in the morning.*

He introduced himself as an art collector and borrowed Ellen's story about finding a painting he thought might be by her in a downtown gallery. "Would you be willing to take a look at a photo of it and tell me if you're the artist?" he asked.

"What gallery?" she wanted to know. Fortunately, he had anticipated that obvious question and had looked up a likely establishment.

"Aegis, on Tenth Street," he lied.

"That schlock house. I wouldn't be caught dead showing there."

"It's on consignment, and it's signed with the initials MCW. It may not be you after all, but I'd be grateful if you'd tell me yes or no."

"How grateful?" That caught him off guard. *Jesus, not another Kligman type. Better steer things in a different direction.*

"I'll be glad to compensate you for your time. Shall we say twenty dollars?"

"No, we shall say fifty. Cash." She hadn't drunk enough to dull her shrewdness. "Bring it to Eighty-Nine East Broadway tomorrow afternoon at two. Third floor. My name's on the bell."

Thirty-Five

TJ spent the morning on the bribery case, a matter of tracking down which employee of an aeronautical engineering firm near LaGuardia Airport in Queens had sold trade secrets to a Japanese competitor. A few suspects' bank accounts had to be discreetly scrutinized, a process at which he was an expert.

After lunch, he went to the bank, drew out two twenties and a ten, and took the subway to East Broadway. As he made his way south from the station, a large rat heading in the opposite direction scuttled along the gutter and disappeared down the sewer.

Fronted by a cracked sidewalk littered with trash, West's building was as decrepit as Ellen had described it. A row of overflowing garbage pails stood in front of the Vietnamese deli. The rumble of traffic on the bridge that loomed over it provided an incessant soundtrack to the general hubbub of street life.

TJ rang the bell marked WEST and was buzzed in. A wide, straight run staircase led to the third floor, where West's door was ajar. He entered the middle of a floor-through loft that had been divided roughly in half by a makeshift wall of plywood and two-by-fours.

"Over here, in front," said the husky voice he'd heard on the phone, not slurring now but just as abrupt. He turned left and saw her sitting in a shabby armchair by the loft's large windows that faced the street. Light filtered through the grimy panes and caught the smoke that curled up from the cigarette in her right hand. Her left hand held a glass half full of a brown liquid that might have been a soft drink, or not.

With the light behind her, it was hard to tell her age, but TJ guessed she was pushing 80. She'd been at the League more than fifty years ago, so she was definitely up there. Her hair was a dull gray, and looked neglected, neither washed nor combed recently. She was wearing a rumpled patterned blouse and a dark skirt spattered with what could have been paint, from which spindly legs protruded. Her feet were in well-worn house slippers.

The room was apparently a combination living-working space, with a single bed, unmade, a chest of drawers, and a wardrobe against the back wall. A makeshift kitchen area boasted an electric stove and fridge, a storage cabinet, a Formica breakfast table, and two chairs with cracked plastic seats. The rest of the space was taken up by the painting studio. Canvases of all sizes were stacked facing the walls. They surrounded a large rolling easel crusted with decades of oil paint. Coffee cans held brushes and other tools on the glass-topped palette table, which was equally paint-laden. But dust covered the surface, and it looked like the pigments had long since dried. Rolls of canvas and bundles of stretchers were leaned in one corner, and cans of sizing and gesso were piled under the table, where boxes of tube paints were also visible. But as far as TJ could tell, there were no cans of liquid enamel. Maybe they were in the room at the back.

Assuming he was in unfamiliar territory, West watched him take in the scene. He decided to reinforce that impression so his curiosity would seem natural.

"Please forgive me, Miss West, but I've never been in an artist's studio before. It's really fascinating, so I hope you don't mind if I look around."

"You're paying the price of admission," she said, waving her right hand in a sweeping gesture, "so help yourself. Want a drink?" She rose stiffly, stubbed out her cigarette in an ashtray on the palette table, and shuffled over to the kitchen area. As she passed him, he got a close look at her lined and sagging face, its former beauty long since erased by age and dissipation. "What can I get you?"

"Whatever you're having, thank you." That was the easiest way to find out what she was drinking.

She returned to the front of the loft with two glasses of brown liquid with ice, handed one to him, and raised the other. "Ars longa, vita brevis," she toasted, with a crooked smile that told him the salute was ironic. The liquid was bourbon, which he disliked even when it was good quality, which this wasn't. He sipped it politely and returned her smile. He was sure that what he left in the glass, which would be almost all of it, would not go to waste.

"Let's see this painting you think I did," she said, returning to the armchair. He had wanted to spend a bit more time looking around, but she was eager to get on with the business at hand. She lit another cigarette as he reached into his jacket pocket and removed the photocopy Ellen had made of the doctored Erich Buchholz.

"It's not a very good picture," he said apologetically, "but you can see the initials clearly. Are you the MCW who painted it?"

She grunted. "Certainly not! It's nothing like my work. I've never used that scumble technique or made such fussy shapes. I always painted with a loaded brush and filled the canvas with pure psychic energy. Look, I'll show you."

Again, she rose with difficulty and led him to the stack of paintings behind the easel. "Go on, take your pick," she directed. He reached for a vertical one, nearly six feet tall, lifted it by the stretcher, and turned it face out. He was confronted by an explosive abstract composition, built of slashing brush strokes that seemed to leap off the canvas, punctuated by spatters of what appeared to be liquid paint—Pollock's favored medium. He pulled out a few smaller ones and saw similar treatments in all of them.

"I see what you mean," said TJ, nodding. "These make the painting by that other MCW look very tame. You're a genuine action painter."

"Past tense, honey. I had a stroke ten years ago and haven't touched a brush since. Nobody wants this kind of stuff anymore. Now it's all either big flat shapes, smooth and slick, or warmed-over German Expressionism, grotesque figures, and garish colors. That's what the dealers tell me they can sell, like I should paint to order. Nuts to that. So now I concentrate on my poetry, equally out of fashion and with no market." She turned her back on the piles of unsold paintings and shuffled back to her chair.

As TJ replaced the canvases, he noticed a date written on the stretcher of the big one, 1965. By then, Abstract Expressionism was passé, supplanted in the marketplace by Pop art and color field abstraction. No wonder she was bitter. But had it made her resentful enough to want to get back at the art world by faking an action painter whose market was still strong despite changing tastes? She certainly had the skill, but did she have the will? If she were really hard up, could she summon the energy? He decided to ask an indiscreet question.

"Please pardon me if I'm out of line, but how do you manage if there's no market for your paintings or your poetry?"

Taking a hit of her drink, she wasn't fazed by his curiosity. "Oh, I get along all right. I have Social Security, with a disability benefit, and I rent out the back of the loft." She gestured toward the makeshift wall. "Course we have to share the bathroom, and it's strictly illegal, but then my living here isn't exactly kosher. This is a commercial space, not residential. I rented it as a studio when my ex-husband and I had an apartment. When we split, I just moved in here. Much more convenient, and I've got a long lease." She chuckled and dragged deeply on her cigarette. "Plenty long enough, if you get me."

TJ understood. She was in poor health and didn't expect to live much longer. So maybe her last laugh would be to put one over on the Pollock experts and cash in while doing it. But if she wasn't lying about the tenant, there was likely no more studio space in back, where house paints and the other necessary materials could be hidden. Although TJ couldn't rule it out. The tenant could be her accomplice. Or maybe the ex-husband wasn't out of the picture altogether.

Just then, the hall door opened, and an elderly Asian woman entered, lugging a couple of grocery bags.

"Hello, Mrs. Tran," called West, giving her a cursory wave.

I guess that knocks out the accomplice theory, thought TJ as the woman nodded politely, unlocked the rear door, and disappeared into the back of the loft.

"Her son runs the deli downstairs," West explained. "She works the register evenings and weekends. Handy for him, and she's quiet as a mouse. I hardly know she's here, except that she keeps the bathroom spotless."

TJ had to suppress a desire to knock on Mrs. Tran's door and offer to pay her to clean West's portion of the loft as well. But the artist's self-imposed squalor was not his concern. His business was to determine whether she faked the Pollocks, and as far as he could see, her past artistic accomplishments notwithstanding, she wasn't capable. She had mentioned a stroke a decade earlier. If her story were true, she had stopped painting before the catalogue raisonné was published.

* * *

"It was very sad," TJ told Ellen over pre-dinner glasses of wine. "Her paintings are really good, full of what she called psychic energy. I almost asked her how much she wanted for one, but then she might have an inflated idea of their value, even if no one's buying them now. So I just gave her the fifty bucks I'd promised and left it at that."

"Maybe we can pick up one of those bogus Pollocks cheap after you've debunked them," said Ellen, with just a hint of whimsy. "That would be a fun souvenir of this adventure."

"Maybe the Stanleys would let me have first refusal after all."

"Once they find out, you'll be persona non grata at Pete and Gloria's cocktail parties. I don't suppose the Fairfaxes and that Rankin guy up in Boston will be any more likely to welcome you, either. And from what you've told me about May Rosenberg's temper, you'd better steer clear of her. But maybe Wagner the packrat would be willing to double his money."

TJ topped up their glasses and reflected. "After what I saw, what with her living conditions and her obvious health problems, I wish I could just outright eliminate West. I don't think she was involved with Thaw—I've taken him off the list anyway—but West and her ex could have cooked up the scheme. How do I know if she really had a stroke? She could have said that to throw me off."

"Why would she need to do that?" asked Ellen. "She wouldn't have any idea you were there to investigate the forgery scheme. Francis kept the whole business quiet, even from the board, so if she is guilty, for all she knows, she's getting away with it."

Then the conversation took the turn TJ was dreading.

"And wouldn't that be true for Kligman, too? You went there to look into her claim to have a real one. What did she say when you told her Francis was having doubts?"

He took a sip of wine to give his answer a chance to form. "Frankly, she was shocked. She didn't think he'd ever question his own judgment, but she put it down to how plausible her story was. After all, she certainly was out there in Springs with Pollock, and he might have wanted to impress her, prove that he still had what it takes, even if the results are not up to scratch."

"You think maybe it is a Pollock after all?"

Desperately wanting to change the subject, TJ punted. "I have no idea. She's still the most likely forger, but I need to follow up with the Matters and either eliminate them or find evidence to implicate them. I'm going to call Mercedes tomorrow. Meanwhile, let's eat."

Thirty-Six

Francis' obituary, carefully orchestrated by Gerry Dickler, appeared in *The New York Times* that morning. The powerful attorney's connections ensured that Francis received the full editorial treatment, complete with a photograph, not merely a paid death notice. It described his rise from a working-class childhood to a prominent position among art historians and his pioneering studies of Jackson Pollock and the New Deal art projects. There were laudatory quotes from Gene Thaw, on behalf of the Pollock-Krasner Foundation, and William Rubin, who extolled his contribution to the 1967 Pollock retrospective at the Museum of Modern Art. It noted that a private service would be held at the Frank E. Campbell Funeral Chapel on Madison Avenue, to be followed by interment in historic Green-Wood Cemetery in his native Brooklyn.

Scanning the paper over breakfast, TJ spotted the obit and pointed it out to Ellen. "Shame there's no mention of his poetry. I bet he'd be furious."

"They probably didn't even know about it," said Ellen. "Didn't you tell me none of it was ever published?"

"Yes, that's what Birdie said. His 1982 will leaves it all to the New York Public Library, but no money goes with it, so they may not take it. Then what will Birdie do with it, not to mention all the stuff that was supposed to go to the Archives but didn't?"

Just then, the phone rang. TJ answered and found himself talking to

Birdie. "Speak of the devil. Ellen and I were just reading Francis' obituary and thinking about what a big responsibility you have as his executrix."

She sighed. "Yes, it's kind of daunting. A certain amount of material is designated, but I'll have a job placing the rest. I need to find out why the Archives deal wasn't finalized. Maybe I can revive it. But first, the funeral, which his parents asked me to arrange. They wisely decided against a church service in his old neighborhood, since none of his friends and colleagues would be likely to travel to the depths of Brooklyn. As the paper said, it's at Campbell's, and as it didn't say, on Saturday at two p.m. The foundation is footing the bill. You and your wife are welcome to attend."

"Thank you for including us," said TJ. "We'll definitely be there."

Half an hour later, Gerry Dickler called to inform Ellen of the funeral and invite her and her husband. She thanked him, told him that Miss Crowe had already notified them, and assured him that they would be going. She wanted to ask him what had become of the overnight delivery from Boston that Francis had been on his way to collect from Dickler's office, but how could she explain knowing about it?

"I was planning to come in today," she told him. "I was about to leave when you called. I really want to keep up with my work on the catalogue, so if you're agreeable, I'll be there shortly." Perhaps she could learn more when she got to the office.

"I was going to ask you to come in," he said. "Charlie and I will be meeting with Gene and Bill later to discuss how to proceed with the board, and you should be present. Of course, we can't replace Francis; he was singular in more ways than one." Ellen detected a sardonic undertone as he finished that sentence.

"But for practical reasons," he continued, "we've been considering expanding the panel to get an uneven number, and now that would involve adding two people. Or we could just leave it at three. We need to consider this matter in confidence. I'm sure you understand."

"I do, Gerry, and thanks for including me in the discussion. I hope you know how much I appreciate it." *And how much I don't look forward to Bill Lieberman's condescension,* she said to herself. *I wish Francis were there to back me up. Damn, I'm really going to miss that stubborn son of a gun.*

* * *

Before heading out, Ellen called TJ at the office and told him her plan. "I'm going to try to find out what will happen to any files or correspondence that arrived or will come in after Francis' death. From what he told you, the board only knows about the Stanley painting. He didn't show them the other four fakes."

"I have his files on all five. I guess I'll have to turn them over to the foundation, tell them about the investigation, and let them decide where to take it. I can just bow out."

"Yeah, right. That would be somebody else, not you," she scoffed. "Let's just see how it goes at today's meeting. I'll give you a full report—that is, if it's not trespassing on your professional territory."

"Okay, I deserved that. But the foundation and the board are on your turf, not mine, so you're my eyes and ears in that department. Meanwhile, I'm going to call Mercedes Matter to see if I can set up a visit to her studio. We can compare notes tonight." They signed off with good-bye kisses.

* * *

Seated at the head of the table, Charlie Bergman called the meeting to order at 3 p.m. Beforehand, Ellen had asked if she could sit on his left, with Dickler beside her, and Charlie had organized that arrangement. Lieberman and Thaw sat opposite them, at enough of a distance so Bill's cigarette smoke wasn't in her face.

Charlie began diplomatically by praising Francis' decades of outstanding work in various capacities on behalf of the Pollock estate, and announcing that a memorial tribute, with contributions by distinguished scholars, was being planned for the fall under the foundation's auspices. He then turned to the issue at hand.

"Gerry has reviewed the bylaws, and it seems there is no specific size required for the authentication board. That is left to the discretion of the trustees, Gerry, Gene, and I. Before we lost Francis, we were considering if, in order to avoid tie votes, an odd number of members would be advisable. The question is whether to proceed with a three-person board, or to add two others." He turned to Lieberman. "What do you think, Bill?"

Lieberman delivered one of his trademark dismissive snorts. "I think we're better off without him and his petty squabbles."

Ellen was taken aback by such callous disrespect. Even Gene was shocked, though he tried not to show it. He opted instead for damage control.

"We had our disagreements, to be sure, but it's unfair of you to call them petty, Bill. Francis was deeply committed to protecting the Pollock legacy, and while his outbursts could be, frankly, exasperating, they were always with that aim in mind. Lord knows I was on the receiving end often enough, but as far as I'm concerned, it was a small price to pay for his expertise and integrity."

Before Bill could retort, Charlie intervened. "Very well put, Gene. We'll be hard pressed to find someone with those qualities who could step up. In fact, we need two of them. Any suggestions, Gene?"

"The only one I can think of is Bill Rubin at the Modern, but that puts us back to an even number. There's really no one else."

"It's a shame Betty Parsons is no longer with us," said Bill. "She had an eye, and in spite of the way Jackson treated her, jumping ship to go with Janis, she believed strongly in his work and knew it well. She would have been an asset, and an amiable one to boot."

That gave Ellen an idea. "How about Sidney Janis? Wouldn't he be just as much of an expert on Pollock's work?"

Without realizing it, Ellen had opened a small can of worms. Gene informed her that Janis had had a falling out with Krasner over the Pollock estate, which she transferred to another dealer, and he was not kindly disposed to the foundation. "You see," he explained, "Sidney had hopes of representing the estate after Lee died, stepping back in, so to speak. Instead, we chose to keep it in the family." Pollock's nephew, a respected art dealer, was now handling the residue. By championing Pop art, Janis had lost favor with the supporters of Abstract Expressionism.

"I'd like to recommend that, at least for the time being, we continue with a three-member board," said Charlie. "Gene, Bill, Ellen, what do you say?"

"Fine with me," said Bill. "I agree," said Gene. "So do I," said Ellen, apprehensive about her new role as the likely tiebreaker. Did either Gene or Bill have enough confidence in her judgment to accept it? She hoped they'd see eye to eye on all the Pollock submissions from now on, and she wouldn't wind up refereeing bouts between two heavyweight egos.

"Let's think about a date in mid-June for the next meeting," said Charlie. "A few more things have come in, both Krasners and Pollocks. In fact, a FedEx envelope came for Francis on the day he died. It's a bit odd. A collector in Boston sent photos of the back of a painting he says is a Pollock, but not of the front."

So they opened it, thought Ellen. *Why not, since it was sent here and was likely an authentication matter?*

"Maybe Francis already had a picture of the front," she suggested, knowing full well that he did. "He probably wanted more documentation before he brought it to the board."

"That reminds me," said Gene, "We need to get hold of any authentication-related files he had at home. Gerry, please contact his executrix and arrange for someone to meet her at his apartment and collect them."

Ellen excused herself and headed down the hall to her office, hoping that TJ was at his desk. She needed to warn him that the files would have to be returned, and quickly. Luckily, he was there and had already copied or photographed everything in them. He assured her that after a cab ride uptown, with the originals and his pick set in his briefcase, the job would be done and no one the wiser.

Thirty-Seven

Friday, May 9

TJ's morning call to Mercedes Matter was greeted warmly. "Certainly I remember you, the handsome young redhead with the pretty wife, who I understand is now a successful fashion illustrator. It's too bad I couldn't persuade her to attend my school, but she's done well in her own field, so I don't fault her."

Matter's high-pitched, slightly breathy voice always disarmed TJ, and he wasn't the only one to marvel at how effectively it disguised her strong, uncompromising character. Without her single-minded leadership and stubborn determination, there would be no New York Studio School of Drawing, Painting and Sculpture, of which she was the founder and dean.

"You may not know it," she continued, "but among my late husband Herbert's outstanding talents was fashion photography. Many years ago, Lee and I used to model for him—we both had beautiful figures, and Lee's hands were especially graceful. There are some charming shots of her posing with jewelry designed by Sandy Calder. I don't know if they ever helped Sandy sell anything, but we loved dressing up with his fantastic wearable sculptures."

"I understand you and your husband were close friends of Lee and Jackson, which is why I'm calling," TJ told her. "As I'm sure you know, Francis O'Connor died last week, and I was working with him on a Pollock-related problem that you may be able to help me solve." Not that he was going to tell her what that problem really was.

"Yes," she said with a sigh, "what a terrible thing. I didn't know Francis well, but he was in touch with us for Jackson's catalogue raisonné. At one time, we owned four of his works. One of them was stolen, and Lee wouldn't help us get it back. And we had another that Lee tried to claim was hers, though she had no legitimate case. She took us to court, you know, and I'm afraid that was the end of our friendship."

This information confirmed Francis' notes in the suspects file, and TJ could hear the bitterness in Matter's tone. What better revenge than to create a brand-new Pollock to replace the stolen one? Then, seeing how convincing the forgery was, why not make a few more and get their middle-aged son, Alex—that would be Francis' AM—to plant them?

But even as those thoughts passed through TJ's mind, they didn't ring true. A single replacement, yes, but not five fakes. Unless there was a financial incentive. He knew the art school had some serious money behind it, but maybe those funds were drying up. That was his next line of inquiry, if necessary. First, however, he needed to look for evidence in Matter's studio.

"May I come over to discuss this problem with you in person?" he asked.

"Yes," she agreed, "if it won't take too long. I'm not teaching today, but I'm getting ready to leave for the country, and I want to get away before noon."

"That's fine," he said. "I'm just off Union Square, so I can walk there in fifteen minutes, maybe less. I remember you're just a little way down MacDougal Alley from Alfonso's old place."

"The alley gate is locked. Come in through the school entrance on Eighth, and the receptionist will direct you."

The New York Studio School comprised a series of adjoining nineteenth-century buildings that once belonged to the blueblood sculptor and art patron Gertrude Vanderbilt Whitney. She had opened a gallery in her studio at 8 West 8th Street in 1914, and a few years later bought the adjoining buildings and established the Whitney Studio Club as an artists' gathering place and showcase for their work. In 1930, it became the Whitney Museum of American Art.

After the museum moved uptown, the complex was leased to a youth hostel and was in danger of demolition when, in 1966, Mercedes and her backers secured the space for the fledgling art school. She and Herbert were already occupying one of the connected carriage houses in the alley behind it, so she only had to walk through a door to go to work.

* * *

An early morning shower had freshened the air, and sunshine peeking through lingering clouds made the streets and sidewalks glisten. As he walked down Fifth Avenue, swinging the umbrella he'd brought along in case the rain returned, and turned right on 8th Street, TJ was looking forward to revisiting his old haunts. He recalled the many times he'd taken this route to and from Alfonso and Ted's MacDougal Alley pied-à-terre and The Bitter End folk club on Bleecker Street, where Ellen and her roommate used to sing in the Tuesday night hootenannies. The club was now a rock 'n' roll venue, and Alfonso had sold Nine Mac, as the carriage house was called, in the early seventies, so he'd had no reason to return to either place.

The Whitney Museum's stylized American eagle frieze still graced the pillared doorway at 8 West 8th Street, above the sign that now identified the art school. TJ entered and climbed the curving, symmetrical staircase to the reception area, where he was given directions to Matter's studio.

He found her standing behind a long trestle table filled with art materials—oil paint in tubes, jars of brush cleaner, plastic tubs of gesso, cans of turpentine, boxes of charcoal sticks and caran d'ache pencils, and brushes of all sizes and shapes. Sketchpads and rolls of canvas were heaped at one end, with several packages wrapped in brown paper and neatly tied with string. Some empty cardboard boxes were stacked under the table. One box was already filled with ring binders and file folders, and Matter was in the process of filling another one as he entered.

"Come in," she said, "and pardon me for carrying on packing while we talk. A friend with a station wagon is picking me up, and I want to take as much as I can while I have the chance. I leave my car in the country. Can't stand driving in the city, never could, but in East Hampton you can't manage without a car."

"Let me give you a hand," he offered, thinking, *this is a great opportunity to find out if she has any vintage materials.* He picked up an empty box and asked, "Is all this stuff going?"

"Yes, if it will all fit in the six boxes I have. And thank you for your help. But how can I help you?"

He had decided that the so-called stolen Pollock painting would be the raison d'être for his visit. According to the catalogue, it had not in fact been stolen but was left unclaimed in storage and was sold without the Matters' knowledge. It had since changed hands a couple of times and was now in a private collection in London. The couple's efforts to reclaim it had failed.

As he began packing, he asked, "Are you aware that the authentication board is working on a supplement to the Pollock catalogue?"

"No," she said, "I didn't know that. Francis hasn't been in touch about it. Or rather, he hadn't been."

"At the time of his death, he was looking into unresolved issues in the original catalogue, and he told me you and Herbert might have a valid claim to the missing painting. He had intended to follow up with you, but then Herbert died, so he held off. He was ready to pursue it when he was killed, and as his research assistant, I'm trying to pick up where he left off."

Mercedes stopped packing, and her eyes widened. "Do you really think I could get it back, after all this time? It's been nearly forty years, and I believe the painting is in England now."

"Francis thought there was a good chance, if you can establish ownership."

"That's what Lee was unwilling to help us with. She knew Jackson gave us the painting—my God, she was in the room when it happened—but she wouldn't sign an affidavit to validate the claim. She couldn't forgive Herbert and me for not giving her another painting she said was hers. As I told you, she sued us for it and lost, so that was her way of punishing us. Oh, yes, she could be spiteful." She shook her head ruefully.

"Haven't you any paperwork at all to prove you owned it?"

"Only a couple of exhibition checklists that identify us as the lenders, but that wasn't considered decisive, like a handwritten note from Jackson would have been. Nobody bothered about things like that back then. In fact, the gift itself was kind of a joke. When he gave it to us, he said it was a wedding present, but we'd been married for two years."

While he listened, TJ continued to pack. Picking up one of the wrapped packages, he noticed the name Pollock written on it. "What's in here?" he asked.

She glanced at the package. "I don't know. It's something of Herbert's, that's his handwriting. There's an awful lot of his stuff to go through, and I just don't have the energy to deal with it. Thank goodness he was very methodical, so his prints and negatives and graphic works are all labeled. But I don't recognize that."

"Mind if I take a look? Maybe there's a note from Jackson after all."

"I very much doubt it, but you're welcome to open it if you like."

TJ untied the string and folded back the paper wrapping. Inside was a pile of small abstract paintings on illustration board, done using Pollock's signature pouring technique. There were a couple dozen of them. He laid them out on the table and studied them in silence.

Either these are the real deal or excellent imitations. If they're real, why didn't Herbert submit them to Francis in the seventies, and if they're fake, did he paint them, or did she?

Matter looked on with apparent indifference, which seemed very odd. Genuine Pollocks, even such small ones, would be worth quite a bit. Phony ones would suggest that one of them was a forger. Either way, some show of emotion was in order.

When she did react, she was as guileless as a Girl Scout. "I thought Herbert had thrown those away. I guess I should have known better, he kept everything, which is the reason I'm overwhelmed."

"Why would he throw them away?"

"They embarrassed him. When he saw the wonderful results Jackson got with liquid paint, he decided to try it himself, so he did a series of what he called Pollock experiments. But they look like miniature copies, and worse, like he was riding on his friend's coattails, so he abandoned the project. It was years ago. I'd forgotten all about it."

* * *

"I spent a couple of hours there," TJ told Ellen later. "She had me working like a stevedore, packing boxes and toting canvases and schlepping the stuff out to her friend's station wagon, but I got to go through the studio top to bottom, and there was no sign of any of the evidence I'm looking for."

"Maybe it's in East Hampton," suggested Ellen. "She's had a place out there for a couple of years, and it would be a lot more private. In the city, someone, like maybe a student, could wander into the studio and catch her at it."

"She told me they'd only just finished building it when Herbert died. That was in eighty-four, and he'd been in and out of the hospital for a year or more. There just wasn't enough time for her to paint five fakes and get them planted while she was taking care of him. Besides, I don't believe she has the—what would you call it—the chops, I guess, for that kind of work. Her paintings are basically cubist, a very different rhythmic structure. On the other hand, from what I saw of Herbert's self-styled Pollock experiments, he could have scaled them up convincingly, but I don't think he did."

"Why not?"

"In order to fit the blank spaces, the fakes had to have been painted after the catalogue came out, and by that time, Herbert was already having serious health problems. Remember Francis' note about medical bills? But he was probably still covered by his health insurance plan from Yale, even though he was retired, and they had enough money to buy land and build a house, so the financial gain argument doesn't work for me. In fact, I think the whole Matter angle is a dead end."

Thirty-Eight

Saturday, May 10

Since 1898, the firm of Frank E. Campbell, known as the undertaker to the stars, had been preparing celebrities for eternal rest—most famously Rudolph Valentino, whose 1926 funeral attracted an estimated 100,000 distraught fans and spawned a day-long riot.

A far more modest and well-behaved crowd attended Francis' service. Several of them lived within walking distance on the Upper East Side, and others arrived by taxi and limousine, while TJ and Ellen traveled uptown on the IRT. In the hall, Ellen introduced TJ to the delegation from the Pollock-Krasner Foundation.

Inside the chapel, Mahler's Symphony Number 6, known as the Tragic, played softly in the background as people filed in and took their seats. Off to the side, Birdie, the priest, and one of the funeral directors were in conference with an elderly couple who TJ and Ellen guessed were Francis' parents. The woman, presumably his mother, kept glancing at the coffin, which was closed, given the condition of the body. Ellen looked on with sympathy, hoping that her ordeal would soon be over. Presently, the funeral director escorted them to their seats, and the service began.

* * *

Once the rites were dispensed with, the mourners were directed to a reception room, where the muted strains of Mahler greeted them again. Floral tributes from the foundation and the Museum of Modern Art flanked a buffet table and bar. TJ and Ellen made a point of offering condolences to the O'Connors, who were accompanied by a few other family members. Most of the gathering was made up of Francis' colleagues, as well as collectors and art dealers he had advised, and a few artists. None of them had ever met his relatives, though several paid their respects politely.

Standing near the bar with a glass of wine in hand, TJ felt slightly out of place. Like the O'Connor family, he knew no one in the room—except his wife, who was chatting with Charlie Bergman, and Birdie, who was deep in conversation with Gerry Dickler. He looked around for Francis' doorman, Louis, but evidently he hadn't been invited. A man standing next to him seemed equally at sea, so he introduced himself as the husband of one of the authentication board members.

"Nice to meet you, Mr. Fitzgerald. I'm Irving Marantz, Jr. My father was an old friend of Francis, from his days researching the New Deal art projects. That's how I knew him."

"Is your father an art historian, too?"

"No, he was an artist. Francis interviewed him about his work on the WPA, and they hit it off. They used to visit museums and art galleries together, and gripe about the sorry state of the art world. Dad died several years ago, but I kept up with Francis. I really enjoyed his company, even though he could be rather, how should I put it…."

TJ finished his sentence for him. "Difficult?"

Marantz nodded with a grin. "In more ways than one. Recently, I was seeing him in a professional capacity, and he was not the most cooperative patient."

"How do you mean?"

"I'm an ophthalmologist. One day, I dropped by his place for a visit, and he complained about eyestrain. He'd recently started using a computer and wondered if that could be causing it. I have no patients who've reported such a problem, but I know there's some evidence that staring at the lighted screen can cause ocular fatigue. He had a habit of getting lost in his work and spending far too much time on the machine, so I advised him to take frequent breaks and made a date for him to come to my office for a checkup, which he did."

TJ was intrigued. "When was that, Dr. Marantz?"

"About six months ago. I ran some tests and adjusted his prescription, and I told him to let me know if there was an improvement. Weeks went by, and I didn't hear from him, so I called him to follow up. He was rather cranky, said the new glasses didn't help at all, so he was going to get a second opinion. As if I weren't competent, which I must say was insulting. But if you knew Francis, you wouldn't be surprised."

"My wife told me about his behavior on the board," said TJ, hedging. "From what she said, he could be quite contrary."

"Exasperating is more like it," said Marantz. "Anyway, I referred him to one of my colleagues at Manhattan Eye, Ear, and Throat. I didn't expect to hear from him again, but he called me back a few weeks later and made another appointment. Without an apology, I might add."

"So you saw him again?"

"Yes, two months ago. I did some additional tests and found an anomaly that I needed to research. Then I had him back in for a couple of more specialized tests two weeks ago. On Friday, I called to set up an appointment to discuss the results with him, but he was out, and of course, he never returned home."

Now, TJ was deeply curious. "If it isn't violating doctor-patient confidentiality, what was the problem? I only ask because I'm wondering if it might have contributed to his death."

"I don't mind telling you, since he's deceased," said Marantz. "It wasn't anything potentially fatal, like encephalitis or a hemorrhage, if that's what you're thinking, but it did interfere with visualization. Are you suggesting that he may have misjudged his position on the platform, not realizing how close he was to the edge?"

"Something like that. I had a hard time believing he fell accidentally, but if he was having trouble seeing where he was, that could account for it."

Marantz shook his head. "No, it wasn't faulty depth perception, or something that would make him dizzy. My diagnosis was morphagnosia, a very rare condition, which is why I needed a while to confirm it."

* * *

It took TJ a couple of beats to react. "What on earth is morphagnosia?"

"As I said," Marantz explained, "it's extremely rare. None of my colleagues at Eye and Ear had ever seen a case, or even heard of one. We're more familiar with other forms of agnosia—the inability to recognize and identify things—even though they're also rare. You may have heard of face blindness. The medical term is prosopagnosia. People who have it don't recognize others, even close friends and family members, by their facial features. They may not recognize their own faces in the mirror, even though they see themselves clearly. There's no cure, or even an effective treatment, so they must learn to live with it."

"Good Lord," said TJ, "how do they function?"

"They work around it, using clues like height, build, voice, and such. Usually, they're so well adapted that those who don't know them don't even realize they have prosopagnosia. There are several other forms that affect vision, as well as one that blocks the ability to recognize words, and another that prevents recognition by touch. We find them most often in association with schizophrenia, bipolar disorder, and dementia.

"In Francis' case, his agnosia blocked the recognition of shapes and patterns, but only new ones. From what I was able to learn from the very limited literature, onset usually occurs as the result of a cerebral trauma, like a concussion or a stroke. Memories formed before the trauma are not affected, but subsequent perception is disrupted. My guess is that Francis suffered a mild stroke, probably without being aware of it, perhaps in his sleep, and that brought it on."

"If it's so rare, how did you know what it was?"

"It happens that I have a patient with prosopagnosia, so I've been reading the journals and corresponding with colleagues familiar with the condition. One of them, a neurologist at Johns Hopkins, is especially interested in various types of visual agnosia, and we discussed symptoms. That's how I knew what tests to conduct."

TJ had become very still and appeared to be looking right through Marantz, who thought perhaps he had gone over his listener's head. "I'm sorry, am I confusing you?"

"On the contrary, Dr. Marantz. Just the opposite."

* * *

"So my guess is," said TJ as he wound up his account of the conversation with Marantz, "that the paintings are real Pollocks. But because of his morphagnosia, Francis couldn't recognize them. He would have no problem identifying Pollocks he'd already seen, but these were new to him, so the shapes and patterns just didn't register."

Seated opposite him at their dining table, Ellen absorbed this revelation before she spoke. "If that's true, you realize what it means. Francis' suspicions were probably groundless. There was no forger with a motive to get him out of the way. If someone did murder him, it was for an entirely different reason."

"Exactly right. But I want to be as sure as I can be that those paintings aren't fakes after all. First thing on Monday, I'm going to start checking back with that New Paltz lawyer who handled the Meert estate and the curator at the University of Chicago. And I need to look into the Art in Trust charity, make sure they're legit. I don't think I'll be able to get anywhere with the Salvation Army donation, unless Isaac Henry's memory improves, but right now I can find out if George Loper, Jr., really is an East Hampton carpenter."

TJ moved to the armchair by the phone, dialed 411, and got the number for a G. Loper in Springs. An answering machine informed him that no one was in, but a message could be left after the beep, which he did.

"That looks like it for now," he grumbled. "Maybe Loper will call back later. Otherwise, we'll just have to wait until Monday."

Thirty-Nine

Consulting his case notes at the office, TJ found the New Paltz number for John G. Sisti, Attorney at Law. Once again, he spoke to the secretary and was connected to the boss.

"Good morning, Mr. Fitzgerald. Still hoping to engineer a windfall for the Meert clan?"

"No, sir. As a matter of fact, I'm not acting for the Meert family, and never was. I confess that I was rather evasive with you a couple of weeks ago because my client wanted to remain in the background. But he has since died, and I'm trying to tie up some loose ends on behalf of his estate. I was researching the Pollock painting for him, and I'd like to clarify its source."

"You're still being evasive," said Sisti. "If you give me the whole story, I'll help you if I can."

"Fair enough," TJ replied, and began describing who Francis O'Connor was and why he wanted to trace the painting, though he didn't mention Francis' doubts about its authenticity. "When you're doing a complete catalogue," he explained, "it's very important to establish the chain of ownership. We need as much information as possible before the work identified as *Number Five, Nineteen Forty-Nine* can be included."

"I understand," said Sisti, apparently satisfied. "I'm Joe's executor, but I have help managing the bequest. This is a one-man office, and I don't have the time or energy to deal with it, so I asked an old friend of Joe's to handle it. He's a retired attorney and his next-door neighbor in Cragsmoor. He kind of took care of Joe after Margaret died. The picture wasn't there when I inventoried the collection, but maybe he knows something about it."

"Will you put me in touch with him?"

"Tell you what. I'll call him, tell him what you told me, and give him your number. If he's willing to talk to you, he'll call you."

TJ was sure he could find a retired attorney living in Cragsmoor, a very small hamlet with fewer than 500 inhabitants. He also thought it likely that this was the lawyer who had approached the Stanleys. If Sisti couldn't persuade him to call, TJ would track him down.

"Thank you, Mr. Sisti. I really appreciate your cooperation, and I'll be expecting to hear from him. What did you say his name is?"

"I didn't say. If he calls you, he'll introduce himself."

* * *

No sooner had TJ replaced the receiver than the phone rang. It was Ellen on the line.

"George Loper called. He said he was away over the weekend and just got your message. He's in now if you want to call him back." She reminded him of the number.

There was no need to be evasive with Loper; TJ got straight to the point.

"Bea Fairfax tells me she and her husband bought a Pollock painting, known as *Number Thirty-Two, Nineteen Forty-Nine,* from you last year, Mr. Loper. I'm researching its ownership history for a new edition of the Pollock catalogue, so I'm following up on their account of how it came into your possession."

"Ain't you the private eye that fingered Mr. Ossorio's killer?" TJ's name had been all over the *East Hampton Star* ten years earlier, and Loper clearly had a good memory.

"One and the same, Mr. Loper. I was hired by the catalogue's editor to track down the former owners of new submissions and get as much documentation as possible."

"Glad to oblige," said Loper, who seemed pleased to be talking to a genuine detective who was also something of a local celebrity. This would be a good story to tell the boys on poker night at the firehouse.

"I don't suppose you have any paperwork from Pollock to your father?"

"Nope, 'cause I looked. Went through all the files, back to the forties. I did find a carbon copy of Dad's bill for the roofing job. Three hundred bucks, it was. That's the price on the back o' the paintin'. I remember Mom givin' him holy hell for not gettin' cash."

"I understand you told the Fairfaxes that your mother wouldn't have the painting in the house, so your father hung it in the workshop."

"He didn't dare leave it where she could get her hands on it," said Loper with a chuckle. "She woulda marched it right back over to Pollock and demanded the money instead. So it stayed in the shop all them years when I was growin' up. Then I got it when Dad passed and I took over the business."

"Did he leave it to you in his will?"

"Not exactly. He left me the shop and the contents, includin' his tools and whatnot. The paintin' was in there, so it was part o' the deal."

"Without a bill of sale, that thirty-year gap in the painting's history is a real problem for the organization that's compiling the catalogue," TJ told him. "Do you think your mother would be willing to sign a notarized statement confirming your account? And since you were a witness, even though you were very young, they'd appreciate having one from you as well."

"Mom has kinda changed her tune since I sold the thing and bought her a condo with the money," said Loper. "Now she's tellin' people how smart Dad was to take it in trade. I'm sure she'd give an honest answer for the record. Me, too."

* * *

After telling Loper that he'd arrange a meeting with an East Hampton notary in the near future, TJ phoned the Smart Museum at the University of Chicago and asked to speak to the director, who listened with interest as he explained why he was calling.

"I was very sorry to learn of Dr. O'Connor's death," said the director. "Although I didn't know him personally, I'm familiar with his scholarship on Pollock and the New Deal. Visionary isn't a term I throw around lightly, but he truly was. I'm glad to know that the foundation is proceeding with the catalogue supplement." Once again, TJ had neglected to mention that his inquiries were strictly unofficial.

"The painting was found in a closet when the professor whose office it was retired last year. One of the cleaning crew brought it to the museum, but we have no record of it in the collection. We thought perhaps the retiring professor had left it behind by mistake, so we contacted him. He told us it was hanging on the wall when he moved in. Turns out he's not a fan of modern art. He couldn't stand looking at it, so he stashed it away in the closet and forgot about it."

"Did you know that the office's previous occupant was Harold Rosenberg?"

"Yes, we confirmed that it was Professor Rosenberg's office from nineteen sixty-six until his death in seventy-eight. As you probably know, he took a leave of absence for health reasons that spring and never returned. He died in July, and the new occupant took over the office in August."

Now, TJ had to ask an awkward question, and he hoped the director would have a plausible answer. "Knowing that the painting was found in Professor Rosenberg's former office, why did you notify Dr. O'Connor rather than Rosenberg's widow?"

"Frankly, I believed it might indeed be ours. The museum's cataloguing system is not foolproof, and I was hopeful that, knowing Professor Rosenberg's relationship with Pollock, he had borrowed it from us to hang in his office. We checked the catalogue raisonné and found that it has been unaccounted for since nineteen fifty-one. Pollock had a show in Chicago that year, so someone might have bought it from that show and given it to the university.

"The museum didn't exist back then—it opened in seventy-four—so the painting could have been hanging somewhere on campus, maybe in the Art Department. If Professor Rosenberg spotted it when he arrived in sixty-six, he could simply have moved it into his office, and it would never have been catalogued. That was perhaps wishful thinking on my part. Naturally, we will turn it over to Mrs. Rosenberg if we can't establish title."

TJ could see the reasoning. Better to let the experts settle it if they can. Assuming it was sold in Chicago, perhaps the buyer is traceable. If so, that person will probably know how it got to the university. Or did Rosenberg locate the buyer? Maybe the buyer found him. If he acquired it for himself, it now belonged to May.

Either way, it seemed likely that the painting in question really was the long-lost *Number 8A, 1948.*

Forty

Returning from the deli with a sandwich and soda, TJ heard Sweeney's familiar grumble summoning him.

"Got a message for ya. Guy named Jeffries up in Cragsmoor said to call him back." He handed over a slip of paper with a scrawled number. Fortunately, TJ had long since become an expert at deciphering his partner's cryptic handwriting. He thanked Sweeney, headed to his office, dialed the number, and introduced himself to Adam Jeffries, who went straight to the point.

"John Sisti told me that you're researching the Pollock painting's provenance. I think I can help you, or at least explain how I came to have it. You see, I was the actual owner."

"I understood you were acting on behalf of the Meert estate."

"Yes, I was, and I wouldn't have taken it on except for my friendship with Joe and Margaret. They moved up to Cragsmoor in the early seventies, after Margaret retired from the Traphagen School of Fashion, and they couldn't afford to live in the city anymore. Joe never had a real job, and his work wasn't selling. I used to buy a picture or two every year, just to help them out. All they had in the way of income was Social Security and Margaret's meager pension, and that stopped after she died.

"Joe went downhill fast after that. He needed medical care he couldn't afford, and the only thing he had of real value was the Pollock. But he had sworn he'd never sell it because he treasured it so much."

"Where did he get it?" asked TJ.

"He told me that Jackson stopped by to see him in the mid-fifties and brought the painting along. Joe said he was shocked by Jackson's condition—he was drinking pretty heavily at that point—and he offered to let him sleep it off on the couch, like in the old days. Jackson said, 'you once saved my life by doing that, and I never properly repaid you. I want you to have this as a token of my gratitude,' and handed him the painting.

"As you can imagine, Joe was deeply touched, but he felt bad about accepting it. He told Jackson that he didn't expect payment for an act of kindness, but Jackson insisted. 'I would never have done this if it weren't for you, I would have died just another unknown artist,' he said. So Joe took the painting, and not long after that, Jackson did die. But, thanks to Joe, he died famous."

"I guess I can understand how hard it was for Mr. Meert to part with the painting," said TJ, "but from what you tell me, he really needed the money. Maybe selling it to a friend was the best alternative."

"Well, I didn't buy it," Jeffries explained. "I paid his hospital bill, and he gave me the painting in exchange. He wanted it that way so it would be like what Jackson did, a gift for saving his life. And it was only in the house next door, so he could come visit it whenever he liked. I do have a receipt, signed by Joe, so there wouldn't be any question that I was the rightful owner of *Number Five, Nineteen Forty-Nine*."

"How long did you have it before you sold it to the Stanleys?"

"About five years. After Joe died, I wasn't in any particular hurry to get rid of it, but when I overheard the Stanleys mention that they were in the market, I got in touch."

"From what Gloria Stanley told me, she was under the impression that the painting was part of the Meert estate."

Jeffries hastened to correct that misunderstanding. "Oh, no, I never said that. I told her I'd gotten it from Joe while he was alive, and about how he got it from Jackson. That helped to explain why it went missing for all those years."

"I guess she didn't give me the full story," said TJ, remembering how reluctant she's been to divulge the details while relishing the opportunity to boast about their good luck. "Anyway, it will be very important to have a copy of your receipt from Mr. Meert, so the piece can be authenticated for the catalogue."

"That won't be a problem," said Jeffries. "It includes a note about how he got it, too. John Sisti can verify his handwriting if necessary. Please give me the foundation's address, and I'll send them a notarized copy."

Forty-One

A call to the Charities Bureau in the New York State Attorney General's office established that Art in Trust was indeed a registered not-for-profit corporation, with Roland Wilson listed as the administrator. The clerk confirmed the address TJ had been given, a New York City law office. That was his next call.

Wilson was cordial, but not as forthcoming as TJ would have liked.

"Our benefactor insists on remaining anonymous," he said, "though I appreciate that the provenance gap is problematic. Nevertheless, I must respect that decision. However, neither the art association nor the buyer had any doubts about the authenticity of *Number Twenty-two, Nineteen Forty-Nine*. What do the experts have to say about it?"

"Perhaps you haven't heard that the leading expert, Francis O'Connor, died recently, which makes the verification of prior ownership all the more important. Given the circumstances, would you be willing to take that information to the donor?" Going out on a limb, TJ added, "I can assure you that the authentication board will keep the donor's identity confidential, as are all their deliberations."

"That's a reasonable request, Mr. Fitzgerald. The donor is out of town just now, but if you give me the board's contact information, I'll let them know as soon as possible."

* * *

At home that evening, TJ gave Ellen a full recap of the information he'd collected.

"I'll have to lay this whole thing out to the foundation," he told her. "When Jeffries and Wilson said they'd get in touch with them, it hit me that the foundation doesn't have a clue about any of this. Although once they get their hands on Francis' files, which they may have done already, they'll know he was holding back four of the five submissions. Naturally they'll wonder why, just like they wondered why Rankin sent pictures of the back of his painting, not the front."

"I think you should talk to Gerry Dickler," advised Ellen. "You can tell him that Francis hired you to do his legwork. You don't have to tell him the real reason."

"Right. It wouldn't be a good idea to show him the suspects list, with Thaw's name on it and Lieberman implicated. I can just say I was doing ownership tracing on Francis' behalf, which is true as far as it goes. That'll explain why I was in contact with the current owners. And I can say, quite truthfully, that I want to continue with the project, and hope the foundation okays it."

Ellen's confident attitude was infectious. "When you show Gerry what you've already got, I bet he does okay it. If they all turn out to be real, which it kind of looks like they will, it's a significant addition to the catalogue."

It would also mean that, much to TJ's relief, he would never have to return to Ruth Kligman's loft. But he was having misgivings. "How can I explain why Francis held them back? He could have shared each one with the board as it came in, unless he had serious doubts about them. Which, if they're real, why would he?"

Ellen gave that some thought. "I see what you're getting at. What would make him doubt them, unless he was having trouble recognizing them? But it would be cruel to undermine his expertise—I can almost hear Bill scoffing, and Gene would probably be just as judgmental, if more polite about it."

"So you don't think I should tell them about his morphagnosia?"

"Absolutely not. Maybe Dr. Marantz was wrong. He said it was really rare, so maybe Francis' eye trouble was something else entirely, nothing to do with being able to authenticate Pollocks."

TJ pointed out the contradiction. "Francis really believed all five are fakes, but the evidence I'm turning up indicates that they're authentic. How do you account for that unless you accept Dr. Marantz's diagnosis? And I think you're wrong about it discrediting him. After all, if he really did have morphagnosia, it isn't like he was making mistakes. He literally couldn't see them for what they are."

"I guess you're right," Ellen admitted. "And they should be told that he wasn't aware of the problem. I wonder what he would have done if he had known."

"Dr. Marantz said there's no cure, or even a treatment. I suppose he would have had to resign from the board. Not only could they no longer rely on his expertise, but he couldn't trust himself. What a devastating blow that would have been for him."

"The end of his career as the leading Pollock expert," said Ellen. "I suppose he could have continued doing research on the Pollocks he already knew, and worked on other projects, like his mural book and New Deal studies. Though that's all moot now."

"Damn right it is. Francis is dead, and it wasn't an accident—at least I don't believe it was. Who killed him, and why? The foundation may decide to hire me to continue the provenance research, but I'll have to hunt for his killer on my own time."

TJ realized he had to learn more about Francis' private life and professional dealings. Could there be someone with a strong enough grudge against him to want him dead? According to Birdie, he wasn't close to anyone, but maybe there was a spurned lover lurking in the background, or a bad business deal that prompted revenge. He decided to return to the apartment and comb through the personal files.

First, however, he needed to get the foundation's backing, which would give him a legitimate reason to spend time in Francis' flat. Louis was beginning to wonder about him, especially after the last visit when he returned the missing files.

Forty-Two

A morning call to Hall, Dickler, Lawler, Kent & Friedman informed TJ that the Pollock-Krasner Foundation chairman would be pleased to see him that afternoon.

"Mr. Dickler was going to reach out to you, Mr. Fitzgerald," said Carla Evans, his personal assistant. "There's a matter he wants to discuss with you, regarding Dr. O'Connor."

That's curious, he wondered. *Why would Dickler connect me to Francis? Because I'm married to Ellen? Guess I'll find out this afternoon.*

* * *

The meeting opened on a friendly note. Dickler thanked him for making himself available at short notice and wasted no time in explaining.

"We've been surveying Dr. O'Connor's papers to determine which material should come to the foundation. Miss Crowe has been most cooperative. My clerk was going through his desk and came across his checkbook. It indicates that he recently wrote two checks to you. We know from your wife's disclosure statement that you are a private investigator, so I'd like you to tell me what Francis was paying you for."

Having decided to be candid, TJ laid it out. "Since you've been combing his files, you know that Francis recently received four Pollock catalogue raisonné submissions that he withheld from the board. He believed they were questionable, and he hired me to trace their provenances. When I asked him why he needed my services, he said he didn't want to do it himself. He was insistent about remaining behind the scenes. He wouldn't tell me why."

"Was Ellen involved in this arrangement?"

"She agreed to introduce us, at Francis' suggestion. He approached her, knowing that her husband was a private investigator."

"What were the results of your inquiries?"

It took nearly half an hour, punctuated by probing questions from Dickler, for TJ to describe his encounters with the owners of the submitted paintings. He elaborated on Francis' doubts, based on their coming in so close together and their dubious histories, though on the face of it, each account was quite believable. He mentioned Francis' regrets about having left blank spaces in the original catalogue—blanks that almost invited forgers to fill them in. Then he got to the crux of the issue.

"Francis thought they were all fakes, and all painted by the same hand. What he really wanted me to do was identify the forger."

Dickler leaned back in his chair. "And did you?"

"I was still working on it when he was killed. I'm sure his death was not an accident, and I assumed the forger had murdered him to stop the inquiry. It seemed like the natural conclusion, so I decided to keep digging, in spite of the fact that I no longer had a client. But at the funeral, quite by chance, I learned something that changed my mind about his death, and about the paintings. I still think he was murdered, but not by the forger, because there isn't one. The paintings are authentic."

Dickler considered this information before he spoke. His tone was querulous. "Are you saying that Francis misjudged them?"

"I don't blame you for finding that hard to believe, Mr. Dickler, considering Francis' reputation. He was the top expert, so I accepted his opinion, but his insistence that the paintings were wrong was leading me up one blind alley after another. What I found out at the funeral is that he was suffering from a neurological condition that prevented him from recognizing Pollock abstracts he hadn't seen before."

Behind his horn-rimmed glasses, Dickler's eyes widened. "What on earth would do that?"

"It's called morphagnosia, and it's very rare. A friend of his who's an eye doctor diagnosed it, and I happened to meet him at the reception. We got to talking, and he told me about it. He said it had probably been caused by a stroke. It explains why Francis couldn't tell that the paintings were genuine—he literally couldn't identify the characteristic patterns. He could recognize the Pollocks he was familiar with, but not new ones."

"Did Francis know about this diagnosis?"

"No. It took the doctor a while to figure it out, and before he could make an appointment to give him the findings, Francis was killed."

Dickler shook his head. "This is astonishing, almost unbelievable, though it explains why Francis kept those paintings from the board. We were perplexed when we found the files, but I see now why, before he presented them, he wanted to establish for certain that they were fake, since they're so convincing. If your conclusion is correct, however, they're convincing because they're *not* fake."

"That's what I think, and I'm prepared to turn over my research material to you, and to continue collecting the necessary documentation if you agree. I would charge the same rate as I charged Francis, fifty dollars an hour plus expenses."

"I'd like to discuss it with the board, but it's agreeable to me," said Dickler. "I'll call you in a day or two and confirm the arrangements. Meanwhile, I appreciate your offer to let us have what you've already done."

TJ smiled as he shook Dickler's hand. "Frankly, I feel obliged to let you have it, since a couple of the former owners will be sending backup documentation directly to you. They're under the impression that my inquiries were on the board's behalf, though I didn't tell them that."

With a knowing nod, Dickler returned his smile. "I understand, Mr. Fitzgerald. In a case like this, we use whatever tools are necessary—as long as they're legal, of course. And once I get the board's okay, you will be acting for us."

Forty-Three

Friday, May 16

Arriving at his office, TJ was met by a messenger delivering a contract from the Pollock-Krasner Foundation authorizing him to act on its behalf in the matter of provenance research and agreeing to his compensation terms. With it was a set of keys to Francis' apartment. He signed the document, copied it, and returned the original to the messenger. As soon as it was received, he'd be officially on the foundation's payroll.

He wasted no time in contacting George Loper to arrange an appointment for him and his mother with an East Hampton attorney. He called the attorney and dictated the statement he wanted them to sign and have notarized, with instructions to send it, and the bill, to the foundation. He made a note to follow up with Art in Trust and the Smart Museum, and to check that Jeffries had indeed sent in copies of his documentation.

Then he went off the clock to work on identifying Francis' killer, which wasn't part of his deal with the foundation. *However,* he figured, *once I get that job done, I don't think they'll refuse to pay for the time I spent on it.*

* * *

With his copy of the contract in his pocket, just in case he needed to establish his bona fides, TJ returned once again to Francis' apartment.

"I'm sorry I didn't see you at the funeral," he told Louis. "Unfortunately, it was limited to family and close associates, but I wish they'd seen fit to invite you."

"That's kind of you to say, Mr. Fitzgerald," the doorman replied, "but I figured it was a private occasion. I did go to Green-Wood on the Sunday and laid some flowers on the grave."

TJ found that very touching. He doubted that many others, apart from immediate family, had taken the trouble to attend the interment, or would ever visit the gravesite. Francis' most visible memorial would be his scholarship, which would enrich the study of modern American art for generations to come.

Louis readily accepted his explanation that he was now employed by the foundation to complete the projects Francis was working on at the time of his death. So once again, he found himself in apartment 11-C, facing a search through the mass of files in the hope of finding incriminating evidence.

He started with Francis' Rolodex, hoping that a name or notation would jump out at him. There were a lot of cards, and he could appreciate why it had taken Birdie so long to notify his many contacts of his death. The list was an art world who's who, including museum directors and curators, art dealers, collectors, critics, academic art historians, philanthropists, state and federal arts administrators, as well as artists he had befriended in the course of his career.

Under K, he found a card for Ruth Kligman. Pricked by his conscience, he quickly flipped to the next one, which ironically happened to be Lee Krasner—with a cross through it. It seemed that Francis didn't bother to remove the deceased. Irving Marantz was there, too, his name and phone number also crossed out, with a note of his son's number.

By the time he got to Christian Zervos, the long-dead Greek art critic and publisher whose name and Paris address were deleted, TJ had drawn a blank. If anyone among the scores of surviving contacts had a homicidal grudge against Francis, the Rolodex wasn't giving it away. He decided to look for personal letters, which he hoped would be as carefully labeled as the other papers and separate from professional correspondence.

In this, he was disappointed. He sighed as he opened each of the four file drawers marked CORRESPONDENCE to find it arranged chronologically. The material related to specific research projects—like the Pollock catalogue raisonné and his New Deal and mural books, as well as Raphael Research, his private consulting firm—had their own filing system, but everything else was simply filed by year. And there was plenty of it.

Better start with the most recent, he reasoned. Since only four months had elapsed between January 1, 1986, and Francis' death, the current year's file was relatively thin. There were a few invitations to dinner parties and exhibition openings, several birthday cards in their own folder, personal letters, and carbon copies of the replies. Evidently, he preferred to use the Selectric typewriter, rather than the computer and printer, for his correspondence. There was a newsy letter from one of his former colleagues at the University of Maryland—whose jaundiced views of his fellow faculty members were quite amusing—with a copy of Francis' equally acerbic reply. But however estranged he was from the university, there was nothing so vicious as to cause lethal retribution, at least as far as TJ could tell. Academics were always knifing each other in the back, though almost never literally.

Turning to 1985, TJ came across the carbon copy of a terse note dated December 15 and addressed to Robin Crowe:

"Dear Birdie, I have considered your request and am inclined to reject it. I imagine that the Hunter College Credit Union can assist you." It wasn't signed, but the signature had probably been added to the original by hand.

There was no corresponding letter from Birdie, so she must have asked for whatever it was in person, or on the phone. Why not respond the same way? He clearly wanted to distance himself from the matter, but this was almost insulting. What would offend him enough to prompt such a curt and impersonal note to his dearest friend?

The answer was obvious. She had asked him for money.

* * *

He took the note to the worktable and switched on the copy machine. It wouldn't be hard to follow up with the Municipal Credit Union, which serviced all City University branches, including his alma mater, John Jay College of Criminal Justice. A call to his contact in the MCU office would disclose whether Birdie had an account, and if so, any recent activity.

His conversation with Ellen about Birdie's possible motive came back to mind. If Birdie was hard up for cash and knew she stood to gain big from Francis' death, it put her high on the suspect list. It would mean she'd lied very convincingly about knowing the terms of the will, though he decided her surprised laugh was probably genuine. She really had no idea about the Pollock painting.

As he waited for the Xerox to warm up, he glanced around the worktable and noticed that the answering machine's red light was on. He decided to check the messages. He sat down, took out a notepad, and activated the playback.

There was Dr. Marantz's call on the day Francis was killed, as well as several messages received since then, mostly from people who clearly weren't aware that Francis was dead. The oldest one, dated April 30, two days before his death, was from a man who didn't leave a name. It was somewhat cryptic, so TJ listened to it a couple of times.

"Please pick up, Francis. I'm back and I must see you. Things are very different for me now, I swear to God. Are you there? Please listen. I need you. Please call me. I have a new number." The caller left his number and closed with "Don't let me down, please."

What's that all about? said TJ to himself, though he could guess. An ex-boyfriend wanting to rekindle the old flame. Who is he? Did Francis call him back? Did they meet? So many questions, leading to the most important one: Did he push Francis in front of the train?

Forty-Four

Putting a name to the number was not difficult. A helpful supervisor at New York Telephone, with whom TJ had regular dealings, informed him that it was unlisted and had recently been issued to James Gruber, living at 241 East 73rd Street, across from Francis. He checked the Rolodex, and there was Gruber, same address, different phone number. There was also a number marked Office. But, as with the deceased, the information had been crossed out.

TJ dialed the office number. "Good morning, Atheneum Books," said the voice at the other end of the line.

"Good morning," replied TJ. "May I speak to Mr. Gruber?"

"I'm sorry, but Mr. Gruber is on leave until the end of the month. Shall I connect you with his secretary?"

"No, thank you. It's not urgent. I'll call back in June."

So Gruber worked in some capacity, senior enough to warrant a secretary, for the publisher of such distinguished authors as Edward Albee, James Merrill, and Nikki Giovanni. TJ looked out the window on the 73rd Street side and saw Gruber's building, a 1910 five-story brownstone, directly opposite on the corner of Second Avenue. Like Birdie's, it had retail on the ground floor and no doorman. He considered calling Gruber at home, or maybe it would be better just to ring his bell and hope to catch him in. But he decided to postpone contact until he learned more about Gruber's relationship with Francis. He was hoping to find something in the correspondence files, though searching them would take a while. At least he now knew what to look for.

* * *

Using his longstanding connections, TJ had no trouble learning about Robin Crowe's history with the credit union. Apparently, she had taken Francis' advice. Early in the year she had applied for a mortgage so she could buy into her building, which was going co-op, but the application was denied. It was notoriously difficult for single women to qualify for loans, and her situation was further compromised by a lack of collateral and substantial credit card and student loan debt.

Only a week ago, however, she had re-applied on the strength of her forthcoming inheritance. Even though the will had not yet been probated, the assets it represented were more than enough to clear her debts and qualify her. The life insurance alone should do it, and if she were to sell the Pollock, she could likely pay off the mortgage and own the apartment free and clear.

TJ wanted to confront Birdie with the note. It hinted that she knew more about Francis' finances than she let on, though she had admitted to being aware of the so-called nest egg that gave him independence. Maybe she asked him to lend her the down payment so she could qualify for the mortgage, or maybe she wanted to borrow the full amount. Whichever it was, his refusal must have been a major disappointment. Did she try him again after the credit union turned her down?

He dialed Birdie's number. This being a workday, he got the expected answering machine and left a message.

"Hello, Birdie, it's TJ Fitzgerald. I'm at Francis' apartment, now officially working on behalf of the foundation to follow up on his catalogue raisonné research, and I came across something I want your opinion about. I'll be here all day. Please call me at his number when you get home, and I'll come right over. Thanks, see you later."

* * *

TJ treated himself to lunch at JG Melon before tackling the files. Procrastinating further, he called Ellen and explained that, if Birdie agreed to see him, he'd be home a bit late.

"How are you going to handle it?" she wanted to know.

"I plan to just show her the note and see how she reacts. The implication is clear, so if she's evasive, it'll mean she has something to hide."

"She may have fooled you once already," said Ellen, not very tactfully, "so you'd better be extra alert."

"I wasn't a hundred percent convinced, remember. Still, even if she was hitting him up for a loan, she may not have known she'd get it all when he died. If she admits she knew, it really strengthens the case against her, which I'm sure she'd realize. But the note might startle her enough to make something slip out—assuming she has something to hide, like being guilty of murder."

"Seems like a long shot to me, but I guess it's worth a try. Good luck, honey pie. See you whenever."

Okay, Juanito, down to business, he told himself as he headed to the file cabinet. Again, he started at the current year and worked backwards. The task was not as onerous as he had imagined, though he knew that if nothing substantial turned up here, he'd have to go through the Raphael Research files and other specialized material as well.

Most of the miscellaneous correspondence was with art world and academic colleagues, fan mail and queries from students, invitations to exhibitions, requests to deliver a lecture or contribute an essay to a journal or art magazine, and needed only a glance.

There were also a lot of birthday cards, for which Francis seemed to have held a special fondness. Each year had a separate folder for them. At first, TJ passed them over in favor of actual letters and handwritten notes, but it occurred to him that there might be notes inside the cards, so he went back and took a closer look.

Since Francis' birthday fell on February 14, many of the cards were modified valentines, while others were specifically for Valentine's Day birthdays. It seemed that a few close friends went out of their way to find specialty cards. Mischievous cupids and arrow-pierced stylized hearts abounded, supplemented by doggerel verses, charming sentiments, and personal expressions of affection from individuals or couples, including his parents. TJ wondered if Francis had reciprocated so sweetly on their birthdays.

In the 1985 folder, he noticed one card that was signed with just an initial: "All my love, J." There were similar cards going back to 1980, but not for 1986.

J for James, as in James Gruber? It could also be for Jane, Joe, Jeff, Judy, or any number of other male or female names. He thought about returning to the Rolodex but opted to wait until he finished combing the files. Maybe there was some matching handwriting that could put a full name to the initial.

Sure enough, on an invitation to the 1983 opening of Shakespeare & Co, a bookstore on Lexington Avenue opposite Hunter College, was a note: "Please come as my guest, James." The handwriting was the same.

In the 1978 file, TJ found the carbon of a short letter from Francis to Gruber, expressing pleasure at having met him at the Yale Club reception celebrating the publication of the Pollock catalogue raisonné. "As we are near neighbors," he wrote, "I hope you will drop by sometime soon to continue our discussion over a glass or two of wine. Please call me at your convenience." His telephone number was added. The letter ended simply, "Yours," with space for a handwritten signature.

TJ considered the implications. *So that's the start of their relationship. A meeting of minds at the reception, maybe even a frisson of sexual attraction. A couple of years go by, and it's blossomed into a full-blown affair. I wonder if Birdie knows about Gruber. She said she never saw evidence of a boyfriend, but she might not have realized what their relationship was. That's something else I can ask her. If I start there, it might ease me into the real question.*

Forty-Five

Birdie returned TJ's call at around half past five and told him she'd be glad to see him now. It took him only five minutes to get to her door, where she greeted him cheerfully. Considering her windfall, she had every reason to be cheerful.

"Your message was very mysterious," she said as she ushered him in. "Come sit down and tell me what you found. Oh, would you like something to drink? A glass of wine?"

He accepted her offer of a seat in the living room and a glass of red wine. When she joined him, he raised his glass and offered a toast: "To Francis. The most willful man I ever met."

Birdie laughed—not as heartily as she had when she saw the terms of the bequest, but with feeling. "I'll definitely drink to that!"

On that positive note, TJ eased into his interrogation. "As I told you," he began, "the foundation has hired me to continue the provenance tracing. I've been going through the files, and I came across some correspondence with a guy named James Gruber. Ever hear of him?" Not that Gruber had anything to do with catalogue raisonné research.

She answered without hesitation. "Isn't he an editor? I think Francis used to consult with him when he was working on an article or a talk. He said he was an excellent sounding board. I never met him, but I remember Francis saying how handy it was that he lived right across the street, so he was a neighbor as well as a friend."

"Do you think he might have been more than a friend?"

Now she hesitated and gave it a moment's thought. "You mean like a lover?

225

Gosh, I really don't know. I think I told you I'm not aware of any romantic partners, though I'm sure that, if there were any, they'd be male. What made you think Gruber might be one?"

"You probably know that Francis kept his incoming letters and copies of his replies. That was essential for his catalogue work and other professional dealings, and it carried over to his private correspondence. It's all filed by year. Interestingly, there's a copy of just one letter to Gruber, back in nineteen seventy-eight, right after they met. From then on, they must have communicated by phone. Living so close, there was no need to write to each other, except for the annual birthday cards, which Francis kept. They're signed 'All my love, J.' That's what made me think the relationship was more intimate. Then I listened to the messages on Francis' answering machine, and what I heard confirmed it."

"Good Lord, the answering machine. I should have listened to them myself, but I was so preoccupied with notifying everyone that I forgot all about it. What was Gruber's message?"

"Seems like they had broken up, or rather Francis had backed off, and Gruber wanted to reconnect. It was a heartfelt plea, only a couple of days before Francis died."

"Speaking of notifying people," said Birdie, "I think I remember calling Gruber, but his number had been disconnected. No, wait, I didn't call him because his name was crossed out, so I thought he was dead. Francis used to leave dead people in the Rolodex. I once asked him if it wasn't kind of macabre to see them every time he flipped through the cards. I said, if you don't want to throw them away, why not put them in a drawer out of sight? He just harrumphed, in classic Francis fashion, and said he enjoyed being reminded that they'd never bother him again."

* * *

Having pointed Birdie in the opposite direction, TJ now turned the tables on her.

"I found an interesting letter in last year's file," he said, and handed her the Xerox copy. "It made me wonder what request he rejected."

He was hoping that the about-face would disarm her, and his radar picked up a mix of alarm, trepidation, and uncertainty as she read the note, taking longer over it than its brief message warranted. She was formulating a reply, calculating how much she should reveal. When she looked up, she had composed herself and had decided that a shield of frankness was the appropriate protection.

"As I'm sure you already realize, I asked him to lend me money. It was very awkward, and I wouldn't have gone to him if I'd been able to get a bank loan. I won't go into the details, but my credit isn't good. If I could get some cash to pay off my debts, I'd be able to qualify."

"Why did you need the bank loan?" He knew why, but he wanted to hear it from her.

"This building is going to become a co-op, and I want to buy in. If I can't, I'll have to move out, and I really don't want to do that. I want to own instead of renting, and this is my chance. But I need a mortgage, and I can't get it while I'm in debt. I had to work myself up to asking Francis, but he was the only person I knew who could come through for me. After all, he trusted me with his estate, so why wouldn't he trust me to pay him back?"

"From the wording of that note, it wasn't a flat-out no. He said he was 'inclined' against it, and suggested you go to Hunter's credit union as an alternative. Suppose you did, and it didn't work out? Would you have tried him again?"

"I did both," she answered, allowing her embarrassment to show. "I got the same response from the credit union that I got from the bank. Clear your debts and we'll reconsider. I told him I'd taken his advice, and it hadn't worked, which is why I was back at his door. Actually, he was at my door— that's to say, I invited him here to dinner. I didn't tell him about the credit union rejection until we sat down to eat."

"How did he react?"

"He started to lecture me about financial responsibility, that I shouldn't have gotten into debt in the first place. As if I could have gone to grad school without a student loan or paid my medical bills before I had Hunter's health insurance without using my credit cards. Jesus, he could be so damned pompous and insensitive. I was offended, and I told him so. He had one of his outbursts and stormed out. End of conversation. I never got to ask him to reconsider the loan."

"When was this?"

"I heard from the credit union in mid-April, so I went back to him immediately. I know it was a Saturday, I think April nineteenth. I even cooked his favorite meal, boeuf bourguignon, which I wound up eating alone, and for two days after."

All this was fine as far as it went, but TJ felt there was more to come. Now he used his intuition.

"That wasn't the end of it, was it?"

She looked apprehensive. "What do you mean?"

"You didn't give up on Francis, did you? There's a message on the machine," he lied. There were no messages from before April 30, and none from Birdie. If she did call, either he had answered when he heard her speak, or he had erased the message.

TJ had guessed correctly. "Okay, I did call him," she admitted, "but he didn't pick up. That didn't surprise me, but I still hoped he'd reconsider. He could be quixotic, you know, so I hadn't quite given up."

TJ emptied his glass and stood. "Thank you for being so forthcoming, Birdie. I appreciate your candor, and especially your take on Gruber. From what I heard on the answering machine, I'm inclined to think he was at the end of his rope, and if Francis didn't respond, he could have lost it. I need to do more digging there. I'll keep you posted on what I find out." He had no intention of doing that, but he wanted her to think she was in his confidence. Also, that his focus wasn't on her—which in fact it was, at least for the time being. He was betting that the phone call she acknowledged wasn't the last time she'd tried to persuade Francis to think again.

Forty-Six

Before heading home, TJ decided to return to Francis' apartment and give Gruber a call. The new number rang for a while, and he was about to hang up when it was answered in a tone that told him the speaker was either half asleep or half in the bag.

"Hello? Who is this?"

"Hello, Mr. Gruber. My name is Timothy Fitzgerald, and I'd—"

Gruber cut him off. "Who the hell are you? How did you get this number?"

"From Francis O'Connor."

Gruber's reply was silence, followed by a muffled sound, either a sob or a groan. *He must have put his hand over the mouthpiece,* thought TJ. Then the voice exploded.

"You're a fucking liar! Goddamn you, son of a bitch, he's dead!"

"Please let me explain, Mr. Gruber."

"Leave me alone! Francis is *dead*. He's dead." He trailed off, and he hung up.

TJ then called Ellen with an update.

"Gruber wouldn't talk to me on the phone, so I'm going to try him in person. Better do it now, when I know he's in, even though I'm pretty sure he's been drinking."

"Think he'll let you in?"

TJ chuckled. "I don't need an invitation, honey." Even though he now had keys to 11-C, the trusty set of locksmith tools was in his jacket pocket.

* * *

The residential entrance to Gruber's building was on the 73rd Street side, with a row of mailboxes and buzzers in the small, unattended lobby. On the off chance that Gruber would admit him, TJ buzzed his apartment, 3-B. There was no reply.

Using his tools with an expert's finesse, he opened the lobby door and made his way to the third floor. Pressing Gruber's doorbell also had no effect, so he used the pick set again, opened the apartment door, and called out as he entered. He was greeted by the stale odor of dirty laundry mixed with the fragrance of an overflowing garbage pail.

"Hello, Mr. Gruber, it's Fitzgerald. I was worried when you hung up. Are you okay?"

He stepped into a short hallway that led to the living room and dining area, with the kitchen and bathroom to the side. He saw no one in those rooms, so he headed for the bedroom, where he found Gruber, unshaven and disheveled, slumped in an armchair next to the unmade bed, staring out the window at Francis' building across the street. Surveying the room, TJ saw a large photograph in a stand-up frame on top of the dresser. It was a full-length picture of Francis standing in front of Pollock's *Number 1A, 1948*, at the Museum of Modern Art. Gesturing toward the canvas, he appeared to be addressing an unseen audience. Perhaps Gruber had taken the picture himself during a gallery talk.

As TJ approached, Gruber turned vacant eyes toward him. "How did you get in here? What do you want?" His voice was as flat as his gaze.

"I'm Tim Fitzgerald. We just spoke on the phone. I let myself in. I need to talk to you about Francis."

He half expected another outburst, but the belligerence had drained out of Gruber, who leaned forward and ran a hand over his eyes, as if to wipe away a disturbing image. His other hand reached down beside the chair and found a half-empty glass of clear liquid, from which he took a couple of large swallows.

Gruber made no move as TJ went into the dining room to collect a chair. The apartment was in disarray, with half-eaten takeout food on the dining table, dirty dishes in the sink, and other signs of dissipation, including several empty gin bottles on the kitchen counter and in the garbage. *He's on a bender,* was TJ's conclusion. *I hope he's coherent enough to answer my questions. Better make some coffee.*

He found what he needed in the kitchen. Waiting for the coffee to brew, he cleared the dining table. When the coffee was ready, he went back to the bedroom, where Gruber was nodding off in the armchair. Easing him up, TJ supported him as they made their way to the dining room, where TJ parked him at the table in front of a large mug of black coffee, with the pot nearby.

It took about half an hour for Gruber to become moderately alert, with TJ comforting and reassuring him the whole time. Once he seemed responsive, TJ explained his purpose—at least the tailor-made version.

He said Francis had hired him to trace the source of the fake Pollocks, and that it was probably the forger who pushed Francis in front of the train. Now he was looking for the killer and wanted Gruber's help.

"I understand that you and Francis were close friends," said TJ diplomatically. "Did he talk to you about his doubts regarding the paintings? Did he give you any clues about who he suspected of forging them?"

Gruber shook his head slowly, as if unsure. But when he spoke, it was with certainty. "I really know nothing of his recent authentication work. I haven't seen or spoken to him in months. We had, uh, drifted apart. And I was out of town for a while, on leave from my job since March. I only got back at the end of April, right before…it happened." He paused. "Excuse me, I need a handkerchief."

He started to rise, but TJ put a hand on his arm. "Here, take mine, it's clean," he said, not wanting Gruber to go back to the bedroom and his glass of gin. Gruber took it with thanks, wiped his eyes, and blew his nose.

"I'm sure Francis' death was no accident, but it may have had nothing to do with the fakes," continued TJ, shifting to another tack. "Can you think of anyone who hated him enough to kill him?"

Suddenly, Gruber's whole demeanor changed as something deep within him welled up and overflowed. He clenched his fists and blurted out, "I wanted to kill him! I loved him, God help me, but he was so cruel! I went through hell for him, and he didn't care. He shut me out when I needed him the most." He began to cry. "You can't imagine the pain."

TJ waited for Gruber to compose himself. Already sure he knew the answer, he asked, "What drove him away from you?"

"He was brilliant, you know, always questioning, digging into things to find their essence, their truth. At first, I was flattered that he was interested in me, but he was never condescending. On the contrary, he told me *I* was brilliant, that we were equally matched. We spent many hours discussing philosophy, criticism, religion, and especially poetry. I'm an editor, and he often turned to me for advice on his own creative writing."

Gruber was apparently having trouble working his way around to the break-up, so TJ pushed him toward it gently. "Your relationship wasn't strictly intellectual, was it?"

"No. There was a physical aspect to it as well, but believe me, that wasn't really important. I think I was Francis' first lover—at least that's what he told me—and he was already forty-one when we met. He said he had always satisfied himself, if you know what I mean, and I'm not highly sexed, so it was just a sidelight that made the relationship that much more intimate and fulfilling."

"Did someone else come between you?"

"Oh, no. Nothing like that." Gruber sighed. "You've probably already guessed. It was my drinking. It took me years to admit that I'm an alcoholic. I'd convinced myself that I could handle it, could stop whenever I wanted to, that it wasn't interfering with my life—all the bullshit fantasies that drunks believe. Francis encouraged me to try AA and psychotherapy, neither of which did any good. I'd be dry for a while, then relapse.

"Finally, he got fed up and told me he couldn't watch me drink myself to death, like Pollock had done, so he wanted nothing more to do with me. That was in January. I hoped he didn't really mean it, but when he returned my birthday card unopened, I knew he was serious."

"I heard your message on his answering machine," TJ said. "That's how I got your unlisted number. Were you telling him you'd been to rehab?"

"Yes. That's why I took the leave. I went upstate to a so-called recovery center, a benign-sounding name for a place where the treatment is anything but benign. I shouldn't say that. They do what's necessary, but the detox process is a nightmare. I was there for six weeks, and at the end I was sure I'd beaten it. I wanted Francis to see that I was sober, that I'd turned my life around, but he wouldn't listen. I'd been telling myself that I did it all for him, but he had written me off."

TJ suspected that, like Birdie, Gruber hadn't accepted Francis' rejection as the final word.

"But you did see him, didn't you?"

* * *

The effect of the coffee was wearing off, and Gruber's hands began to twitch. He put one on top of the other to calm them, and he studied them as he answered.

"When he didn't take my call, I wanted to go to his apartment, but I was sure he would have told the doorman not to let me go up. I knew he often went shopping at Citarella on Friday, fish day, though he wasn't observant. The fish is nice and fresh on Friday. Anyway, I was across the street, and I saw him come out at around three and head west, but not to Citarella. He crossed Third Avenue and turned down Lexington. I followed him, hoping to catch him at a light.

"He had crossed Sixty-Ninth Street and was about a block ahead of me when he met someone coming out of Hunter. A woman. She stopped him, and they talked for a few minutes, so I hung back. The conversation got quite heated. She tried to take his arm, and he pulled away and shouted at her. I couldn't hear what they were saying, but he was very angry. He marched off and left her there, but in a moment, she went after him. He went down into the subway station, and so did she."

"Did you recognize her?"

"No. I wasn't really paying attention to her, and I mostly saw her back."

"Did you follow them?"

"Yes. I went into the station, but I didn't have a token, so I went to the booth to buy one. It was pretty crowded, so I had to wait on line. Then the train pulled in, and I heard the brakes squeal and people started yelling and running out. It was chaotic. I looked for Francis, but I couldn't see him. Then I heard people saying that someone fell in front of the train, and I knew it was Francis. I was praying I was wrong, but I just knew he was dead. I haven't drawn a sober breath since then."

Forty-Seven

id Francis really issue an order not to admit him, or was Gruber just being paranoid? As he left Gruber's building, TJ decided to check his story with Louis, who confirmed it.

"Yes," said the doorman, "Dr. O'Connor told me that if he came here, I should not let him go up. He told the night man the same thing. It wasn't my place to ask why, but I gather they had a serious falling out. The only thing Dr. O'Connor would say was that he never wanted to see him again."

"When was that?" asked TJ.

"Late April, I believe it was," said Louis. "But I saw Mr. Gruber hanging around watching the building a couple of times, I guess waiting for him to come out. On the day Dr. O'Connor was killed, he followed him up the block."

Gruber had told TJ as much, but Louis amplified the account.

"When he caught up with him, they had a terrible row, right on the street, in front of several other people. Dr. O'Connor was shouting at Mr. Gruber, so loud that I could hear him from a few doors away."

"Could you make out what he said?"

"Not most of it, but Dr. O'Connor pushed Mr. Gruber away from him, screamed, 'You're dead to me,' and stormed off. I think Mr. Gruber was shocked, because he just stood there for a few moments. Then he went after Dr. O'Connor and followed him across town."

* * *

Setting the table while Ellen put the finishing touches on dinner, TJ reviewed what he'd learned from Birdie and Gruber. Ellen summed it up succinctly.

"So neither of them is telling the whole story, and from what you've learned they each had a motive and the opportunity. Birdie lied about the will. She knows she's going to inherit a bundle. Gruber is mortified by Francis' very public rejection and wants to get back at him."

"Gruber was determined to confront Francis, hoping he'd soften up if they could talk face to face, but it backfired," said TJ. "He didn't mention that the meeting did take place and went horribly wrong. He opened up a crack when I asked him who hated Francis enough to kill him, but he made it seem like just a figure of speech."

"How do you feel about the rest of his story?"

"Did he see Francis argue with a woman outside Hunter? Probably. He didn't know her, but it must have been Birdie. Did he follow them into the subway? Again, probably. Question is, was he really waiting on line at the token booth when Francis was killed? Suppose he's already on the platform when the train approaches, and he suddenly decides to get even. I'm dead to you, so you'll be dead to me—for real.

"Meanwhile, Birdie said nothing to me about meeting Francis that day. From what Gruber told me, she just bumped into him as she was coming out of the building while he was passing. She couldn't have known he'd be there, whereas Gruber was stalking him."

Ellen considered the circumstances. "She must have asked him about the loan again, and he blew up. Her timing was terrible—since his fight with Gruber, he's already in a bad mood—but why would she go after him?"

"That's my next question to her. Right now, the question is, when do we eat?"

* * *

Approaching Birdie again was going to take some maneuvering. It had to be in person, not on the phone, since he wanted to watch her reaction. But setting up another visit so soon might spook her, make her wary. He needed a reason. Fortunately, the Pollock-Krasner Foundation gave him one.

He was at the office on Monday morning, still trying to make headway on the bribery case, when he got a call from Carla Evans.

"Mr. Dickler would like you to have Miss Crowe sign an affidavit affirming that she has no claim to the material related to the authentication process. We want to have it collected from Dr. O'Connor's apartment, and we need her authorization. The affidavit will also authorize both you and Miss Crowe to supervise the removal." Adept at forestalling disputes, Dickler wanted to ensure there would be no question that only what the foundation was entitled to was taken.

TJ said he'd be glad to handle it, and Evans told him a messenger would bring him the document within the hour.

He decided to arrange to meet Birdie at her bank, where the form could be notarized, then suggest they stop for coffee before he headed to Dickler's office. A coffee shop would be as good a place as any to confront her with Gruber's story.

He called her at the Hunter College Library and explained his mission. She agreed and told him she could be at Citibank on East 72nd Street at noon.

"Is that your lunch break?" he asked, and she said yes. "In that case, I can treat you to lunch after we get the paperwork out of the way. We can go to Neil's on Lexington. Right across from Hunter, so you won't be late getting back."

She agreed. "That's fine for me, TJ. I think I know the menu by heart."

* * *

With the affidavit duly signed and notarized, TJ and Birdie settled into a booth at Neil's and ordered sandwiches and coffee.

"I did follow up with Gruber," he told her. "I went to his apartment. He's in a bad way, really broken up over Francis' death. My hunch was right, they were lovers, but Francis had dumped him."

Birdie shook her head. "I can't believe I didn't know about their relationship. I should have realized there was someone. I told you Francis kept his private life quiet, but we were very close."

"You said he trusted you, yet that was something he couldn't share, even with you."

"I guess I should feel hurt, but it just makes me sad to think that he couldn't come out to me. I wouldn't have disapproved or thought any less of him for being gay. I assumed he was anyway, only one of the celibate ones. It shows how little we really know about other people, even those we're closest to."

"I also found out that Gruber's an alcoholic, which is why Francis called it quits. He couldn't put up with the self-destructive drinking. Gruber dried out and wanted to get back together, but Francis wouldn't have anything to do with him."

With her coffee cup halfway to her lips, Birdie paused and considered the implication. "Are you saying that Gruber might have been so deeply hurt that he'd kill Francis? That what he's feeling now is remorse rather than grief?"

"It's a real possibility," TJ replied, "especially since he told me himself that he followed Francis into the subway that afternoon. What he didn't tell me was that they'd had a heated argument on the street just before."

Birdie was stunned. "Oh, my God. Hell hath no fury like the scorned lover, female or male."

"It's a strong motive, I agree," said TJ, "but something else Gruber told me suggests another option."

"What do you mean?"

"While he was following Francis, Gruber saw him encounter a woman coming out of Hunter. He said they argued, and she also went after him into the subway." He let that sink in, then asked, "That was you, right? What did you and Francis fight about?"

She lowered her eyes and spoke very softly.

"It was just a coincidence. I had to go across to the bookstore to pick up an order, and I ran into him. He wasn't pleased to see me and tried to brush me off, said he had an appointment. I guess I should have let him go, but on impulse, I asked him again about the loan. No, I didn't ask, I pleaded. He got angry and said if I didn't leave him alone, he'd change his will, and I'd get nothing."

"You weren't just his executrix. You were the beneficiary, and you knew it."

"Okay, I knew about the money. When he said he trusted me, he explained that he wanted to set up a fund to support modern art scholarship, but he hadn't decided how to do it. He didn't think his nonprofit corporation was the right vehicle for it, and he was going back and forth with the Archives, which could administer it, so if something happened to him before he made up his mind, he'd leave it up to me to decide how to handle it. But I had no idea I would get all the money outright, and that there was a major Pollock painting as well. That was a shock."

"That's why you laughed when you read the will. Too good to be true."

Her hazel eyes leveled on him. "That inheritance will change my life. Having it is a godsend."

"Sent by the devil is more like it," he countered. "Why did you follow him?"

"He said he was going to Dickler's office, and I was afraid he might carry out his threat to change his will. I didn't know that Dickler wasn't his personal attorney. Like I said, it was all on impulse. I kept my distance and walked to the other end of the platform so he wouldn't see me. The idea was to follow him, head him off once he got up to the street, and convince him that I'd stop bothering him. I just wanted to cool him down. I was nowhere near him when he went under the train. When the brakes squealed and people started screaming, I panicked and ran out. I didn't even know it was Francis until I got home and heard it on the news."

Forty-Eight

After he delivered the affidavit to Dickler, TJ returned to the Sweeney & Fitzgerald office, where his partner was devoting himself to the *Daily News* sports page.

"Sorry to interrupt, Pat. I can see how busy you are, but I could use your advice."

"Can the sarcasm, sonny," grumbled Sweeney. Even after fourteen years together, eleven as full partners, he still liked to remind TJ who had seniority.

"You're right. Sarcasm is the last refuge of the defeated, and I ain't beat yet. But I do have a dilemma."

"On the O'Connor case? Not still a freebie, I hope."

"No, I'm on the foundation's payroll, officially to continue the provenance research, but I think I'm homing in on his killer."

Sweeney set the paper aside and pointed to the chair beside his desk. "Okay, plant it there and gimme what ya got." Out came a Chesterfield, which he ignited as he settled back to listen.

TJ described his visit to Gruber and his lunch with Birdie. Now he knew they both had strong reasons for wanting Francis dead. They had admitted to being in the subway station. Either of them could have pushed him, and he was sure one of them had.

Gruber said he was still at the token booth, but he might be lying. Birdie said she was at the other end of the platform, but she might be lying. His dilemma, he explained, was that without a witness able or willing to point a finger, there was no way to pin it on either of them.

"Yeah," said Sweeney, "I see your problem. Unless one of 'em fesses up, you got no case. It's just guesswork, no real evidence." He exhaled a fragrant Chesterfield cloud. "What's your gut tell you?"

"My money was on Birdie. She had a lot to gain, and she did cash in royally. But that was before I met Gruber. I could see him snapping when Francis pronounced him dead, which put the idea into his brain. Birdie was desperate for money, but Gruber was destroyed. So now the two of them are running neck and neck."

* * *

Back on the job for which he was being paid, TJ called Roland Wilson to find out if the mysterious Art in Trust benefactor was willing to divulge the source of *Number 22, 1949.* Wilson reported that his boss was still out of town on business but assured TJ that he would raise the matter with him as soon as he got back. At least he now knew it was a man.

From the Smart Museum director, TJ learned that they had not been able to trace *Number 8A, 1948,* to any donor or to find a record of its purchase. Reluctantly, he said, he had to admit that the university couldn't establish title. In all likelihood, Rosenberg acquired it privately, probably from a Chicago collector, so he would arrange for it to be turned over to his widow. Without saying as much, TJ felt it would be well-earned compensation for her husband's infidelities.

He could follow the trail back to the Museum of Modern Art's lending service—which, according to the catalogue raisonné, sold it around 1951—though Francis had already covered that ground without success during his original provenance research. Nevertheless, maybe a more thorough combing of the records would turn up a lead, so he dialed the museum and made an appointment to visit the archives.

On the phone with Adam Jeffries in Cragsmoor, he confirmed that the attorney had indeed sent copies of his documentation to the authentication board, backing up the claim that *Number 5, 1949* was a gift from Pollock to Joe Meert. The statement by George Loper and his mother regarding *Number 32, 1949,* was already in the works, and the East Hampton lawyer would call him when it had been notarized and mailed.

Unless Isaac Henry had a brainstorm, the backtracking of Richard Wagner's *Number 23, 1950*, still ended at the Salvation Army Donation Center on West 8th Street. Then TJ had a brainstorm of his own. Maybe a classified ad in *The Village Voice* could get results. It was a long shot, but what other choice was there? He called the newspaper and bought a notice asking the person who donated a square drip painting on a baseball game board to the thrift store last year to contact him. He hoped it wouldn't make trouble for Wagner. If the former owner found out it was a valuable Pollock, he might try to get it back.

* * *

Tuesday, May 20

As was their habit, Ellen and TJ woke up at seven a.m. to the sound of the clock radio delivering the morning news on WNYC. Dozing and half listening as they cuddled under the covers, they were suddenly wide awake when they heard a local bulletin:

"For the second time this month, a man was killed by a subway train at the Sixty-Eighth Street IRT station. According to witnesses, the victim, identified as James Gruber, a senior editor at Atheneum Books, threw himself in front of the downtown local as it entered the station just after midnight. Unlike the previous fatality, which occurred on May 2nd and was officially declared accidental, this one was apparently a suicide, but a police investigation is in progress."

TJ sat up with a start. "Holy shit! My visit must have triggered him. Jesus, what have I done?"

Ellen put her arms around him. "Don't say that, sweetheart. You don't know what set him off. Okay, it's more than two weeks since Francis died, but he may have been working himself up to it ever since then. You just don't know, so please don't blame yourself."

He jumped out of bed and pulled on his robe. "I've got to talk to someone at the Nineteenth. Samuelson, if he's in this early. Whoever's on the case." He headed to the phone.

"I just heard about James Gruber's death on the morning news," he told the desk sergeant at the precinct. "I'm a private investigator, and he was helping me with inquiries. Can you tell me the status of the case?"

"It ain't really movin' yet," said the sergeant. "Guy was a jumper, no question. Not many folks on the platform at that hour, but them as was agree he done it on purpose. Samuelson's gonna handle it, but he don't get in until nine. Then we can start tracing next of kin. You know anything about his family or friends?"

Not about to reveal the relationship between the two deaths, TJ said no. It now looked to him like Gruber killed Francis, was overcome by guilt and remorse, and took his own life. Did he leave a note? TJ needed to get to his apartment before Samuelson showed up.

* * *

Seven stops from 14th Street on the Lexington Avenue local found TJ in the 68th Street station, which was beginning to feel jinxed. He got to the street as quickly as possible and headed east to Second Avenue. His pick set, miniature camera, and a pair of latex gloves were in his pocket.

He entered Gruber's building without difficulty and walked up to the third floor, where the apartment door was also opened easily. Slipping on the gloves, he began to search. There was a desk in one corner of the living room, but there was no note or envelope on it, or on the dining table.

He found what he was looking for in the bedroom.

On top of the dresser, the framed photograph of Francis had been turned on its face. TJ picked it up. Under it was a piece of paper, on which Gruber had scrawled,

God forgive me

Forgive me for killing Francis, or for killing myself? Or both.

TJ photographed the note, replaced it where he found it, and left.

* * *

He called Ellen from a phone booth on the corner of Second Avenue.

"That note comes as close to a confession as we're likely to get. I suppose, like you said, he was working himself up to it, but I can't shake the feeling that my questioning was what pushed him over the edge, literally."

"Please don't beat yourself up. He was drinking himself to death anyhow. By the way, are you going to tell Gerry about the note? If you do, you'll have to admit to breaking into—I mean, entering Gruber's apartment without permission. How do you think he'd react?"

"I think I'll leave Dickler out of this," said TJ. "The foundation isn't paying me to investigate Francis' death, so I don't need to tell them about Gruber. If he did kill Francis, and he probably did, he paid the price. If I were a believer, I'd say he's burning in hell twice over."

"So you're just going to carry on with the provenance research? Charlie wants to schedule a board meeting to consider the new Pollocks, so I guess you'll have to wrap it up soon."

"I think they have what's needed for the Stanley and Fairfax paintings. I still need to keep after the Art in Trust guy and hope I can turn up something on the Rosenberg picture at the Modern. Wagner's is the long shot, but maybe my *Voice* ad will flush out the donor."

"I probably won't get to weigh in on them," said Ellen. "I guess it'll just be Gene and Bill duking it out. Not that I mind being a fly on the wall for that, could be fun. And maybe there won't be any fireworks. After all, if they're real Pollocks, what's not to like?"

"Right," agreed TJ. "The materials are correct, the histories are plausible, and they look genuine. I'm sure Dickler's told the others about Francis' morphagnosia, so his doubts can be ignored."

He went quiet for a moment. "Are you there, honey?" asked Ellen.

"Speaking of doubts, why am I not a hundred percent convinced that Gruber killed Francis? Suppose I take his story at face value. He goes to the subway station, more or less witnesses Francis' death, and is so devastated that he spirals down, decides he can't live without him, and does a copy-cat.

What's wrong with that scenario?"

Ellen considered the alternative. "Nothing, especially if you don't believe Birdie's story. Was she really at the other end of the platform, or was she standing right behind Francis when the train pulled in?"

Forty-Nine

Friday, June 20

"Yes, to all five," was Gene Thaw's emphatic decision, seconded by Bill Lieberman. Ellen added her affirmative vote, with the caveat that she was not herself an expert on Pollock's work but accepted the majority opinion, as well as the evidence collected by her husband on behalf of the board. She felt it was important to acknowledge her relationship with TJ for the record, in case a future dispute questioned her judgment.

As a formality, given the circumstances, Charlie Bergman had asked Gerry Dickler to sit in on the meeting. The board had never before weighed evidence collected by a private investigator.

In addition to the deed of gift for *Number 5, 1949* from Joseph Meert to Adam Jeffries, together with Meert's statement and the bill of sale from Jeffries to Peter and Gloria Stanley, there was the notarized affidavit by Mrs. George Loper and her son swearing to her husband's acceptance of *Number 32, 1949* in payment for carpentry services, and the bill of sale to Gordon and Beatrice Fairfax.

At the Museum of Modern Art archives, TJ had managed to uncover a misfiled loan form for the 1951 Pollock show at the Arts Club of Chicago. It included *Number 8A, 1948*, which was not on the published checklist. A letter to the club had yielded the information that the painting had been bought by a local collector, whose family confirmed that he, now deceased, had sold it to Rosenberg in 1969. They supplied a copy of the receipt.

The Art in Trust benefactor had finally returned from his business trip, and TJ had persuaded him to divulge how he came to own *Number 22, 1949*. His reluctance was due to the fact that it had been given to him by a lover—the owner of record. Since they were both then married to other people, the affair was clandestine, and he had kept her secret. But she had died a few years ago, so he agreed that, if the catalogue would omit any reference to the affair, he would acknowledge the gift.

Against all odds, the donor of *Number 23, 1950,* had responded to TJ's *Village Voice* ad. He was an estate liquidator who had found it in a West Village brownstone he was cleaning out after the owner's death.

"Fella named Goodman," TJ was told. "He was an artist, painted landscapes. The abstract didn't sell, so it went to Sally's with the rest of the leftovers." He said he only remembered the painting because of the baseball game on the back—he thought that was where any value might be.

"Are you a baseball collector?" he had asked TJ, who answered yes, he went for anything with a baseball theme, especially games and toys, and said to call him if any more baseball stuff came his way.

Checking Francis' files, TJ found references to Job Goodman, a buddy of Pollock's at the Art Students League who later worked with him on the WPA. Like Joe Meert, he had kept up with his old friend and may also have been the recipient of a gift. Or perhaps he did Pollock a service for which the painting was payment. Without documentation, the provenance was a bit shaky, but there was enough in its favor to make the case.

All five paintings had been subject to materials testing and had passed easily. And on aesthetic grounds, neither Gene nor Bill had any doubts that they were looking at genuine Jackson Pollocks.

* * *

"Well," said Gerry, "the board has unanimous agreement. I'm just an impartial observer, but given the evidence so ably collected by Mr. Fitzgerald,"—here he gave Ellen a nod and a grin—"I believe there won't be any challenges to your findings.

"However," he continued, "I strongly advise you not to mention or discuss Francis' neurological condition with anyone outside this room. Any suggestion that his opinions were not based on expert connoisseurship could be highly detrimental to the board's credibility."

"That's sound advice, as always, Gerry," said Gene, casting a glance at Bill, who was widely known as a world-class gossip. "Whatever our differences with Francis may have been, it would do the Pollock legacy no good to expose his disability."

"To be fair," said Ellen, recalling what TJ had told her, "we don't know when his morphagnosia began. The eye doctor said it likely came on suddenly, probably after a stroke he didn't even know he'd had, so it may have been quite recent. Perhaps we should review the things he vetoed in the six months before his death, which is when Dr. Marantz said he complained to him."

"A very sensible suggestion," agreed Gene. "Most of what we've seen in the past year has been obvious fakes or misattributions, about which all three of us concurred. There was only one painting he questioned, *Number Five, Nineteen Forty-Nine,* that looked right to Bill and me, and it's now been authenticated. Oh, yes, he also didn't like that small painting on paper we looked at in March, the one that belongs to my very good client. I've already told her we need to see the original at our next meeting, so that won't be a problem."

* * *

To celebrate the successful end of TJ's provenance investigation, he and Ellen decided to splurge on dinner at the St. Regis, where she and Francis had had their fateful meeting in April. Over Bloody Marys in the King Cole Bar, she amused TJ with the story about the flatulent monarch.

"Tell you what," she said, "let's come here every February fourteenth and toast Francis on his birthday."

"An excellent idea. It'll be our annual Valentine's Day celebration."

"I hope someone will continue his research on the history of American murals. There's a book begging to be written. Maybe Birdie will take it on. She has access to all his files, and the Hunter College art library."

TJ sipped his cocktail. "Speaking of our favorite librarian, a little birdie tells me that we still don't know the truth about Francis' death. Okay, Gruber has your vote, and I can't argue with your reasoning, so why am I not satisfied?"

"Because his suicide note was so ambiguous," she replied. "If only he'd written, 'God forgive me for killing Francis,' there'd be no question. Or 'God forgive me for killing myself. I can't live without Francis.' Then Birdie would be the one. Even so, how could you prove it? And maybe neither of them did it. It's just possible that he really did fall off the platform by accident."

"No way," he insisted. "This case is going to stick in my craw."

"Better not unload your doubts on Sweeney, or you'll never hear the end of it."

He took her hand and kissed it.

"I promise to do all my unloading on you, my sugar plum, if you'll promise to ignore me when I do."

She gave him her most radiant smile. "If unloading is your new code word for making love, I promise you my undivided attention."

Epilogue

Last Will and Testament
of
Robin Crowe

I, Robin Crowe, resident in the City of New York, County of New York, State of New York, being of sound mind, not acting under duress or undue influence, and fully understanding the nature and extent of all my property and of this disposition thereof, do hereby make, publish, and declare this document to be my Last Will and Testament, and hereby revoke any and all other wills and codicils heretofore made by me.

I. EXPENSES & TAXES

I direct that all my debts, and expenses of my last illness, funeral, and burial, be paid as soon after my death as may be reasonably convenient, and I hereby authorize my Executor, hereinafter appointed, to settle and discharge, in his absolute discretion, any and all claims made against my estate.

I further direct that my Executor shall pay out of my estate any and all estate and inheritance taxes payable by reason of my death in respect of all items included in the computation of such taxes, whether passing under this Will or otherwise.

II. EXECUTOR

I nominate and appoint Raymond White, of 2 Larchmont Avenue, County of Westchester, State of New York, as Executor of my estate.

III. DISPOSITION OF PROPERTY

I direct my Executor to liquidate all securities, real and personal property and any other assets I may own at the time of my death and bequeath the funds therefrom to the Archives of American Art, Smithsonian Institution, Washington D.C. to create an endowed fellowship, to be called the Francis V. O'Connor Fellowship for the Study of New Deal Art. Instructions for the administration of said fellowship are appended to this Will as a sealed document, to be opened following my death.

IV. OMISSION

Inasmuch as my parents are deceased and I have no known living close relatives, I have intentionally, and not as a result of any mistake or inadvertence, omitted in this Will to provide for any family members or other individuals.

V. GOVERNING LAW

This document shall be governed by the laws in the State of New York.

I, the undersigned Robin Crowe, do hereby declare that I sign and execute this instrument as my last Will, that I sign it willingly in the presence of each of the undersigned witnesses, and that I execute it as my free and voluntary act for the purposes herein expressed, on this 14th day of February 1988.

Robin Crowe Testator Signature

Robin Crowe Testator (Printed Name)

The foregoing instrument was, on this 14th day of February 1988, signed, sealed, published and declared to be the Last Will and Testament of Robin Crowe, in the presence of us and each of us, who thereupon, at her request, in her presence, and in the presence of each other, have hereunto subscribed our names as attesting witnesses thereto.

Catherine Bell 240 East 75th Street, New York, NY

Witness Signature, Address
**Martin Lopez** 912 President Street, Brooklyn, NY
Witness Signature, Address

To be opened after my death

FELLOWSHIP INSTRUCTIONS

The Francis V. O'Connor Fellowship for the Study of New Deal Art, an endowed award funded by the income from my bequest, shall be given annually to a graduate or postgraduate student or independent scholar for study at the Smithsonian Institution's Archives of American Art in Washington, D.C., or at one of its branches.

The Archives shall solicit applications in accordance with its established procedures, and the awardee shall be chosen by a panel of no fewer than three recognized scholars in the field of 20th-century American art, nominated by the Archives. The amount and duration of the award shall be at their discretion.

This fellowship is established in memory of my dear friend, the distinguished art historian Francis V. O'Connor, Ph.D. (1937-1986), whose death I caused.

Acknowledgments

As in my earlier historical fiction, many of the characters are real people who might have figured in the story if it had been true. Chief among them is Francis Valentine O'Connor, Ph.D., my longtime friend and mentor and the foremost scholar of Jackson Pollock, the New Deal art projects, and American mural painting, who died of natural causes in his apartment at 250 East 73rd Street in November 2017. He was 80 years old.

I was inspired to kill him thirty-one years before his actual demise by his executor, Avis Berman, who had to deal with his multiple wills and the ensuing complications. Avis told me that if I were to write another art-world murder mystery, I must do away with Francis! With this book, I grant her wish and thank her for her able administration of his estate.

In constructing the premise for Francis's efforts to discredit the five purported Pollocks, I have relied heavily on the artist's four-volume catalogue raisonné, published by Yale University Press in 1978, which contains the empty rectangles described in the narrative. Since then, four of the missing works have been found, including *Number 22, 1949*, which features in my story. They are documented in the catalogue raisonné supplement, published by the Pollock-Krasner Foundation in 1995, after which the authentication board was disbanded. The foundation's primary mission is to provide financial support to artists. Since its establishment in 1985, it has given grants to thousands of artists around the world.

In the 1990s, after years out of sight, Pollock's *Number 17A, 1948*, emerged in the collection of media mogul David Geffen. He sold it to hedge fund CEO Ken Griffin in 2015 for $200 million.

While there are several arcane forms of agnosia, there is no such neurological condition as morphagnosia, which prevented Francis from recognizing the missing paintings. I invented it on the advice of my medical consultants, Robert J. Singer, M.D., and Maryann Melucci, C.R.N.A. I am grateful to them, to Verena Rose of Level Best Books for her editorial acumen, to Ellen T. White for setting the wheels in motion, and to my agent, Paul Bresnick, for being intrigued.

A year before Francis died, I gave him a copy of my first art-world mystery, *An Exquisite Corpse,* and asked for his opinion of my maiden voyage into fiction. To my surprise, he told me I had a "flair" for it—high praise from a very judgmental critic. I like to think he would have been delighted to find himself as my latest victim.

About the Author

During her career as a director of the Pollock-Krasner House and Study Center in East Hampton, New York, Helen A. Harrison began writing mystery novels set in the New York art world. A widely published author of books and articles on art, she enjoys making up stories in which fictional characters interact with real people from her own background and experience as a *New York Times* art critic, NPR arts commentator, museum curator and practicing artist. Her second novel, *An Accidental Corpse,* won the 2019 Benjamin Franklin Gold Award for Mystery & Suspense. A New York City native, she and her husband, the artist Roy Nicholson, live in Sag Harbor with the ghost of Roy's beloved studio cat, Mittens.

AUTHOR WEBSITE:

helenharrison.net

SOCIAL MEDIA HANDLES:

Facebook: artworldmysteries